KEEPER CHANCE
AND THE CONUNDRUM OF CHAOS

EVIL VILLAINS INTERNATIONAL LEAGUE

KEEPER CHANCE
AND THE CONUNDRUM OF CHAOS

ALEX EVANOVICH

SIMON & SCHUSTER BOOKS FOR YOUNG READERS
New York   London   Toronto   Sydney   New Delhi

SIMON & SCHUSTER BOOKS FOR YOUNG READERS
An imprint of Simon & Schuster Children's Publishing Division
1230 Avenue of the Americas, New York, New York 10020

This book is a work of fiction. Any references to historical events, real people, or real places are used fictitiously. Other names, characters, places, and events are products of the author's imagination, and any resemblance to actual events or places or persons, living or dead, is entirely coincidental.

Text © 2024 by Alex Evanovich
Jacket illustration © 2024 by Christina Chung
Jacket design by Laura Eckes
All rights reserved, including the right of reproduction in whole or in part in any form.
SIMON & SCHUSTER BOOKS FOR YOUNG READERS and related marks are trademarks of Simon & Schuster, LLC.
Simon & Schuster: Celebrating 100 Years of Publishing in 2024
For information about special discounts for bulk purchases, please contact Simon & Schuster Special Sales at 1-866-506-1949 or business@simonandschuster.com.
The Simon & Schuster Speakers Bureau can bring authors to your live event. For more information or to book an event, contact the Simon & Schuster Speakers Bureau at 1-866-248-3049 or visit our website at www.simonspeakers.com.
Interior design by Laura Eckes
The text for this book was set in Adobe Garamond Pro.
Manufactured in the United States of America
0824 BVG
First Edition
10 9 8 7 6 5 4 3 2 1
Library of Congress Cataloging-in-Publication Data
Names: Evanovich, Alex, author.
Title: Keeper chance and the conundrum of chaos / Alex Evanovich.
Description: First edition. | New York : Simon & Schuster Books for Young Readers, 2024. | Series: Evil Villains International League ; book 1 | Audience: Ages 10 up. | Audience: Grades 4-6. | Summary: When sixteen-year-old Keeper Chance receives an invitation to join E.V.I.L., a society of villains, he embarks on a journey of low-grade villainy until members begin to disappear and Keeper races against time to save his newfound friends and uncover his true nature amidst the chaos.
Identifiers: LCCN 2023056218 (print) | LCCN 2023056219 (ebook)
ISBN 9781665960045 (hardcover) | ISBN 9781665960069 (ebook)
Subjects: CYAC: Good and evil—Fiction. | Villains—Fiction. | Missing persons—Fiction. | Friendship—Fiction. | LCGFT: Novels.
Classification: LCC PZ7.1.E8576 Ke 2024 (print) | LCC PZ7.1.E8576 (ebook) | DDC [Fic]—dc23
LC record available at https://lccn.loc.gov/2023056218
LC ebook record available at https://lccn.loc.gov/2023056219

For Max

CHAPTER 1

THE man known as Chaos had entered Peachmont High School through a back door. It hadn't required a key or a crowbar. All that was needed was a chain of mildly catastrophic events causing the lock to fail and rendering the security system inoperable.

His footsteps echoed throughout the halls, and his boots squeaked on the tile floors. "Why do empty schools always feel like a haunted, abandoned mental institution?" Chaos whispered to himself. The idea was probably left over from the irreparable psychological damage done around four decades ago, when he suffered through the horrors of high school.

Chaos's penlight flickered across painted concrete brick walls, illuminating flyers for chess club and theater tryouts. He found his destination, language arts room 347, at the end of the hall. Chaos opened the door, went straight to the teacher's desk, and started rifling through the drawers, searching for papers belonging to the fifth-period class. He opened the period five folder and thumbed through it until he found Keeper Chance's story. It had an 80 percent grade, and written in red pencil was *Great effort!*

Chaos read the story and rolled his eyes. "Puh-leaze!" He was hardly the literary type, but he knew a slapdash job when he saw one. The paper was solid C material, and this teacher's comment was completely insulting to Keeper's lack of effort.

Chaos put the paper back inside the folder and left room 347 in search of precalculus, room 102. He had already hacked into the school's systems and seen Keeper Chance's schedule, report cards, and individual grades for assignments and tests. For that matter, he had been following Keeper's educational career for quite some time, but there had been a particular comment on a recent report card, from this year's math teacher, that interested Chaos. *Keeper seems to rush through and finish early but doesn't take the time to double-check his work.*

Chaos was confident that Keeper didn't need to double-check his work to know he had a solid 75 percent on a test. Based on Chaos's observations, Keeper Chance could have finished a math test early, without double-checking, and received an A+ if he wanted.

Chaos found room 102. It wasn't an internal room, so he turned off his penlight before he entered, not wanting to be seen through the windows. The moon was bright enough that he wouldn't need the extra light.

Chaos followed the same motions as he had in room 347. He found the test, looked it over for corrections, folded it, and placed it in the messenger bag he wore across his chest. He couldn't help but smile as he put the desk back in order, then left the math room in search of the nurse's office.

Yes, indeed, Chaos had a good feeling about Keeper Chance. Not that he'd ever actually met Keeper. "Soon enough," Chaos said to himself as he headed to the front of the school. "Soon enough."

The nurse's room was just past the main office. One door in and one door out.

Chaos searched through his bag and removed a screwdriver, along with a new door handle. It looked the same as the one currently on the door, but it had a lock that operated through an app.

He set to work removing the handle from the nurse's door and replacing it with his own. He was halfway through tightening the new handle into place when headlights from a car flashed through the windows behind him. Chaos immediately flattened himself on the floor and waited. It was hard to say if it was school security or the police. Was it a routine drive-by, or had someone come to investigate the broken alarm situation?

The water fountain twenty feet away began to groan. Sparks

shot from the wall where it was mounted, and water spouted out of the fountain's bubbler, spilling over the side and causing a pool to form on the floor.

"Get it together, Chaos," he whispered to himself. "You control chaos. It doesn't control you." Chaos closed his eyes and focused on his breathing.

The headlights disappeared. The sound of car tires faded into the distance. Chaos picked himself up, dusted off his coat, and pushed his half cape back behind his shoulders. The smell of smoke from the sparks began to fade, but there was no hope for the water fountain. There would be a major mess to clean up in the morning.

Chaos finished his handiwork on the nurse's door, placed his tools back in his bag, and tested the handle.

"Excellent. Phase one complete." Chaos looked at his watch. It was getting late, but that was no reason to not exit through the cafeteria in hopes of finding a post-midnight snack. He didn't have to start watching the Chance house on Willow Street for another few hours. He wanted to be sure Keeper made it to the last day of school before spring break.

At 7:20 a.m., Chaos stood outside, in the shadows of parked cars, watching the front door to a small two-story house. The house was built in the fifties, like the rest of the little bungalows lining the street. Four steps leading up to a covered porch. Two

floors, pitched roof, paint starting to peel off the wood siding. No garage. Street parking only. It was like stepping back in time.

Chaos shivered as a lone voice escaped the confinements of the home's walls and filled the still air. It was the type of voice that clawed at eardrums and made your stomach go sour. "Did you brush your teeth? Did you use toothpaste? How much toothpaste? Enough to actually clean your teeth? Did you wash the sink out when you were done?"

There was never a reply to the voice. Mostly because there was never an opportunity.

"Don't just walk out that door without taking the garbage. Don't drag it across the floor. Pick it up. And don't just throw it in the can. Put the top back on. Stop slouching!"

The front door opened, and sixteen-year-old Keeper Chance emerged with a bag of garbage. He was still growing at a pace that assured him his pants would always be too short and his shoes too small. He was lean, with dark blue eyes and unruly, wavy black hair. His jeans had seen better days, and he wore an inside-out gray T-shirt under a red sweatshirt. A well-used backpack hung over his shoulders.

The screen door closed behind him. His nana's face appeared behind the screen.

"I'm watching you," she said. "Don't forget it." The front door slammed shut, followed by the sound of a lock being turned.

Keeper took the garbage bag around to the side of the house

and placed it in the can. He stood motionless for a moment, debating what he was about to do. He pushed any doubt aside, bent over, and rummaged through the garbage, pulling a partially consumed fish carcass out. Keeper gagged and tried to blink back tears. He took a plastic freezer bag out of his pocket, slid the half-eaten fish in the bag, zipped it closed, and placed it in his backpack. He turned on his heel and walked down the street toward the bus stop. His shoulders were back and his head up, thanks to years of Nana's thoughtful reminders, but his eyes were narrow slits of annoyance.

"Wait for it," Chaos murmured as he repositioned himself between two large holly bushes for a wider view of the street.

Sure enough, Keeper Chance returned. This time in a crouch, skillfully weaving his way between hedges and parked cars until he made it to his nana's ancient, but perfectly maintained, Caddy. He took a secret copy of Nana's car key out of his pocket and inserted it into the car's keyhole. He carefully opened the driver's door just enough to slip the fish carcass out of the baggie and under the driver's floor mat. He closed the door, inserted the key again, relocking the door so Nana would be none the wiser until it was too late, and crept back the way he came.

Chaos couldn't tell if Keeper Chance was smiling, but it didn't matter. Chaos was smiling enough for the both of them. It was a wonderfully evil smile.

CHAPTER 2

SINCE Keeper had neither a car nor friends, he was forced to succumb to the smell and indignity of public-school transportation. To make matters worse, the bus driver was a retired math teacher and demanded that equations be solved as fare to board.

Keeper walked to the corner and watched the Peachmont High bus pull to the curb and open its doors. He climbed aboard, answered the equation of 405 divided by 9, took an empty seat closest to the front, and stared at his cruddy, falling-apart sneakers for fifteen minutes.

Sitting up front meant Keeper was first off the bus. He squinted in the bright April sun and joined the mass of teenagers mindlessly following the call to migrate into the giant brick-and-mortar building. He didn't notice Coach Martin standing at the bottom of the stairs, keeping students in line, until there was no escape.

"Happy Friday, Mr. Chance. How nice of you to join us on

time today. I'm guessing it's so you can make up all the laps you missed in PE this week. If you actually decide to run, instead of walk, you might just pull it off."

Keeper was pretty certain Coach Martin was a vampire. He had unusually long canines, was too pale for any type of actual blood flow to be happening, and had to be at least 290 years old. Word in the halls was that he had retired three times already but just couldn't give up making teenage boys miserable. Keeper suspected Coach Martin kept coming back to the high school so he could easily feast on young blood. If he calls you into his office, don't go. You're literally lunch.

"Sorry to disappoint," Keeper said, "but I won't be in gym class today. College reps are here, and I'm on the list to talk to State."

"What's that going to take? Five minutes? I'll give you ten. Get your brochure, a free pencil, or whatever garbage they're giving away, and I expect to see you on the track." Coach Martin grabbed hold of the whistle around his neck. It was a nervous gesture. "If you can't make it to class, I'll have to issue a detention. I'd hate to do that on the last day before spring break."

Keeper hooked his thumbs into his backpack straps. "I understand completely. If I don't make it to PE, please call my nana and tell her I have to stay after school. She expects me home promptly."

There was a pause, and for the first time that morning

Keeper smiled. It wasn't a big smile, but a smile nonetheless. There was an upside to every down, and in the case of Nana, this was the upside. The administration, teachers, and half the town were terrified of her. The last time Coach Martin called home about Keeper, Coach couldn't even get out two words before Nana landed a way-too-personal verbal assault centered around proper enunciation and phone etiquette.

Coach Martin visibly swallowed. It wasn't physically possible for him to get any paler. "Just . . . try your best to get to class today."

Keeper smiled sympathetically. "Will do, Coach Martin, but if I don't see you later today, enjoy the week off. I promise I'll be in class on Monday when we return."

Keeper felt kind of bad playing the Nana card but not bad enough to run laps. Over the past eleven years of his educational career, Keeper had learned where the line was drawn on what he could, and could not, get away with. The last thing the school wanted to do was make a phone call, and they would have to because Nana didn't have e-mail or a cell phone. She claimed the internet and most modern technology made people lazy and stupid. She didn't need a computer—or anyone else—correcting her spelling or reminding her to breathe.

Keeper moved past Coach Martin and squeezed his way through the crowded halls to his locker. He exchanged some books from his backpack for the ones he'd need for the next three periods of profound boredom.

At lunch, he ate in a corner by himself. Being alone wasn't a big deal to Keeper. After reigning eleven years, and counting, as the Cootie King of Peachmont's various educational institutions, he often found relief in the solitude. It allowed him to avoid the misery of overhearing whispered rumors and gossip about Nana and himself, which were plentiful. Though much of it was true, some of it was exaggerated, and occasionally a tidbit was completely unsubstantiated.

When the bell rang for fourth period, Keeper made his way to the library to meet with State College. It was the only college Nana had agreed to foot the bill for *if* Keeper graduated with a degree in accounting.

A number of other colleges and universities had representatives visiting Peachmont High. Each had a small room off the library to talk privately with prospective students. Keeper found the door with a sign for State taped to it and entered.

The room was empty except for a pile of brochures and free pencils on a plastic table in the middle of the room. Keeper took a seat at the table and waited, hoping no one would show. Doing nothing still beat going to PE.

After ten minutes Chaos entered the room and closed the door behind him. He was of average height and build. Brown eyes with laugh lines. He wore dark gray canvas cargo pants with forest-green bands around the knees and cuffs. His fitted long-sleeve dark gray T-shirt matched, but the green stripes went vertically down from his shoulders and circled back at the waist. The strangest, and best, part of Chaos's outfit was the short cape attached at his shoulders. It was black on the inside and dark green on the outside.

Keeper figured the man must be part of State's theater department.

Chaos sat down in the chair across from Keeper, placed his hands on the table with his fingers interlocked, and stared at him.

"So, you want to go to State?" Chaos asked after a minute of uncomfortable silence.

"Um. Yes, sir," Keeper said.

"That's a complete and outright lie." Chaos leaned back and crossed his arms over his chest. "You are hardly State material, and it would be a waste of four years of your life in that post-pubescent glorified day care they call higher education."

Keeper felt his mouth drop. State really needed better representatives.

"Look," Chaos said, leaning forward again and resting his elbows on the table. "I'm not sure how much time we have, so let's get to the point. I'm not with State."

"No joke." Keeper's eyes went to the stack of pencils. And back to the man sitting across from him. "What happened to the State rep?"

"Mr. Meeks? He was part of an unfortunate series of events that caused him to make a sudden visit to the nurse's room.

Equally unfortunate for him, someone—and that would be me—snuck into the school last night and installed a lock on the nurse's office door. School maintenance is currently trying to figure out how to free Mr. Meeks and Nurse Whitmore without breaking down the door."

A smile tugged at the corners of Keeper's mouth. Chaos took it as a good sign.

"I'm head of the local chapter of an elite organization. We are currently looking to recruit two more members, and I would like you to try out for one of those spots."

An elite organization? "The CIA?" Keeper asked.

The man rolled his eyes. "I said elite."

"Um, no offense, sir, but I think you have the wrong person—"

"No. I don't. You're Keeper Chance." Chaos reached into his messenger bag, pulled out a manila school file, and threw it down on the table. CHANCE, KEEPER was printed on a label that was attached to the tab. Across the entire front, in thick, red Sharpie was written BEWARE OF THE GRANDMA. "You match the photo on your school records."

Keeper stared at the warning message on the folder. "Crikey! Did you steal that?"

"Of course I stole it. I'd appreciate it if we didn't waste time with ridiculous questions. I'm fully in the know about how extraordinary you are."

Keeper's brow furrowed. "You definitely have the wrong person. I'm a straight C student."

The man smiled. "Yes. Extraordinary. I've noticed that C of yours is always a perfect seventy-five percent. Every test, every homework, every paper turned in." Chaos removed the math test from his bag, unfolded it, and placed it in front of Keeper. "You know exactly what is worth two points and what is worth one. Always a seventy-five. Except once, recently, when a language arts teacher took pity on you and gave you an eighty on a story you wrote. You had to compensate on a grammar quiz to not ruin your GPA. Why you choose to get seventy-fives, I don't know. Bored? For fun? To tick off your grandmother? All of the above? Doesn't matter. They're all fantastic reasons. You're an excellent fit for the organization."

There was the sound of someone trying to open the door to the room, but the door was locked. Both Keeper and Chaos turned to look. There was some swearing and a lot of rattling coming from the other side. That was replaced with the sound of what seemed like a bookcase falling over, a mishap involving chairs, a lot of yelling about fluorescent lights, and finally the fire alarm going off.

Chaos calmly rose from his chair and pulled a business card from a pocket in his cargoes. He handed it to Keeper. "It seems our time is up. My card. I'll be back in touch."

Keeper took the card and watched Chaos unlock the door. He walked out into the commotion as if there were nothing to see and disappeared out of view.

Keeper turned the card over. Handwritten in green marker was one word. *Chaos.*

CHAPTER 3

THAT Nana expected Keeper home promptly from school couldn't have been any further from the truth. Nana had no desire for Keeper to come home, and Keeper had no desire to go home. As long as he was back in time for dinner, mostly because it was his job to wash the dishes, Nana kept her nagging to a minimum.

When the dismissal bell rang for the day, Keeper left school grounds, walked four blocks, and waited for a city bus. The bus took him outside the town of Peachmont, through the historic theater district, to the edge of the city of Durian, where a history museum, art galleries, and hip coffeehouses resided. Keeper liked coming here because it felt modern compared to Peachmont. The coffee shop was always filled with college kids and young professionals, happily chatting away or working on assignments, too busy to notice him.

Durian was a relatively young city. Office buildings and parking garages were creeping their way toward the northeast boundaries. Financial bigwigs and corporate headquarters fought over cubic floor space in prime locations that gave them visibility and a sense of success. Towns and suburbs of various sizes spread like wildfire to the southwest of Durian. When Nana had first bought her house in Peachmont, the development was surrounded by farms. Now it was surrounded by strip malls, freeways, and ever-changing neighborhoods, some with gates and pools.

Keeper disembarked the bus and walked toward the Natural History Museum until he came to his favorite coffee shop. The coffee was decent, but what he really liked was that they sold grape soda and had free Wi-Fi. He pushed his way through the shop's door, paid for a soda, and found an empty table and chair in the corner.

Once he was settled, he opened his grape soda, took a sip, removed a book on accounting from his backpack, and began reading. He had borrowed the book from the school library after the fire alarm stopped. He was only a few pages in, but the book was horrible. Way worse than he had ever imagined. So many columns of numbers and mentions of liabilities and accruing things. His eyes were burning with the blandness of the language. His mind filled with images of cubicles and the sound of computer mice clicking.

"Is this soy milk or almond milk? I specifically said almond."

Keeper's eyes strayed from the paragraph about the importance of balance sheets and focused on the man complaining at the counter.

"I won't accept it!" the man shouted, shoving his cup back at the barista. "I know it's soy. Make it again."

Keeper raised his book to shield the man from his line of sight and tried to shrink into his shoulders like a turtle. This guy was totally ruining Keeper's happy place.

The barista placed a new cup on the counter in front of the man. The man slid it back in annoyance. "I said hot. This is barely lukewarm. And I saw you put it together. Two-thirds should be almond milk, not half."

Keeper peeked over the top of the book. The man was still going on and on and on. What was his damage?

"Be more careful! Almond milk froth is very delicate, and I want froth."

Keeper glanced around the room. Everyone was staring at the unpleasant scene unfolding. Keeper had enough. He closed his book, chugged down his soda, and stood.

The man snatched his cup from the poor barista and took it to the sugar, cream, and stir stick station. "Obviously you don't live on tips," the man said, putting his cup down on the small counter. He turned to look through the packets of sugar and sugar substitutes. "What, no organic?"

Keeper passed by the man and noted the BMW car key he was holding. Keeper grabbed the almond milk latte from the counter and walked unnoticed out the door. He removed the lid and took a sip. It was no grape soda. He approached a BMW convertible, top down, that was parked at the curb, threw the contents of the drink onto the driver's seat, and continued walking down the sidewalk.

Keeper made it about a hundred yards when a squirrel fell out of a tree onto the hood of a moving car. The car swerved and took out a fire hydrant. Water shot up, raining down a shower of heavy drops, soaking Keeper and sending four other people running around screaming, knocking into one another, like a bunch of raccoons caught in a car's headlight.

Keeper stood frozen, focused on the melee, when a body slammed into him. Keeper dropped his book and staggered back. A man's hands grabbed at his T-shirt, holding him upright.

"So sorry," the man said. "I didn't see you there." He picked Keeper's book up, wiped the soggy side off with his sleeve, and handed it back to Keeper. "Are you all right?"

Keeper took the book and used his fingers to rake his wet hair away from his face. It was the man from school.

"Fine," Keeper said. "I . . . I'm fine. Thank you."

Chaos smiled at Keeper and then continued walking past

him, down the street toward the coffeehouse and the Museum of Natural History. Keeper watched. On the back of Chaos's cape were thin gold bands, like threads, in the shape of ellipticals. The ellipticals seemed to move as the man walked. Was it a butterfly? Keeper blinked. Not a butterfly, but there was a pattern. Keeper blinked again. No. It was his imagination or maybe an optical illusion. The elliptical shapes made no sense.

Keeper put his book back in his backpack and thought about the man and his cape. He touched his chest. He was wearing his favorite T-shirt. It was inside out so his nana wouldn't see it. On the inside of the shirt was Euler's equation, $ei\pi + 1 = 0$.

Nana would wholeheartedly disapprove of such a nonsensical theory. To Keeper, it gave him hope, and wearing the shirt, even inside out, brought him a sense of comfort. The idea that all these strange numbers, including one that wasn't even real, could combine gave him faith that the universe knew what it was doing. He just needed to pay attention.

Sixteen-year-old Whylene "Y" Love stood outside the coffee shop's doorway, watching Keeper Chance and Chaos. Her curly dark red hair was pulled up into a ponytail, and her hazel eyes were focused on the encounter. She wore a sparkly Hello Kitty T-shirt, a short black skirt over black capri tights, and red Vans high-tops. She hated the name Whylene, she hated the cards life had dealt her, and for many reasons, she was currently hating the situation that had just unfolded in front of her. Her phone buzzed with a text message. It was her father.

Just do your best to not let everyone down. It's okay if you fail. There are skilled people who can do the job.

*S*ince there was no emoji to accurately convey the sentiment of where her father could shove it, Y chose to ignore the message. She was completely capable of doing the job. She was just having serious doubts about whether it was the right thing to do. She watched Keeper Chance standing in the middle of the sidewalk, water pouring down on him, and she was certain he was gorgeous, brilliant, and completely clueless.

Keeper finally pulled himself together and sloshed down the street. Y had been observing Keeper for over a week, and wherever Keeper was, more than likely so was Chaos. Often hiding behind a magazine or a tree. Once she saw Chaos secretly slip five dollars into Keeper's backpack so he could get something to eat with his grape soda.

I've been living in a rose-colored cesspool of lies and self-serving misconceptions, Y thought to herself. *Keeper Chance deserves the right to make his own choices, for better or for worse.* Y looked down at the message on her phone. She deserved the right to make her own choices too, and the time had finally come for her to choose. She just needed to be calculating, cunning, and most importantly, deceitful.

Y sent a text out to her father. Three minutes later a white sedan pulled up to the curb. Y opened the door on the passenger side and climbed in.

"Well?" her father asked. "Did you make contact?"

Sensei Love was tall and muscular with wide shoulders, all the better for carrying the burden placed upon them. His head was clean shaven. He wore white breeches, a fitted white tunic, white wraps about his shins and forearms, and white shoes with a split toe. Everything he wore was white, except for the ever-present black belt about his waist.

Y diverted her attention out the side window, avoiding eye contact. "No. Chance wasn't even there for a full minute before a situation arose and he left."

"I see." There was a barely audible sigh out of her father.

Y knew exactly what he was thinking. Why couldn't I have had a son? Why couldn't I have had a child with a skill? Why me? Why, why, why? She was pretty certain "why, why, why" was her father's meditating mantra.

"You've been hanging out at that coffee shop for over a week, and still nothing," Sensei Love said. "I blame myself."

Y did a mental eye roll, careful to not show any emotion. If she didn't want to return home, to the dojo, she was going to have to play her cards very carefully.

"I thought I was doing the right thing, giving you all the best," her father continued. "The best education. The best training. That despite your shortcomings you could make something of yourself."

It wasn't entirely true that Y didn't have any abilities. She worked hard to keep most of her talents secret. For example, she was an excellent spy. At the dojo she was rarely noticed as she observed private lessons, secret classes, and people who came and went. Y was also an accomplished liar, though she mostly only lied to her father. She lied about wanting to please him, being committed to the family business, and about being unskilled. There wasn't much point in lying to her mother, Vogue, who designed and created clothing for the best of the best. It had been painfully clear early on that Y had absolutely no aptitude for anything within the fashion industry. She couldn't sew, she couldn't draw, she couldn't design, and she couldn't care less about properly accessorizing. Therefore, Y was pretty much invisible to her mother. Often it was preferred over not being invisible to her father.

"It wasn't my fault this time. I swear," Y said. "Chance was totally preoccupied with a book, and then this dingus started making a scene about his latte, and I use the term latte loosely—"

"No need to make excuses. I shouldn't have encouraged false hope," Sensei Love said matter-of-factly. "It's just that when I saw you flirting with the Mallet boy back home, I thought perhaps you had your mother's gift of allure, despite obviously lacking her fashion sense."

Y tried to not gag. Mallet was the worst. All he did was talk about how big his hands were. She would have felt bad about using him the way she did if he hadn't been such a loser.

"Sorry that didn't work out for you," her father said, patting Y's knee as an insincere afterthought. "I know how much you liked him."

Y looked at her father and forced a small smile. She hoped it came off as heartbreak and not nausea.

"No point in dwelling on failures," her father said, returning his attention to the road. "The weekend is here, and I'm going to let you try one more time. After that, I'll have no choice but to turn the job over to someone else. The condo here is only rented for the month. I can't be away from the dojo—upstate—any longer than that. I know giving you this extra chance makes me seem weak and like a pushover, but you are my daughter."

Y refrained from thanking him for his generosity. "I promise I can get Keeper Chance," she said. Except this time she was going to do it her way, and then she'd keep him for herself and be free of Sensei Love and the dojo forevermore.

CHAPTER 4

KEEPER was happy to find Nana not home. She was probably somewhere cheating at bridge or shopping for cabbage that she would make into so-called soup.

He slogged up the stairs, trying to leave as little of a water trail as possible. His room had originally been his father's. Both of Keeper's parents had died when he was a baby, and Nana and Pop-Pop had taken on the task of raising Keeper. Keeper had fond memories of his pop-pop, even though they were few. He had been a quiet man who would secretly take Keeper out for ice cream every now and then and claim Nana didn't need to know because it was "secret business." Pop-Pop had passed on when Keeper was four. Since then, it had been a battle of wits and mental fortitude between Keeper and Nana.

Keeper's bedroom was sparse. His mattress was on the floor, a worn wood desk and chair against a wall, and an old dresser against another. The dresser had a couple of secret drawers with false bottoms. Keeper used them to hide inventions he was working on and the parts he'd pilfered from people's garbage to build them. Stacks of library books on chemical compounds, artificial intelligence, and quantum physics were next to the mattress, along with a table lamp circa 1970. Keeper didn't mind the old furniture and lamp. He suspected they had been his father's.

Keeper removed the accounting book from his bag and threw the book on the desk. He kicked off his sneakers and peeled off his soaked socks. He looked mournfully at the book on his desk and noticed a piece of paper sticking out. He opened the book, removed the folded paper, and read it.

KEEPER CHANCE,

THANK YOU FOR YOUR TIME THIS AFTERNOON. YOU ARE CORDIALLY INVITED TO ATTEND A QUESTION-AND-ANSWER SESSION FOR POSSIBLE MEMBERSHIP IN THE EVIL VILLAINS INTERNATIONAL LEAGUE (E.V.I.L.). IF YOU ARE SO INCLINED TO ACCEPT THIS INVITATION, PLEASE COME TO THE FORSHAM THEATER IN THE HISTORIC DISTRICT,

> TONIGHT AT MIDNIGHT. WAIT IN THE ALLEY, IN THE SHADOWS OF THE GREEN DUMPSTERS. REGARDLESS OF YOUR DECISION, PLEASE EITHER BURN, EAT, OR FLUSH THIS LETTER DOWN THE TOILET (IF PLUMBING ALLOWS).
>
> WITH GREAT RESPECT,
>
> CHAOS
> HEAD OF CHAPTER 626
> E.V.I.L.

Villainy was a vocation? Keeper wasn't even sure what being a villain would entail. He thought about the man with the green cape. Does being a villain mean you get to wear a cool outfit like Chaos?

Keeper looked at the accounting book on his desk. Maybe villainy wasn't so bad. After all, he wasn't very comfortable in conventional society. Maybe the smart thing to do would be to stick with and embrace unconventionality.

Not to mention, the possibility that life would be any better for him at the local state college was slim to none. Keeper would have to live at home, and that meant another four-plus years before he could escape the clutches of his nana.

The real problem was that Keeper didn't think he was evil.

At least he didn't feel evil. Of course, he also didn't think or feel like an accountant. He could always attend the meeting and make up his mind later.

Keeper looked at the letter. Burning it would attract Nana. Eating it would probably be the equivalent in texture to Nana's pork chops. The house plumbing would have a total meltdown if he flushed a wad of paper down it. Keeper smiled. It wasn't like Nana needed her savings to pay for State anymore. Flushing it was.

Chaos entered a diner two blocks east of the museum and found Slasher already in a booth, waiting. Slasher was in his late forties and dressed as if he had been living on a deserted island in the Caribbean. He wore a Hawaiian shirt, flip-flops, and what appeared to be homemade jean shorts with a paper clip as the zipper pull. For most of Slasher's life, he had maintained the physique of a string bean, but lately age had gotten the better of him, and a small potbelly was beginning to form.

Chaos slid onto the vinyl bench across from him.

"Order whatever you want," Slasher said. "It's on me."

A waitress appeared at the end of the table and took Chaos's order. Hamburger, no bun, extra pickles, and a diet Cherry Coke.

"I saw your text," Slasher said. "Tell me about these two new possible villains."

Chaos straightened the silverware in front of him. "Both very different, but I think they have potential."

"How'd you find them?"

"One found me," Chaos said. "Multiple times. Very enthusiastic. The other one I invited."

Slasher watched his friend. He'd known Chaos long enough that he could tell there was something he was keeping to himself. Chaos had a terrible poker face. "Chaos, what are you hiding?"

Chaos picked up a fork and jabbed the table a couple of times. "Nothing." He laid the fork back down and forced his hands to his lap. "Well, maybe not nothing. Showboater should be here soon. Let's wait for him."

The door to the diner swung open, and heads snapped up to stare. A figure, blinding in bedazzled sequins and glitter, stood in the opening, sending sparkling rays of light throughout the room like a human disco ball. Showboater did a little victory dance, and all the eyes that were staring in his direction turned away. Business returned to normal.

Showboater strutted his way into the diner, stopped at a booth, and looked down at the table.

"Tch!"

Showboater turned in the direction of the *tch* and saw Chaos and Slasher in their booth. Chaos *tch*ed Showboater again and pointed at the empty seat next to Slasher.

Showboater slumped his shoulders, looked up toward the

heavens, and did an overly dramatic and overly loud sigh. He walked over to the table and slid onto the bench next to Slasher.

"They had real maple syrup on their table," Showboater said. "It would have been an easy swipe, and we'd all be enjoying it with pancakes."

"For crying out loud, Showboater," Chaos said. "You know I'm having a gluten issue these days. I can't eat pancakes."

Showboater frowned, furrowing his brow. "Still, huh? That's a shame."

"No Frog today, Showboater?" Slasher asked.

The Frog was Showboater's sidekick. He dressed entirely in green spandex, was six foot four, and had size 13 feet. He claimed he wore the green so he could hide better from security cameras. Most of the villains thought the Frog just liked green.

"No, he's washing his tights," Showboater said with an eye roll. "I thought we might need a bottle or two of wine tonight. Frog created a diversion in the boxed wine aisle, puncturing all the boxes, while I broke into the locked case. Sadly, Frog chose the red boxed wine and will have to soak the stains out before he can be seen in public again. On the plus side, I got us a nice red from Italy and a white from France."

"Very thoughtful, Showboater. We just might need a couple of drinks after the meeting," Chaos said.

Showboater raised his eyebrows. "The applicants are that bad? Please tell me no one's skill is burping the alphabet. Remember that guy?"

"Nothing that bad," Chaos said. "The first recruit is Tobias 'Toby' Boggs. Sixteen and a junior in high school."

"What's Toby's skill?" Slasher asked.

"He seems to have an extraordinary sense of hearing and is a master tracker," Chaos said. "I couldn't get away from the kid. There was no hiding place hidden enough. I suspect he also has computer skills and hacked his way into the E.V.I.L. database. He knows everything about the current members of 626. Best I can describe his personality is Pillsbury Doughboy. He seems happy, but I suspect his high school career is less than stellar and involves a lot of swirlies."

"It would be nice to have a computer expert in the chapter," Showboater said. "I can't seem to sync my calendar to my phone. I can go phone to computer, but not the other way. It's maddening."

"Tell me about it," Slasher chimed in. "When I delete an e-mail off my computer, it won't delete off my iPad. I must have a bazillion pieces of spam sitting in my iPad's inbox. This Toby kid seems promising. What's the deal with recruit number two?"

"Also sixteen and a junior. I invited him." Chaos swallowed and cleared his throat slightly. "Keeper Chance."

Showboater and Slasher froze. Incapable of even blinking.

"Karaoke's kid?" Slasher asked.

Chaos nodded. "Yes."

Showboater sounded nervous. "Does he take after his mother or his father?"

"Father, most definitely," Chaos said. It might have been a lie. Best to push on with the positives. "The kid is brilliant. Invents things."

Slasher looked Chaos in the eye. "That's not exactly a skill. How long have you been watching him?"

Chaos used a napkin to dab at the sweat forming on his forehead. "Since birth."

Slasher rolled his eyes. "Chaos . . ."

Chaos held up his hands. "Thomas Chance was a good man. And his mother is every bit the hideous she-devil he claimed. Someone needed to make sure Keeper was okay under her watch. It wasn't until six or so months ago that I started seriously thinking about offering him a place in 626."

Slasher thought about it for a moment. "Does the kid know his father was an E.V.I.L. villain?"

Chaos stirred his drink with his straw. "No. He knows nothing about his parents. His grandmother won't speak of them. Either one. Told Keeper they died of disappointment. I'll give the old hag the benefit of the doubt in that it was his parents' wish Keeper know nothing. That he be raised with the hope of being 'normal.'"

"That's everyone's wish," Slasher said. "But he's not?"

"No. I don't think so. As a matter of fact, I think he might have a skill that is . . . special."

Slasher and Showboater leaned in.

Chaos glanced about the room to make sure no one was paying attention to them. "It's possible his skill is luck, but I think it's more refined. I think he has a skill for finding things or maybe helping people."

Slasher and Showboater pulled back. Showboater let out an enormous sigh and looked toward the heavens.

"For the love of Loki," Slasher said. "Please tell me you're joking. You said Keeper was like his father. This is just bad. Really bad. We don't help people, and we don't *find* things."

Chaos held up his hands. "No, we don't. *But* I can't think of any group of people more constantly in need of help than Chapter 626. Just last week Barricade lost his E.V.I.L. identity medallion."

Slasher's brows knit together. "And Keeper Chance found the medallion?"

Chaos took a sip of his drink in triumph. "Yes. I don't know how, but the medallion somehow made its way to Keeper. I was sitting outside the boy's favorite haunt, having a cup of coffee on a bench, and he dropped the medallion into my cup. As if I was begging for change. I don't think he even knew he did it. He was pretending to have his nose in a book but was actually looking at a redheaded girl."

Slasher shook his head. "I don't know, Chaos. Could just be crazy luck."

Chaos shrugged. "Whatever it is, I'm telling you Keeper Chance is special. Besides having an enchanting singing voice, his father was a genius, and his mother was . . . well, I don't like to speak ill of the dead. She was highly skilled. Their son is worth keeping an eye on."

CHAPTER 5

TWO years prior, Keeper had rigged the bathroom window to open silently when pressure was applied to the top right corner, which Nana was too short to reach. At 11:30 p.m. he snuck into the bathroom and climbed out the window. He pulled himself up onto a tree branch, inched across the limb to the trunk, and shimmied down the far side. He was wearing the same worn jeans and sneakers, now dry, a once-black T-shirt with frayed edges that had been washed to gray, and a black hoodie. Nana wasn't big into fashion. She said it led to vanity, and she wasn't interested in spending her money on the development of a fat-headed fancy pants.

Keeper would have to walk to the historic district. If he kept up a good pace, he could make it in half an hour and avoid some of the more questionable nighttime streets. It wasn't Keeper's first time heading to the historic district late at night. Every now and then the Forsham Theater would show a classic film. Keeper would sneak out of the house and try to talk his way into the theater. He would claim his parents were already inside and he'd forgotten to take his ticket when he went back to the car for his phone. It was a double lie. Keeper didn't have parents or a phone. The person taking tickets usually bought the story or just felt sorry for him. Either way, Keeper got in and saw a movie.

He approached the theater with five minutes to spare. The streetlights were yellow and dim, and the spring air was still and cool between the buildings. Keeper made his way toward the alley in the back of the theater. There was just enough light to see a figure standing between the dumpsters. He was softer than Keeper, about the same age, around five foot ten, with brown hair and brown eyes. The boy was practically vibrating off the ground with excitement. He nodded a hello at Keeper. Keeper nodded back. They stood in silence for a few minutes, staring at the theater's back door.

"Toby," the boy blurted out. "I'm Toby. Are you here for 626 too?"

"Yeah. I'm Keeper."

Toby seemed to bounce up and down a bit in nervous apprehension. "Cool."

They went back to staring at the door.

"What's your skill?" Toby asked.

Keeper turned his head and looked at Toby. "My what?"

"Your skill. Something special that you can do."

Keeper thought for a moment and shook his head. "I don't have one."

Toby continued watching the door with unblinking eyes. "I have a crazy sense of smell. I can hear things too. There are three villains on the other side of the door. Senior members. They're talking in hushed voices. Something Tex-Mex just came out of a toaster oven. You wouldn't be here if you didn't have a skill. Omigosh. Omigosh. They're going to open the door."

Keeper's palms were beginning to sweat, and his heart was racing. His mind filled with thoughts about what was behind the door. Doc Ock? The Joker? Voldemort? This was a major mistake.

Chaos stepped out into the dim light. Behind him a guy in a Hawaiian shirt and another in a suit lined with sequins filled the doorway.

Keeper couldn't tell if he was relieved or disappointed. This was the "elite" organization?

"Welcome," Chaos said. "I'm glad you made it. Please, come inside where we can talk freely. We have taquitos." He looked at Keeper. "And grape soda. Help yourselves."

Keeper and Toby walked through the doorway, shaking hands with Slasher and Showboater. The door closed, and

Chaos remained in the alley. The lights slowly went out. Chaos stood still, listening.

"Did you want to apply?" Chaos asked into the darkness.

There was no reply.

"You've been standing there a long time. Watching the boys."

Y Love stepped out of the shadows at the end of the alley. How did he know she was there? "No," she said. "I'm not interested in joining."

Chaos turned his head to look at her. "Are you sure?"

"Yes."

Chaos smiled and slowly approached Y, as if she were a wild animal he didn't want to startle. He extended his hand. "Chaos."

She couldn't tell him her real name. She needed a name and fast. She thought about good and evil. She thought about where she came from and where she was now standing. She tried to not think about the inner conflict she was having. "YinYang," she said, shaking Chaos's hand. "Most people just call me Y, like the letter."

"It's a pleasure to meet you, Y." Chaos held her gaze. Studying her. "If you should change your mind . . . I'm sure you have the skills to find me." He turned and walked back down the alley, opened the theater's rear door, and disappeared inside.

He found the other villains and recruits in the small break room. It wasn't an area of the theater the villains often used. Showboater's private lair was hidden behind racks of old costumes and boxes of ancient props. It was a series of secret rooms used back in the time of Prohibition and since forgotten behind a false panel. The rooms linked to passages Showboater more frequently used as an exit. They came out across the alley in an abandoned space that used to be a five-and-dime store.

Chaos held up a hand. "If I could have everyone's attention. I would like to keep this get-together under an hour. It's important that our young applicants return to their homes before they are missed. This meeting is to answer any questions the applicants have. If, at the end of the hour, an applicant wishes to join Chapter 626 of the Evil Villains International League, we will proceed with the process.

"Toby. Keeper. I'd like to introduce the two most senior members of 626, after me." Chaos motioned toward the man in the Hawaiian shirt. "This is Slasher. He has the unusual skill of being able to talk down the price on anything. Since the age of ten, he's gotten everything he has ever wanted for pennies on the dollar, if not for free."

Showboater appeared with a plate piled high with taquitos. Toby helped himself to a handful, and Keeper took one, not sure what a taquito was.

"The man with the Tex-Mex midnight munchies is Showboater," Chaos continued. "The more flamboyant he is, the more he demands attention, the more he disappears."

"It's both a curse and a blessing," Showboater said. "I made sure to get the corn tortilla taquitos, Chaos, if you're feeling peckish."

Chaos held up a hand. "Thank you, Showboater, maybe later.

"There are currently eight members, total, in our chapter. A chapter typically consists of eight to thirteen members. Villains aren't overly social. Meetings are typically called for one of three reasons. An evil emergency, recognition of an outstandingly evil deed, and the holiday party. No one likes to be alone over the holidays. Your chapter, and the league, are family. If you are ever in trouble, you can count on someone showing up to help. That being said, no one likes a problem child, so don't go getting yourself into a pickle over and over again. Any questions?"

Keeper half raised his hand.

"This isn't grade school," Chaos said, rolling his eyes. "No need to raise your hand. What's your question?"

Keeper wasn't sure he wanted to ask the question. Or more accurately, he wasn't sure he wanted to hear the answer. "I'm . . . I'm just wondering, sir, what being an evil villain entails and why I've been invited to join."

"You know exactly why you've been invited. That T-shirt you love so much but wear inside out—how did you acquire it?"

Keeper was pretty sure he was about to be in deep doody. "I stole the money for it, sir. But I tried to only take a dollar here and there, so it wouldn't go noticed or hurt anyone too much. It's just . . . I really needed the shirt, emotionally speaking, and

I had no way of getting the money. Nana won't let me get a job, and I don't get an allowance. It seemed better than stealing the shirt from the store. It was a small store, and it probably really needed the sale."

Chaos held his hand up for Keeper to stop rambling. "It's okay. You hit on a key element of being an evil villain. At least an E.V.I.L. evil villain. We don't hurt people or animals. At least we try not to do so. We might annoy them—"

"Oh, we definitely annoy them," Showboater said.

"I like to think of ourselves as necessary evil," Chaos continued. "We're the sock that goes missing in the dryer. We're the kid who won't stop screaming on the plane. Life isn't meant to be perfect every day. And let's be honest, some people are really asking for a less-than-perfect day.

"To be even more honest, villains are often people who have certain . . . traits . . . that keep us from fitting comfortably into conventional society. Often those traits make us awkward or undesirable to be around."

"You made the fire alarm go off at my school and that squirrel fall out of the tree," Keeper said.

"Yes." Chaos stood a bit straighter. "And the chain of events that followed. I'm still working on controlling the release of chaos, and I suspect I will have to work on it for my entire life, but I have learned how to set it off when I want."

"I have exceptional hearing and smell," Toby said, stuffing a taquito into his mouth.

Chaos raised an eyebrow. "Are all of your senses heightened?" he asked Toby. "What about vision and taste?"

"Twenty-twenty, and I'll pretty much eat anything."

"What's my skill?" Keeper asked.

Chaos shrugged. "We're still waiting to see it develop. It's my belief that everyone has a skill. Sometimes they develop later in life or aren't recognized until there is a necessity. What I do know is that you are quite the inventor."

Keeper shook his head. "I just tinker a bit. Mostly I turn things into new things or improve them. But I do have ideas."

"Yes, well." Chaos smiled. He had just found Keeper's weakness. "As an evil villain, the world is yours to tinker with. Something you need for a particular invention? Find it and go get it. Make amazing creations without some senior corporate nitwit telling you it can't be done or it's not what you're being paid to do or it's not safe."

Keeper's eyes had glassed over with the possibilities. He had a notebook full of plans, just no resources to turn the dreams into reality.

Chaos took a step closer to him and lowered his voice. "Of course, if you're not comfortable with villainy, we understand. You are free to return to your nana's house and continue your pursuit of a life in accounting. An ergonomic chair in every cubicle. I hear computers are programmed to do most of the work these days. Should give you plenty of time to daydream about what you'd rather be doing."

Keeper snapped out of it. His eyes shifted to Chaos. "I'm in. Where do I sign?"

Toby emphatically nodded in agreement.

"No need to sign anything. This isn't the military. However, you will both have to pass a small test. It will allow us, and you, to be sure that you possess the correct disposition for such a career choice."

Showboater stepped forward and handed Keeper and Toby each a small, insulated black lunch sack.

"Don't open it until you get home," Slasher said. "It's for your eyes only. Not your nana's. Not your mom's. Not your cat's. Understand?"

Keeper and Toby nodded.

"Bring the bag to Myer Distributions," Slasher continued. "We'll meet you on the far side of the parking lot for the warehouse at one a.m. That's about twenty-four hours from now. Don't be late. I suggest you wear black."

Keeper and Toby left the same way they came, through the theater's back door. Chaos locked the door behind them and returned to Slasher and Showboater in the break room.

Showboater handed Chaos a glass of wine. "I think that went fairly well. Toby didn't ask for any autographs, and I see what you're saying about Keeper Chance. He's worth watching."

Chaos took a sip of his wine. "We aren't the only ones watching him."

"What do you mean?" Slasher asked.

"Before the meeting began," Chaos said. "I ran into the Love girl in the alley."

Slasher choked on his wine. "As in Sensei Love's kid? Are you sure?"

"Oh, yes. She looks a lot like her mother, Vogue. The girl has been watching Keeper for at least a week now," Chaos said. "You know, I'm kind of impressed. Considering what an anti-villainite Sensei Love is, it's downright evil to send his pretty teenage daughter out to convince a teen boy into joining the Love dojo of holier-than-thouers."

"Has she had any interactions with him?" Showboater asked.

"Once," Chaos said. "She approached Keeper at his favorite coffeehouse and asked if the empty chair at his table was taken. Keeper was totally clueless, or maybe he panicked. Hard to say. Told her the seat was free, and he was just leaving. Then he got up and left. Grape soda and all."

Slasher and Showboater cracked up, laughing.

"So, what are we going to do about Love's kid?" Slasher asked.

Chaos took a sip of his wine. "Nothing. I get the feeling Whylene Love, who told me her name was YinYang, but prefers Y, is not fully committed to the task she's been assigned."

"You don't think she wants to get involved with Keeper?" Slasher asked.

Chaos laughed. "Oh, I suspect that part she's committed to fully."

A slow smile grew on Slasher's face. "You think it's going to go the other way. That Keeper Chance will bring Y Love over to Chapter 626."

Showboater topped off the wineglasses. "You know, if 626 managed to recruit Keeper Chance and Y Love, you'd be legendary. The greatest head of a chapter the league has ever seen."

Chaos held up his glass in a toast. "To young love."

CHAPTER 6

KEEPER and Toby made their way out of the alley and down the main street, filled with knickknack shops and cafés. All closed, lights off, waiting for a new day to begin.

"I'm really glad you decided to join," Toby said. "It was a no-brainer for me. Chances of finding a college where I wouldn't get emotionally scarred for life were nil. Plus, my grades are atrocious. I miss a lot of classes because I'm locked in a locker or janitorial closet. Once the girls' bathroom. You wouldn't believe what they talk about in there.

"I've been studying E.V.I.L. and Chapter 626 for over a year now. I found them when I was home from school for a week with an eye infection due to toilet water splashing up during a swirlie. To keep my spirits up, my mom kept sending me funny memes, reels, and videos that would pop up on her social account. I started noticing the same people passing through the background in many of them.

"Did you know Chaos was recruited when he was our age? Not all villains join just out of high school, so we have that in common with him. This is going to be great. Am I talking a lot? I'm really nervous."

Keeper stopped walking at the next intersection. "No. You're fine," he said. "I need to cross here. I'll see you tomorrow at Myers Industries."

"You're not going that way, are you?" Toby was staring into the darkness across the street, a death grip on his lunch bag.

"Yeah. My nana's house is in Peachmont."

"You don't want to go that way." Toby sniffed the air. "There's trouble."

Keeper followed Toby's gaze down the dark streets leading out of the historic district. He couldn't see or hear anything.

"You should come with me. My mom is picking me up outside of the Natural History Museum. I told her there was some sort of Night at the Museum thing going on. We can give you a ride home."

Keeper decided to trust the knot in his stomach and Toby's instincts. "Are you sure your mom won't mind? I don't want to get you in trouble."

Toby tugged at Keeper's shirtsleeve, pulling him down the lit main street. "Seriously? My mom will be more than happy to drive you home. She's a full-on-mom mom. Come on. We just need to arrive before she does. I don't want her knowing I wasn't at the museum and worrying about me."

Keeper forced himself to stop staring into the darkness, looking for the trouble Toby sensed. "You're a good son, Toby."

Toby smiled. "Thanks, Keeper."

They continued walking toward the museum and arts district that bordered the historic district. "What's your mom like?" Toby asked.

"I don't have a mom. My parents died when I was a baby. My nana raised me. She's a walking, talking hobgoblin."

Toby quickened the pace. He had his lunch bag clamped tight to his chest, and he looked pale even under the yellow streetlamps.

"It's following us," Toby said. "The trouble."

"Maybe it's not trouble," Keeper said. "Maybe it's just an evil villain following us."

Toby bit his lip. "No. E.V.I.L. evil villains don't smell like trouble. Not like this. You know, Keeper, I thought if I became an evil villain, I wouldn't ever have to worry about trouble again. I mean, if you are the trouble, you don't have to worry about it, right?"

"Makes sense to me. Don't worry. There are two of us, and we're almost on Fulton Row. I can see the light increasing ahead."

Keeper and Toby practically ran down Fulton, past statues

and strips of gardens, the Science Exploration Center, and a government building until they were standing in front of the Natural History Museum's entrance. Keeper's heart was pounding in his chest. He looked around the museum's grounds, trying to see past the ring of lights.

"It's getting closer," Toby whispered.

Keeper wanted to tell Toby not to freak out, but it would have been totally hypocritical. Headlights made their way down Fulton, and a red Kia Sorento pulled to the curb in front of Keeper and Toby. Toby opened the passenger-side door and jumped in. Keeper followed, hopping into the back seat, locking his door behind him.

The woman in the driver's seat was wearing sweatpants and a nightshirt that said NEED MORE COFFEE with a sloth holding a mug.

"Hi, Jelly Bean," Toby's mom said to him. "Did you have a good time?" She looked at Keeper in the back seat. "Did you make a friend?"

"Yeah. This is Keeper, Mom." Toby glanced nervously out his window. "He was going to walk home, but I didn't think it was safe. Can we give him a ride?"

"Of course. That's some smart thinking." Toby's mom pulled away from the curb and looked at Keeper through the rearview mirror. "Where do you live, honey?"

Keeper tightened the grip on his lunch bag. "Willow Street in Peachmont."

"I know exactly where that is," Toby's mom said, making her way around the block. "It's not too far from here. Are you a big history buff too, Keeper?"

"Yes, ma'am."

"And aren't you adorable. The kind of hair girls go crazy for. I bet the girls just love you."

Keeper was rethinking walking home.

"Mom! Stop! You're embarrassing him." Toby turned to face Keeper. "Get your phone out. I'll give you my number."

Keeper swallowed. "I don't have a phone."

Toby looked horrified. "Oh. Okay. No worries." He turned forward and rummaged through the glove compartment. He took out a pen and paper. "I'll write down my number for you."

Toby handed Keeper the piece of paper as the Kia came to a stop in front of Nana's house. Keeper took it and climbed out of the car. He waved goodbye, watched the car disappear, and read the message.

> I'll pick you up in the Kia, at the corner of Willow and Maple, at midnight.

Keeper and Toby had escaped the trouble, but Y had not. She stayed in the shadows, outside the museum's circle of light, and waited for the trouble to show itself. She wasn't sure if the trouble knew she was there, but she suspected the trouble would look for her. If she wanted to escape, she would have to be patient, quiet, and careful about her every move. She concentrated on slowing down her breathing, controlling her emotions, focusing on the museum, and then . . . it came into the light.

Sensei Love's eyes searched the perimeter. He ran a hand over the top of his bald head.

Y waited for her father's gaze to pass her before she began making her way in the opposite direction. She broke into a run, moving as silently as possible through the grass, toward the side of the museum. There were a number of alleys running around the building that Y could hopefully use to escape.

"Y?" Sensei Love's voice floated across the still night air like an annoyed hiss.

Y ignored it. She made it to the museum, jumped onto an abstract metal sculpture, and pulled herself up to a stone ledge that bordered the second-floor windows. The museum's security lights were mounted underneath the ledge, and Y quickly made her way along the top, careful to not set them off. She took the corner of the building and hung at arm's length from the ledge, dropping into the museum's back lot. It was used mostly for loading, unloading, and trash removal. A motion sensor caught Y landing on the pavement and turned on. It turned off just as fast. Hopefully her father hadn't seen the burst of light.

She moved behind two large green dumpsters and noticed a partially hidden manhole cover under one of them. There was enough exposed for her to fit through, but her father would have to move the dumpster if he chose to follow.

Y grabbed a piece of broken rebar from a pile of debris and used it to pry the manhole cover up. She placed the rebar as far under the dumpster as she could and climbed down into the sewer, moving the cover back into place.

Y descended the rusted metal ladder, almost slipping in the slime and muck at the bottom. The smell was unbearable but not as unbearable as being subjected to another one of Sensei Love's "you need to do better" lectures.

She used the light on her phone to illuminate the concrete tunnel. She would follow it back, under the museum, and find an exit through another manhole cover on the other side.

"Stupid sewer tunnel. Stupid mission. Stupid shoes are probably ruined. Keeper Chance and his stupid rockstar hair. Why does he have to be so stupidly wonderful? Now I have to come up with a stupid lie about where I was. Stupid. Stupid. Stupid."

Y continued slipping and sliding through the sewer, taking a couple of turns so she could continue north, until she found an exit. She pulled herself up, through a manhole, brushed herself off, and took a moment to get her bearings before jogging back toward the theater district, where she had left her ride.

Keeper had emerged from the meeting with a bag in hand. Dollars to doughnuts, he was going to meet up with Chaos again in less than twenty-four hours, and Y had no intention of missing it. She was going to do whatever she could to help

Keeper get into 626 and keep him, and her, out of the dojo.

Y began to forge a lie that would appease her father and keep his guard down. Once the sun set, she would need to be outside Keeper's house, watching, ready to follow. One way or another, she would finally get Keeper Chance's attention.

CHAPTER 7

KEEPER stood at the corner of Willow and Maple, watching for a red Kia. He wore the same outfit as the previous night, lunch bag in hand.

At exactly midnight, the car appeared and rolled to a stop in front of him. Keeper opened the passenger door and slid in. Toby looked ecstatic to see him. Keeper was certain that if Toby had a tail, it would be wagging.

"Thanks for the ride," Keeper said.

Toby put the car into gear. "No problem. I was worried you might have a hobgoblin issue as a result of last night. Although I suspect it wasn't the first time you've snuck out."

Keeper clicked his seat belt into place. "No, it's not. But it feels like something has changed. Nana knows, or suspects something.

Shouldn't be an issue tonight. When she wasn't looking, I kept refilling her wineglass. Two glasses and she's out like a light."

Toby pulled away from the curb and headed toward a small industrial area near the airport that contained warehouses used for everything from moving companies to granite slabs to distribution centers. "What's in your bag?" he asked.

Keeper opened the lunch bag on his lap and looked inside. "Night-vision goggles, wire cutters, a pair of gloves, and Reese's Peanut Butter Cups."

"Sweet! I got an iPad, a screwdriver, petroleum jelly, gloves, and a Kit Kat. Want to swap the Kit Kat for the Reese's?"

Keeper looked over at Toby. "Are you insane?"

"How about sharing?"

Keeper let out a sigh. "Maybe. What kind of screwdriver? Philips or flathead?"

"Flathead."

"Nice."

"Oh!" Toby reached behind Keeper's seat and produced another lunch bag. It was green and had dinosaurs on it. "This is for you. From my mom. She says you're too skinny and need to eat more."

Keeper opened the bag. A grilled cheese, wrapped in aluminum foil, still warm, a brownie with chocolate frosting and dinosaur sprinkles, a small snack bag of carrot sticks, and a juice box.

"Don't worry about the carrots," Toby said. "I'll feed them to my neighbor's dog for you."

Keeper dug into the sandwich. Toby could have the peanut butter cups. Keeper had never had a homemade brownie before. Actually, that wasn't entirely accurate. Nana had made so-called brownies when he was eight. She used carob instead of chocolate and prunes instead of sugar because sugar will rot your teeth. It was an incredibly traumatic moment in Keeper's youth. It wasn't until five years later he learned what a real brownie was and that he had been totally hoodwinked.

They arrived at the Myers warehouse fifteen minutes early. Toby backed the Kia into a dark corner of the lot, and they left the doors unlocked. Just in case a hasty exit was needed.

"I did a little research this afternoon," Toby said as they walked to the meeting spot. "There are two exits to the parking area. If there's a problem, we'll take the one we parked near and hope for the best. It's partially dirt, and there is a chain-link fence lining it. Hopefully no gate. It exits to a service road for the airport."

"What's the deal with this warehouse?" Keeper asked.

"Mostly serves as a local and citywide distribution center. Everything is done by truck. Offices are on the other side."

Keeper and Toby waited for the three senior members of 626 under a tree, away from the security lights. At exactly 1:00 a.m. Toby swatted at a moth that was attacking him but missed and slapped Keeper. Keeper instinctively slapped Toby back. Toby let out an impressive burp that, in the nighttime silence, echoed off the cement building. Keeper was overcome with a combination of awe, respect, and horror. Toby burst out into a laugh that sounded more like a hound on the hunt. Chaos emerged from the darkness, followed by Slasher and Showboater.

"Ready?" Chaos asked.

"Yes, sir," Toby and Keeper said, trying to choke down the last of their laughter.

"Open your bags and put on your gloves. Take any other items in the bag and place them in your pockets. The candy is optional. It's just in case you're hungry."

Keeper placed the goggles on top of his head and everything else in his pockets. Toby did the same but kept the iPad out and ate his Kit Kat. They handed their lunch bags to Slasher.

"As an evil villain, you will find you need things," Chaos said. "Things you don't have the financial bearings to afford. That will leave you with two choices: steal the finances or steal the item." Chaos began to slowly pace back and forth in front of Keeper and Toby. "In this case, we—and by *we*, I mean you two—are going to steal the item. In order for us to have an E.V.I.L. initiation ceremony, we need cookies, and not just any cookies—good cookies.

"By unanimous vote, it has been decided that Chapter 626 would like Cookie Maven cookies."

"Ah, Cookie Maven," Showboater declared with an air of theatrical drama. "Smells like heaven, line out the door and down the street. Once I sent Frog in to hop-skip the line. He came out with oatmeal raisin. Oatmeal raisin!"

Keeper and Toby stared at Showboater. He was waving his arms in outrage, and glitter was flying everywhere.

"Is there a point to this story?" Slasher asked.

"As a matter of fact, there are two," Showboater said, trying to regain his composure. "One, never send a sidekick in to do a villain's work. And two, don't come back with oatmeal raisin! We said *good* cookies."

Keeper raised his hand. Chaos groaned. "Keeper. You have a question?"

Keeper put his hand back down. "Yes, sir. Why are we at a warehouse if you want Cookie Maven cookies? Shouldn't we be at the store?"

"Actually, that's a good question for a new villain," Chaos said. "Nothing is ever as simple as it seems. If you don't want to waste your time or get caught, research things first. In this case, our research has shown that the number of cookies in the shop at the end of the day is limited. Not nearly enough for an event as important as an E.V.I.L. initiation. However, we also discovered that a number of corporations within the city limits receive weekly shipments distributed from this warehouse.

"Your job is to break into the warehouse and return here,

undetected, with a crate of Cookie Maven cookies. I stress the undetected part. You two aren't evil villains yet, and if you're caught, the only ones who can bail you out are your mom and nana."

A sense of dread washed over Keeper. The idea of calling his nana to bail him out was less than ideal.

Toby leaned in toward Keeper. "Don't worry. My mom would bail us both out," he whispered.

Keeper smiled. Toby could definitely have his peanut butter cups. "Thanks, Toby."

"All right, then," Chaos said. "Off you go. We'll be waiting for you here. Unless security or the police show up. In that case, we'll be long gone."

Keeper and Toby made their way around the perimeter, making sure to stay away from the lights illuminating the cargo bays. Toby woke up the iPad and dimmed the screen down as much as he could.

"Our first issues are where to enter and what kind of security they have," Keeper said. "I think there is a door next to the cargo bay at the end."

Toby tapped the pad a few times. "I've already checked out the preinstalled apps. There's one showing the camera feeds for the warehouse. All the bays have cameras on them, although some are distant shots. The door has a camera on it as well. It looked to be taking a picture from the right."

"What about inside?" Keeper asked.

"I suspect there is an alarm. The door has a glass window, and I could see the reflection of a little light inside. Keypad, maybe?"

"If it's an older keypad system, I can use the wire cutters to cut the callout line and then disable it before it goes off or tries for cellular. That being said, once the central station notices there is a callout issue, they'll alert the owners and possibly the police."

"How long will we have?"

Keeper shrugged. "Ten minutes to three hours? It's all about when and how often the warehouse system checks in. I'm not an expert on this. I found an old security keypad in an electronic store's recycling once. I took it apart and did some research on how they work."

Toby was staring at Keeper. "Why would you do that?"

Keeper shrugged. He was starting to feel awkward. "I don't know. I was curious."

"Wooooow. You're like some sort of genius, aren't you? You're like Tony Stark, but evil."

Now Keeper was really feeling awkward. "I'm not a genius. I just like making things, and to do that I need to know how other things are made."

"Uh-huh. Uh-huh. I like to play video games in my free time," Toby said.

"Nana says video games poison your mind and make you fat and lazy."

Toby nodded. "I'm starting to see why you go through people's garbage for fun."

"I'd like to play a video game."

"I'll make that happen, but first we need to finish this cookie heist."

Keeper looked at the iPad's screen. "There are no cameras on the other side of the building." He pointed to one of the camera feed squares. "If we blur out the camera for the door with your petroleum jelly, we just have to get the door open, and I'll disable the alarm."

"Door isn't a problem," Toby said. "I can do it with the screwdriver. At least I think I can. I watched some videos on YouTube when I saw the screwdriver in my bag. If that doesn't work, I brought my lockpicks."

"You have lockpicks?"

"I told you, I've been looking into a life of villainy for a year now. Picking locks seemed like something a villain would need to know how to do."

Keeper and Toby jogged past the end of the warehouse, staying in the shadows, then doubled back to the side of the building with no cameras. There was a light on the corner that couldn't be avoided, but if no one was around and they stayed tight to the building, it shouldn't matter. Keeper knelt down, and Toby climbed onto his shoulders.

"Remember," Toby said. "Lift with your legs, not your back."

Not a problem since Keeper's vertebrae felt like they were

fusing together under the strain. Toby was a lot heavier than he looked.

Toby reached from underneath and put an enormous glob of petroleum jelly on the lens, and Keeper brought him down again.

"Just use your picks," Keeper said, cracking his back. "Let's get this over with."

Toby inserted his tools into the lock and swung the door open. Keeper went straight to the keypad. The light was green.

"Um, Toby? I'm pretty sure this light should be red if the alarm is on."

"Yeah," Toby said. "And I'm pretty sure that door was unlocked. I'm not that good. I've been practicing, but it usually takes me a couple of tries."

"I have a bad feeling about this. Do you think Chaos set us up?"

Toby shook his head. "No. It's an E.V.I.L. rule that villains don't go after other villains in E.V.I.L. I would think that would apply to us, as well."

The warehouse lights were on low. No need for the night-vision goggles. "Let's find these cookies and get out of here," Keeper said, heading into the maze of crates and boxes. "Cookie boxes shouldn't be very large. They're perishable and more than likely they come in and go out same day or next day. Let's start looking next to the loading bays and work our way inward."

Keeper and Toby had made it through two of the four bays

when they came around a pallet, piled sky-high with boxes of printer paper, and Keeper slammed into a figure dressed all in black. Black tights, black sneakers, black cap with red strands of curls escaping, a black neck gaiter, hazel eyes, and a black fitted shirt that made it apparent the figure was female. The figure lowered her gaiter, and Keeper could now see her perfectly beautiful mouth.

"What the barf?" Y said. "If you can't see in the dark, put those night-vision goggles on."

Keeper took a step back and tried to regain his composure. "They can't see around corners. Who are you, and why are you even here?"

"YinYang, but I go by Y. I'm doing some warehouse shopping. What's your story?"

"I'm Keeper. This is Toby. We're stealing cookies. Are you an E.V.I.L. villain?"

"No. Are you?"

Keeper was feeling more uncomfortable by the minute. "No. Not yet. We need cookies first."

Y seemed to soften. Her body was less tense, her mouth softer.

"Oh." Her eyes dropped to Keeper's feet and slowly made their way up to the goggles tangled in the waves of his hair. "Cookie Maven cookies? They're near loading bay six. I can show you." She turned on her heel and began making her way down the aisle.

"Dude," Toby whispered to Keeper. "She just totally checked you out."

"That's crazy," Keeper said. "She's a girl. Girls don't do that type of thing. Do they?"

Toby shrugged. "This one did."

CHAPTER 8

KEEPER and Toby followed after Y. Keeper judged her to be around five foot eight. She had long athletic legs, and she walked through the warehouse with confidence and ease. She didn't seem to be in a hurry or have any concerns about getting caught.

Y stopped near a stack of medium-size boxes and pointed to the one on top. "This is the only Cookie Maven box I've seen so far. Is one enough? There are some other snacks. I think the one on the bottom is biscotti."

"This one box should be fine. Thank you." Keeper went to move the box to see how heavy it was when Y's hand shot out and pushed back on his chest. Keeper would have been concerned that she could feel his heart racing, but he was pretty sure his heart had moved up into his throat.

"You owe me," Y said. Her eyes darkened, and her mouth had a hint of a smile.

"For what?" Keeper said.

"Who do you think turned the alarm off? Who unlocked the door and turned the lights on? Who just showed you where to find cookies?" Y moved into Keeper's space.

Keeper tried to stand up taller, but she was practically pressed against him, looking up. Keeper opened his mouth to say something when her hand grabbed hold of the top of the peanut butter cup wrapper and pulled the package from his front pocket.

Now Y was smiling, and her mouth was inches from Keeper's. "Thanks." She stepped back, turned around, and walked away to continue her shopping. "Make sure you close the door on your way out. I'll take care of the lights and security."

Keeper waited until Y was out of sight before he relaxed and remembered to breathe.

"Holy smokes," Toby said.

"Sorry about the peanut butter cups," Keeper said. "I was going to give them to you."

Toby nodded. "Maybe you should go find her and get them back."

Keeper looked at Toby as if he had sprouted a second head. "Are you bananas? That girl is totally unhinged."

Toby burst out into his hound dog laugh. Keeper couldn't help but smile.

"Let's just grab this box of cookies and get out of here before she returns," Keeper said. He lifted the box off the stack. "What the fudge? This is freakin' heavy. Who knew cookies weighed so much?"

"They must use real butter," Toby said, sniffing the box. "Doesn't smell like cookies. I can only smell paper."

"Judging from the weight, they probably had to use heavy-duty cardboard for this box." Keeper started walking in the direction Y had gone.

"Keeper," Toby said. "Exit is this way."

"Seriously?" Keeper asked, looking back at Toby. "I have a terrible sense of direction. You lead. I'll carry the box."

Within ten minutes Keeper and Toby had exited the warehouse and returned to the meeting point with the cookies. Keeper placed the box down in the grass and wiped the sweat from his forehead onto his T-shirt sleeve. Chaos, Slasher, and Showboater came out of the shadows and inspected the box.

"There was only one box," Keeper said. "Hopefully they aren't oatmeal raisin."

Showboater took a box cutter out of his sequined pants pocket. "Only one way to find out." He sliced through the tape and opened the box. "What the bat guano is this? We can't eat this."

The box was filled to the brim with money. Tens and twenties all neatly stacked without an inch to spare.

Chaos took out a penlight and inspected the label on the side of the box. "It says Cookie Maven cookies. Chocolate toffee coffee chip."

Showboater fell to his knees and looked up to the heavens. "Whhhhhy? Those are my favorite, and now all we have is this worthless box of money. It's like the gods hate me."

Chaos was frowning and staring at the box. "The way I see it, we have two problems. One, how are we going to get our cookies? And two, I have an insatiable need to know where this box of money is going. Why would Cookie Maven be shipping a box of money?"

Keeper half raised his hand.

Chaos pinched the bridge of his nose with his fingers. "For the love of . . . stop raising your hand, Keeper. What's your question?"

"Why don't we just use the money in the box to buy cookies directly from Cookie Maven? Put in an order."

"Because a box of money, labeled as cookies, is trouble. Big trouble," Chaos said. "Someone is going to be seriously cheesed off if they don't get their delivery. And then that person will come looking for it. We—and by *we*, I mean you two," Chaos said, looking at Keeper and Toby, "need to put the box back." He sighed. "I wish we had a tracking device. Currently, the only delivery info on the box is in the form of a barcode."

Keeper started to raise his hand, then lowered it. "Um, sir, I have a tracking device."

Chaos raised an eyebrow.

"It's nothing fancy." Keeper reached into his pocket and pulled out what looked like the felt pads that go on the bottom of furniture feet. "The chip is inside. It's based on pet GPS ID tags. Technology is a bit vintage, but I use it to keep Nana from sneaking up on me. I have an app on my computer at home that lets me know when the chip is within a hundred feet. I can put the app on Toby's cell phone."

Chaos smiled.

"I can probably hack into Myers's delivery schedule," Toby said. "Find out where they are going tomorrow. Keeper and I can borrow my mom's car and see if we can pick up the tracker along a delivery route."

Chaos was still smiling. Slasher was not.

"Chaos," Slasher said, motioning for him. "A word in private with you and Showboater."

Chaos, Slasher, and Showboater walked about five yards away and huddled together. Slasher lowered his voice. "I think we should put the box back and forget about it. I also think Keeper Chance is trouble. If anyone else went in for this box of cookies, it would be filled with cookies."

"Are you suggesting Keeper turned the cookies into money?" Chaos asked. "That would be a phenomenal skill."

"I'm serious, Chaos. You yourself said that the kid's skill might be finding things. This isn't a good find."

"I like him," Showboater said. "I find Keeper oddly innocent and endearing. I'm not saying the money *is* his fault, but we have all had mishaps with our skills. I think Keeper Chance deserves . . . well, a chance. I like the Toby boy too. Reminds me of a puppy."

"When the Ghost was head of 626, he always said, *Don't let fear and the unknown guide you. Follow your heart*," Chaos said. "My heart doesn't think finding things is Keeper's skill."

Slasher went quiet for a moment. "The Ghost was a great man. I miss him."

Chaos placed his hand on Slasher's shoulder. "As do we all."

"Okay," Slasher said. "Let's see what Keeper Chance can do. Did anyone bring tape?"

"I have some duct tape in the car for emergencies," Showboater said.

Chaos and Slasher returned to Keeper and Toby while Showboater strutted off to retrieve the tape. When he returned, they put one of the felt pad trackers inside the box, closed it, and resealed it. Keeper lifted it up off the ground.

"Put the box back exactly where you found it," Chaos said, "then go home. Do your best to track the box tomorrow. Toby, I sent a text to your phone so you can keep in contact. The text came from Eddie Farlow. Slasher, Showboater, and I will work on the cookie disaster."

Keeper and Toby made their way through the parking lot to the warehouse's door. Keeper was torn between hoping the girl was still there and hoping she was gone. If she was still there, the alarms would be off and it would be easy to return the box, assuming they didn't run into her again. If she was gone, they were going to have to try to dismantle the security system, and the way things were going, Keeper was feeling less and less confident about everything he was doing.

"You know they were talking about you," Toby said to Keeper.

Keeper glanced at Toby. "Good or bad?"

Toby shrugged. "They aren't sure what your skill is. I think Slasher is worried it's finding trouble."

Keeper smiled. "As much fun as that would be, I don't think that's my skill."

Toby tried the warehouse door's handle. Still unlocked. The lights were dim inside, and the security pad was green.

"Y's still here," Keeper said. "Must be some shopping trip."

"You know girls," Toby said.

Keeper followed Toby down an aisle, toward the far loading bay. "Not really. Nana's worn the same outfit for as long as I can remember. I suspect her underwear is older than me."

Toby stopped at the box's return location and turned toward Keeper. "Not to overstep any boundaries, but it sounds like your childhood was a bit traumatic."

"A valid observation," Keeper said, placing the box back in its spot. "Speaking of traumatic experiences, let's try to avoid running into Y again. This night has been long enough."

Toby's eyes were wide and unblinking. He did a couple of slight jerks to the right with his head.

Keeper felt every muscle in his body tense, and he used all his willpower to not break out into a cold sweat. He turned and came face-to-face with Y. She was finishing the last of Keeper's peanut butter cups with one hand. The other hand was on her hip.

"That's hurtful," Y said. "What's the matter? Out of candy? I'm sure we can figure out another form of payment."

"There is nothing to pay you for. We're just returning this box and leaving." Keeper did his best to keep his voice level. "Happy shopping."

Y stared at Keeper for a few seconds, ratcheting up the feeling of awkwardness. "Why are you returning the box?"

This wasn't going well. "No real reason," Keeper said. "Not my favorite flavor."

Y kept staring at Keeper. "Okay. I'll take them. I love cookies."

"No!" Keeper watched Y freeze, except for her mouth. Her mouth was breaking out into a full-on smile.

Keeper closed his eyes, tilted his head back slightly, and took a deep breath, hoping for a moment of zen. Or at least hoping that when he opened his eyes, it would all be a bad dream and Y would be gone. No such luck.

"The box is filled with money," Keeper said.

Y's eyebrows raised. "Money? Isn't that better than a box of cookies?"

"No," Keeper said. "It's not. It's trouble. Especially for Cookie Maven if this box doesn't get to its destination. And I think we can all agree that the end of Cookie Maven cookies would be a disaster of epic proportions."

Y's mouth dropped open, her eyes never leaving Keeper's. "No way. You put a tracking device in the box."

"What? *Psht.* No. Why would we do that?"

"I don't know," Y said. "You tell me."

"You don't need to know," Toby blurted out. "It's E.V.I.L. business."

Y's attention left Keeper and turned toward Toby. She took a couple of steps toward him. Toby took a couple of steps backward, away from her.

"Toby, right?" Y said.

"Y-yes, ma'am." Toby swallowed. "Please don't hurt me."

Y studied Toby. Her eyes switched to Keeper. Then back to Toby. Then she turned and walked away in the opposite direction. "Good luck with E.V.I.L.," she said. "Enjoy the rest of your night, boys."

Keeper and Toby watched Y until she disappeared around a corner. They waited a few seconds to be sure she wasn't returning.

"Do you think she's going to take the box of money?" Toby asked Keeper.

Keeper shrugged. "I don't know. But if she does, we can try to track down her lair. That might be fun."

Smiles grew on Keeper's and Toby's faces. Full-on evil smiles.

CHAPTER 9

IT was early afternoon when Y rode her red Vespa Primavera scooter down Willow Street, counting off house numbers and trying to make sense of why E.V.I.L. villains would not take a box of money, much less why would they track it. For her entire life, her father had told her that E.V.I.L. villains were lazy, cruel, and ruthless, lacking a moral code and compassion. They were tricksters and opportunists and undisciplined. And they were all ticking time bombs to become something even worse.

None of those words described Keeper Chance. At least Y didn't think they did. For that matter, Toby also didn't seem to fit the mold. Chaos might be undisciplined and a bit of a trickster, but she had yet to see him actually hurt anyone, and Y was 99 percent certain Chaos would put his life on the line for Keeper or any member of his chapter.

She brought her scooter to a stop in front of the two-story clapboard house that read 7989. Y removed her open-faced helmet, hung it on the scooter's handlebars, and stared at the vintage home, trying to imagine Keeper Chance living there. The lawn was neatly trimmed, and flower beds lined the stairs up to the covered porch. She knew Keeper lived with his grandmother, but she didn't know much more about him than that. Y envisioned homecooked meals of roast chicken and mashed potatoes followed by nightly games of Scrabble and Parcheesi.

She swung her leg over the seat, rolled the scooter onto its center stand, and made her way up the stairs to the front door. Y straightened her skirt and smoothed out her T-shirt in hopes of making a good first impression. She tucked a stray strand of hair behind her ear and knocked on the door. Nana opened it.

Nana was about five five on a good day, slender and perfectly put together. She wore a matching blue skirt and jacket that was probably from the 1950s but looked brand-new. Her blouse was white and crisp and neatly ironed. Her Mary Jane heels were the only thing showing their age despite being polished and still fashionable. Nana's light gray hair was thick and pulled back into a loose French braid. Two perfect strands curled down from her bangs to frame her face.

Y smiled. "Hi. Is Keeper here? You must be his grandmother."

Nana's eyes narrowed slightly, judging Y. "And you must be a colossal disappointment to your parents."

All the vintage beauty seemed to melt off the woman and spread like black muck around Y's feet.

"Are you? Do you always dress that way?" Nana said. "Does your mother know you go out in public looking like this?"

Y's feet seemed to be stuck in the muck. She opened her mouth to say something, but there were no words. Nana had them all.

"Do you honestly think you have a chance with my grandson? Do you? Do you? Do you? How dare you poison my doorstep."

Y's eyes were wide and unblinking.

"Your skirt is too short. Your shirt is too tight. Your shoes are inappropriate."

Y involuntarily looked down at her outfit. She had worn capri tights under her skirt. Her T-shirt had a giant cartoon bumblebee on it. And Y had saved all her chore money to buy the Vans on her feet. Her mother had been horrified at the footwear choice. Cripes, had she been right?

Keeper barged through the doorway, knocking Nana out of the way with his shoulder. He grabbed Y by the arm and dragged her down the stairs back to her Vespa. Nana stood her ground, watching.

Keeper released Y's arm and shoved his hands into his jean's pockets. "What are you doing here?" he asked in a low voice.

Y looked at Keeper, then at Nana glaring at them, and then back at Keeper. "Holy horse apples!"

"Y . . ."

She dropped her voice to a whisper. "No. I mean H-O-L-Y horse apples! You live with that?"

"You have to think of it like a chess match. You just entered unprepared to play the game. You shouldn't be here at all. Why are you here, Y?"

Y looked past Keeper at Nana again. Nana's mouth had practically disappeared, and every muscle in her face was tense. Then the worst of the worst happened. Nana silently mouthed the word *Love*. She knew who Y was. Unrelenting misery was going to rain down on Keeper, and it was all Y's fault.

"Um, no reason." Y's mind was racing. She had to do something. "I have to go."

"What? I . . ." Keeper was only partially confused. Y wasn't the first person Nana had run off, but she was the first girl. He desperately wanted to know what Y was doing at his house.

Y already had her helmet on and the Vespa running. She took off, doing a tight U-turn in the middle of the street. Y made a mental note that when her dad finally disowned her and took his Vespa back, she would get something faster.

Keeper watched Y tear down the road. He took a deep breath and slowly turned toward the house and Nana, hands still in his pockets.

"Wash my car," Nana said. "*Inside* and out. And stop

slouching. Stand up straight. No wonder you have no friends."

The front door slammed shut, and Y's words echoed in Keeper's head, *holy horse apples*. They almost drowned out Nana's voice coming from behind the closed door.

"I'm watching you."

Keeper was hosing the last of the soap off Nana's Caddy when Toby pulled up in his mom's Kia. He parked on the opposite side of the street and bounded across the road, out of breath.

"Hey," Toby said, panting. "Y just came to my house and said you needed rescuing ASAP. She said it was a 911 type of situation. No real details, but I'm guessing it has to do with nana-hobgoblin. I thought, since it's spring break, you might want to come do an extended sleepover at my place."

"Y was at your house?"

Toby wiped some sweat from his forehead. "Yeah. It was awful. My mom got super excited that a girl came to see me. Totally embarrassing. Offered her chocolate milk and cupcakes and then started grilling her. Where did you meet my Jelly Bean? How long have you two known each other? Do you like Star Wars? What wizarding house are you in? Toby's a Hufflepuff." He shook his head, his eyes wide with the horror of the memory. "It was essentially like one of those dreams where you show up to school naked."

Keeper looked at Toby in disbelief. "Whoa. You're a Hufflepuff?"

Toby held his arms out to the side, palms up. "Dude. Look at me."

"Nothing wrong with Hufflepuffs. Loyalty and compassion are hard to come by."

"Thanks, Keeper. I appreciate that. They also have the badger."

Keeper nodded. "Badgers are cool."

Keeper and Toby both looked at Keeper's house. Nana's figure pulled away from a window and disappeared.

"We need a plan," Keeper said. "What are your strengths?"

"Hearing and sense of smell, and I could probably fear tinkle if I really had to."

Keeper threw the hose nozzle he'd been holding onto the road verge. "That's it? Hearing and smelling are the last two things you want amplified around Nana. We're doomed."

"When I'm really nervous I can ramble on and on and on about total nonsense," Toby said.

"That might work. Come on. You talk nonstop to Nana while I run upstairs and get my stuff. Don't let her get a word in or you're done for."

Toby trotted after Keeper. "Wait, wait, wait. I need a subject. I can't go in cold turkey." Toby's eyes were scanning the house as if it had been moved to Peachmont from Amityville. "Something I can get really heated about."

Keeper looked at Toby. What would Toby get heated up about? "Have you tried that new no-meat meat sandwich at the SubHub?"

Toby rolled his eyes. "Please. Don't get me started!"

"Too late," Keeper said, opening the front door. "You can tell Nana all about it."

Keeper and Toby stepped into the house. The stairs were on Keeper's left, and Nana was standing in the living room to the right. She was balancing a cup of tea on a saucer. She looked ready to destroy someone's will to live.

"Hey, Nana." Keeper spoke in rapid fire. "This is my friend. I'm going to sleep over at his house tonight, maybe more since it's spring break. Okay? Great. He'll tell you all about how we met at SubHub while I get my stuff." Keeper gave Toby a slight shove toward Nana, signaling it was go-time.

"Hi, Mrs. Keeper's Nana lady. I've heard a lot about you, and I'm thinking you can't really be that horrible."

Nana took it as a compliment. A thin smile grew on her face.

"I mean not horrible as in hobgoblin horrible. You're not a hobgoblin. I don't know why I said that. Hobgoblin hahaha. I meant horrible as in a horrible cook. You know like that no-meat meat sandwich at SubHub. No one could cook anything that bad. It was like eating boiled bacon without the bacon taste. All gelatinous . . ."

Keeper was already halfway up the stairs and racing to his room. He grabbed his severely worn school backpack off the back of his desk's chair and started collecting clothes off the floor. Favorite T-shirt, his only other pair of pants, socks and underwear, dirty or clean. He could deal with that later. He looked around in a panic at the stacks of books. Most of them were town library books that he hadn't "officially" checked out, since they had a three-book limit. He couldn't take them all with him, and returning them was going to have to wait until after spring break. A code red situation was about to go down in the living room between Toby and Nana. He took a book on chemical compounds and one on sound waves.

"Sometimes I put peppers on my sub, but in general I try to stay away from green things. Seems unnatural. Except for banana peppers. I like them. Not that they are green-green, more a yellow-green, but they start green . . ." Toby's voice carried up the stairs. Keeper needed to abandon the idea of retrieving any bathroom items. Even Toby couldn't ramble on forever.

He zipped the bag closed, slung it over one shoulder, and tucked an ancient laptop under his other arm. Hopefully Toby had an extra toothbrush.

Keeper flew down the stairs, two at a time. He grabbed hold of Toby's upper arm and sprinted for the door. "Okay, we're off, Nana. See you later. Bye."

The front door slammed shut behind Keeper and Toby. Nana walked to the front window and watched the two boys sprint to the Kia, dive inside, and take off with skidding tires. She raised her teacup, took a sip, clanked the cup back down on the saucer, and swallowed. "Just like his father."

CHAPTER 10

KEEPER looked over his shoulder and watched the house he grew up in disappear from sight. He would pay dearly for taking a week's vacation from Nana. Keeper had no doubt she would spend the rest of the week plotting her hobgoblin revenge. In hopes of minimizing the damage, he would check in with Nana once he was sure she had calmed down . . . maybe. Right now he had a bigger problem to deal with.

Keeper shoved his backpack into the back seat, clicked his seat belt into place, and opened his laptop.

Toby tried not to stare at the ancient piece of equipment. "Dude, is that a Commodore 64?"

"I wish. It'd be worth a lot more," Keeper said. "Internally, I've done some decent upgrades. Screen is still garbage. As long as we're out and about, do you want to see if we can track down that box of money?"

"It's like you read my mind." Toby dug his cell phone out of a side pocket on his cargoes and handed it to Keeper. "You can hotspot. Phone's passcode is 112710. It should open to a list of delivery locations for us to check out. Most of the trucks going out today were big—eighteen-wheelers—but there was one smaller truck. Maybe the size of a package van. The smaller truck had a list of stops that were relatively close to the warehouse. I'm hoping that the box of cookie money wasn't meant to go far."

Keeper and Toby circled blocks and went down alleys, hoping to see something ping on Keeper's laptop. A couple of times Keeper had to get out of the car and walk through office buildings, riding the elevator up and down. After two hours the thrill of the chase was wearing off.

"Next location on your list is 43 Martingale Avenue," Keeper said, entering the address into the Kia's navigation system. "According to the list, the truck made a couple of other stops nearby."

"I think Martingale is in the new designer district," Toby said. "The one where all the stores have medieval names. My mom was thinking about renovating the kitchen last year. For a month she dragged me out to look at tiles and faucets and cabinets. It was brutal."

"Does the new kitchen look good?" Keeper asked.

"Never happened. My mom finally decided the whole process was too emotionally exhausting. I tried to assure her that eventually avocado green would come back in style."

Keeper nodded in understanding. "You're a good son, Toby."

"I try." Toby pulled the car up to the curb of a large, bowl-shaped building. "I think this is it. Getting anything?"

"Not yet. Let's circle."

Toby drove around the building. When they got near the back, a red dot pinged on Keeper's computer.

"I think we found the box," Keeper said.

"Seriously?" Toby sounded a bit panicked. "I didn't think we really would. What do we do now?"

Keeper shrugged. "Call Chaos?"

Toby pulled into 43 Martingale's little gravel lot and parked in a spot that said PORCELAIN PALACE CUSTOMER PARKING ONLY. ALL OTHERS WILL BE TOWED. Keeper handed Toby his phone and Toby called the number attached to Chaos's alias, Eddie Farlow.

"He's not answering," Toby said. "Now what?"

Keeper shrugged again. "We go inside?"

"You can't be serious. The person who owns this store is extorting money from someone who makes cookies. Cookies! Who knows what else this person is capable of?"

Keeper had already unbuckled his seat belt and opened his door. "No one knows that we know about the box of money. We'll just tell them our parents sent us in to get a brochure, and then we'll say we want to browse and do our best to snoop around."

Toby was jogging to keep up with Keeper. "Okay, but you do all the talking. I'm worried I'll start rambling and say something I shouldn't."

"No problem." Keeper pushed through the double doors and entered the showroom. His eyes glazed over, and his legs froze in shopper paralysis.

For as far as Keeper and Toby could see, the showroom was filled with various models of bathtubs, toilets, sinks, towel bars, and showerheads. In the center of the bathroom fiefdom, a golden toilet sat atop a fake mountain of gold, reigning supreme over all of the other more inadequate toilets. A sign was stuck into the mountain that read NO SITTING ON THRONE.

Keeper tried to scan the room, but his eyes kept returning to the golden spectacle.

"Welcome! Welcome!" A man stepped out from behind a faux wall, covered in peacock wallpaper that showcased the opulence of a Swarovski-crystal-adorned bathroom hardware and fixture set. The man was not nearly as glamorous as the fixtures. He had on maroon sweatpants with the knees permanently stretched out, as if from hours on end of sitting. His gray T-shirt had coffee stains, and the vest that covered it was frayed at the edges. The golden plunger he carried was shined to perfection. "Welcome to the Porcelain Palace," the man said. "What type of picture-perfect porcelain can I send you home with today? I carry products for bathrooms and kitchens."

After a moment of uncomfortable silence, Toby elbowed Keeper, signaling it was his turn to talk.

Keeper cleared his throat. "Um, yes. We need a new toilet."

"Delightful." The bedraggled man's eyes lit up with hopes of a sale. "Two fine young men like yourselves are probably interested in something modern and sleek. I have a whole section of minimalist toilets this way."

Keeper tried to wrap his head around what a minimalist toilet might be, while he also tried to figure out how to get away from the king of commodes. "Um, actually it's a gift. Maybe."

The golden plunger fell limp at the salesman's side. "A gift?"

"For my nana. Her birthday is coming up, and I want to get her something super special. Since her current toilet is circa 1950, I thought a new one would be a thoughtful surprise."

"1950?" the salesman asked. "Really? Is it pink?"

"Yellow."

The salesman was clearly impressed. "A collector's piece! Are you sure she'll want to replace it? We could always bedazzle it with a new handle or a magazine rack."

Keeper shrugged and began to slowly walk around the displays, as if browsing, heading toward the back of the building, where the tracking device had shown up. "That might be better, and far more affordable. It's just the bathroom is so dated, and Nana has been talking about moving into a retirement home. All the home improvement videos I watched online said how important bathrooms and kitchens are when you go to sell. I can't do much about the kitchen, but maybe she'd like a new showerhead. Are those easy to switch out?"

The salesman followed after Keeper and Toby. "I'm afraid I don't install. I only sell the pieces. However, if you aren't purchasing the matching knobs and body sprayers, you might be able to handle it on your own."

Keeper searched for security cameras and motion sensors. He was only half listening. "Body sprayers sound pretty exotic. Are they expensive?"

The salesman's eyes lit up enthusiastically. "Oh, yes! Very!"

They circled around a bathroom display that was made to look like it was out of the mid-1800s but with all the modern conveniences, to find a door with an EMPLOYEES ONLY sign leading to the backroom storage. There was a numbered keypad lock on it and a slender rectangular window. Keeper and Toby exchanged a quick glance.

"Would you mind showing the sprayers to me?" Keeper asked the salesman. "Maybe I can get my parents to chip in on the present."

"Of course," the salesman said, directing Keeper back toward the center of the showroom. Toby stayed behind, pretending to be interested in a wilderness-themed bathroom display.

Keeper continued firing question after question about shower systems and payment plans until he was certain that it was getting suspicious. He hoped Toby had had enough time to try the door or at least see through the window to get some sort of an idea about what nighttime security they would have to circumvent.

Keeper headed back to the front of the store with a selection of brochures in hand and the salesman on his heels. Toby was waiting by the front door, phone in hand, texting.

"Sorry it took so long," Keeper said to Toby. "Ready to go?"

Toby put his phone into his pants pocket. "Yup. Whenever you are."

The salesman held the front door open, calling after Keeper and Toby as they climbed into the Kia and peeled out of the parking lot. "Remember, the Porcelain Palace is open seven days a week, nine to five, for all your necessary needs! Or by appointment. Call or come by anytime!"

Sensei Love sat in his white sedan, parked across the street from the Porcelain Palace. He watched Keeper and Toby run out of the Palace, jump into the Kia, and leave the gravel parking lot. When Love was certain the boys weren't returning, he exited the sedan, crossed the street, and pushed through the Porcelain Palace's front doors.

"Welcome! Welc—oh, my sweet Grim Reaper . . ." The salesman was backing up, stumbling over displays, his hands up. "I didn't do anything. I swear! I swear!"

Sensei Love continued approaching the distressed

salesman. Love's posture was perfect, his gray eyes unblinking, and his footsteps silent. "Hello, Polyp."

The salesman's back was plastered against the fake mountain of gold, making it impossible to retreat any farther. A bead of sweat ran down the side of his face. "Polyp? *Psht.* Who's that? You have the wrong man. I'm not with E.V.I.L. Never even heard of it."

Sensei Love towered over Polyp, studying him. After the longest three seconds of Polyp's life, Love's body relaxed slightly. He stepped away, approached a display of novelty toilet paper, picked up a roll printed to look like money, and looked it over without interest. "Word on the street is that Chapter 403 kicked you out, Polyp."

Polyp righted himself and pulled back his rounded shoulders as best he could. He was feeling relatively certain he wasn't about to have all his teeth knocked out by Love, but only time would tell. It seemed Love wanted something. "I assure you it was a mutual kicking to the curb. It's well known that 403 lacks vision. Plus, I may or may not have broken some so-called rules."

Love's dojo served a higher purpose, at least Love liked to think so. But the higher purpose had rules too, and that worked well for Love. He liked rules.

One of the rules was that he was not allowed to actively recruit for the dojo. That job belonged to other people. The problem was that the other people refused to recognize Keeper

Chance and what he offered. If Y could have befriended the boy, it would have been a legitimate way around the recruiting rule. Sadly, she had failed, and time was short. Love needed another legitimate way to circumvent the situation. After all, it was for the greater good.

Polyp used his sleeve to rub a smudge off his golden plunger. "Chapter 403 and I went our separate ways before the official vote on my expulsion was complete."

"The vote was leaning toward a unanimous decision?" Sensei Love asked.

Polyp's face distorted into a look of disgust and annoyance. "Bunch of jealous posers."

Love liked the direction this conversation was going. Polyp seemed angry, desperate, and lacking in morals.

"And how's the new life treating you?" Love looked around. "Is the toilet business a royal flush?"

Polyp smirked in irritation. "Potty humor? From you? Really? I've had better days. Want to help? Buy a toilet, or sink, or forty."

"How about a new costume?"

Polyp narrowed his eyes, worrying it was a trick. "A Vogue Love original?"

Sensei Love smiled a bit more.

Polyp tried to control his voice. He didn't want to sound desperate. "Will it have a cape?"

"Do you want a cape?"

"I wouldn't *not* want a cape."

"Then it will have a cape," Sensei Love said.

Polyp felt like he was having heart palpitations. Hard to say if it was a warning about doing business with Love or excitement over a costume with a cape. Polyp leaned forward and tried to study Sensei Love. The guy was totally unreadable. It must be part of his skill. "What's this new outfit going to cost me?" Polyp asked.

"I want you to bring me Keeper Chance," Love said. "He's involved with Chapter 626."

Polyp leaned back, thinking, tapping his head with the golden plunger. "Why don't you get Keeper Chance yourself?"

"It's against the rules. But if you were to capture him, there's no rule against me liberating him. . . ."

Polyp narrowed his eyes, incapable of hiding his contempt. "Seriously?"

"It's in Keeper's—and everyone else's—best interest that he trains at my dojo," Love said. "I'm just looking for an audience with him. Keeper isn't to be hurt, but the experience might help him decide on his own to follow a virtuous path. You help me recruit Keeper Chance, and you will be dressed like a king. Do we have a deal?"

"We have a deal," Polyp said.

Sensei Love turned to leave. "Good. We never had this conversation."

Excellent, Polyp thought. *Excellent.* It felt as if the wheel of fortune had begun to spin, and his peg was on the rise. Except something was bothering him. Something . . . Maybe it was that he had no idea who Keeper Chance was and had forgotten to get details. Didn't really matter. Polyp had no intention of wasting time with finding Keeper Chance. He had bigger fish to fry.

CHAPTER 11

KEEPER and Toby stood outside of the twelve-thousand-square-foot house with detached guest house, mouths agape. The Kia was parked in a driveway that circled around to the front door and led down the side of the house to a four-car garage. A spotless, custom-built black Range Rover Autobiography was parked in front of the Kia. A sporty Rolls-Royce with the license plate SLASHR was next to the Rover.

"Are you sure this is Chaos's lair?" Keeper asked. "I can't tell if it's a hotel or a house."

Toby held up his phone and checked the text Chaos had sent. "This is the correct address. Someone should ring the doorbell."

Keeper was afraid to put his dirty sneakers on the white marble stairs leading up to the door, much less touch the glowing golden doorbell. He was pretty sure the landscaping alone cost more than Nana's whole house.

The front door opened, and Chaos stuck his head out. "For the love of all that's evil, what are you two doing standing there? Get inside before the neighborhood security comes around, drags you off, and blabs about you in their monthly newsletter."

Keeper and Toby entered the home to stand in a large foyer that was decorated in modern minimalism. White marble lined the floor and surrounded two floating staircases.

"Shoes," Chaos said, pointing to an old beach towel by the door that already held three pairs of boots belonging to Chaos, Slasher, and Showboater.

Keeper and Toby removed their sneakers and followed Chaos through the house.

"Um, Chaos, sir?" Keeper said. "Is this your house?"

"No. Many years back I discovered that I don't really need a whole lot, but I do like nice things at the end of my day. Must be the Leo in me. About six years ago I discovered this neighborhood. A number of the homeowners on this street go on monthlong vacations. One or two are only in-house briefly, for a week here and a week there. I move around to stay in whichever house is currently empty, enjoy their cars and Italian linens."

"So, you're squatting," Keeper said.

Chaos sighed. "More like house-sitting. The neighborhood has gotten wise to me. The last house I stayed in, I found a full fridge and a bottle of champagne on the counter with a note that said 'Car keys are in the drawer by the garage. Be back in two months. Thanks.'"

Chaos led the boys into a kitchen that could have served food for forty people. At least Keeper assumed it could. All the appliances were hidden behind glossy, navy cabinetry that lined the walls floor to ceiling. Slasher and Showboater were sitting on stools at the corner of one of two giant, white quartzite islands. They stopped talking as Keeper and Toby approached.

"Nice car, Slasher, sir," Toby said.

"You look at it, you breathe on it, you touch it, you wax it," Slasher replied. "It's better than nice."

"Now that we're all here," Chaos said, "who would like a drink? There's plenty of sparkling water." He walked over to a shiny wall and started knocking on panels. "Took me two days to figure out how to open things in this kitchen. Thought I was going to starve to death." Chaos's knocking finally paid off, and the panel hiding an enormous refrigerator popped open. Chaos swung it open the rest of the way, pulled out a drawer full of canned drinks, and removed a few. He closed the door and brought the cans over to the collection of E.V.I.L. villains and E.V.I.L. villain wannabes. "I have lime, orange, and . . . pamplemousse? What the Green Goblin is pamplemousse?"

Toby took the pink can from Chaos, popped the top, and took a sip. "Grapefruit?" He went to put the can down on the counter.

"Coaster!" Chaos yelled, grabbing one from a stack nearby and placing it in front of Toby. "We're E.V.I.L. villains, not ungrateful slobs."

Chaos handed out coasters and drinks, claimed the free stool next to Slasher, and adjusted his cape. "Now that I've completed the obligatory host garbage, let's hear about the box of cookie money."

Keeper glanced at Toby. Toby had been smart enough to busy himself with his pamplemousse, leaving the floor to Keeper.

"Well, we found the box," Keeper said. "It's in the designer district in a store that sells porcelain products. Mostly bathroom fixtures, hardware, and accessories, but there is a decent selection of kitchen sinks."

Silence. Not even a cricket. Just stares from the senior members.

Keeper continued. "We entered the showroom. I kept a disheveled, yet enthusiastic, salesman busy while Toby examined the door to the back storage room. I didn't see any motion sensors or cameras in the showroom. I'm guessing not many people want to steal a toilet or bathtub."

Chaos slowly turned his gaze away from Keeper. "Toby?"

"Yes, sir! The door had a keypad lock. The code to enter was 55555. Took me four tries to figure it out. I did the typical 12345 and then 11111, then I doubted myself and thought it could be six numbers, or maybe four, but the pad wasn't old enough—"

"Toby," Chaos said. "Get on with it."

"Storeroom was empty of people. No employees in the building other than the salesman—he might also be the owner. Did some googling while I waited for Keeper to come back to the front door. It's a relatively new business. The building used to belong to a lighting store...."

Chaos pinched the bridge of his nose with his thumb and index finger. "Toby! The box."

"Oh, yes. I found the box in the back storeroom. Hadn't been opened yet. There is another door in the storeroom that leads to a rear lot for parking and deliveries. The dead bolt on the door is basic and can be picked from the outside. There is a keypad alarm next to it. My guess is the back door and front door set it off."

"Windows?" Chaos asked.

Keeper shook his head. "Nothing on the ground level. They were all high, like skylights, circling the dome."

Chaos's eyebrows raised. "A dome? The one on Martingale Street?"

"Yes," Keeper said. "Do you know it, sir?"

Chaos took a sip of his drink. "More or less. I was at the Carpet Castle a while back, when, through a series of unfortunate events, one of their one hundred percent New Zealand wool carpets caught on fire. I remember the building across the street being a dome shape, but I couldn't tell you what it sold. I was a bit preoccupied on that day."

Slasher turned his attention to Toby. "Were there other boxes in the room?"

"Yes. Typical storage room stuff," Toby said. "The cookie money box was the only one on the folding table next to a cot with a sleeping bag."

"Fantastic!" Showboater said, throwing his hand up over his head in an overly dramatic and glittery display. "He's the owner, salesman, and full-time occupant. If he's sleeping on a cot in a forest of bathrooms, at least we know why he's extorting money. He clearly has none. Personally, I would have extorted cookies over the cash, but to each his own."

"The situation gets worse, I'm afraid," Chaos said. "I went by the Cookie Maven's store today, hoping to form a plan B for obtaining cookies. It's closed. There wasn't a going out of business sign, but the lights were off and the cases empty."

Silence followed while everyone digested the idea of no more Cookie Maven cookies.

Showboater slammed his fist down on the countertop and jumped off his stool. "I'm going to say it! I'm going to!"

There was an audible groan and a highly visible eye roll from Slasher.

"I'm declaring an evil emergency!" Showboater finished with a small victory dance that ended with the imaginary dropping of a microphone.

"Well, that's that," Chaos said, standing. "You called it, Showboater, so you're in charge of contacting all members of

Chapter 626. Emergency meeting at your place tomorrow, midnight."

"Huzzah."

Keeper and Toby left Chaos's lair through the front door, shoes in hand. Once their shoes had been put back on and the Kia had cleared the gated entrance, Keeper turned to Toby.

"I have to agree with Showboater," Keeper said. "I don't like it. Something seems off about the whole thing. Why would someone blackmail the Cookie Maven? And what could possibly be so bad in the Cookie Maven's past that she would pay to the point of losing her business?"

"Everyone has something in their past," a voice said.

Toby slammed on the brakes. Keeper's seat belt locked, and his arms braced on the dash. He whipped his head around to see Y sitting in the back seat.

Y looked from Keeper to Toby and back again. "What? It's true. Mistakes allow us to grow emotionally and intellectually. It's inherently human. Like thumbs."

"Where did you come from?" Keeper asked. "Have you been here the whole time?"

Y looked at Keeper like he had sprouted a third eye. "Not the *whole* time. I was only waiting about ten minutes for you to come out. You really should lock your car doors, Toby."

"I did!" Toby took his foot off the brake and continued

making his way through the neighborhood. "Where do you want me to drop you off?"

Y motioned with her head. "In three blocks take a right. There's a country club down that street. I left my ride there. Back to the Cookie Maven . . ."

"Why are you so concerned about the Cookie Maven?" Keeper asked.

"Because, like you, when I started thinking about the box of money, something seemed off. So I tried to do an internet search on who the Cookie Maven was, but that type of thing isn't really in my skill set. All I could find was a name."

"What is your skill set?" Toby asked.

Y had hidden her skill her whole life. It was the worst, most embarrassing skill ever. Her parents already thought she was a pathetic no-skill loser. Being a pathetic skilled loser would be even worse. The subject needed to be dropped immediately. "Let's just say I don't start fights, but I'm good at finishing them."

Keeper and Toby exchanged glances. It was quite possibly true.

Toby swallowed and looked at Y in the rearview mirror. "I'm really good at tracking. If you give me her name, I can find out where she lives, what kind of debt she has, family members, all kinds of stuff."

"Great! The Cookie Maven is Joanne Josephine Larbole, but you probably want to double-check my work." Y unbuckled her seat belt as Toby parked next to her Vespa. "I'll meet you outside Toby's house tonight. We can do some drive-bys and maybe break into the shop. It will be fun. What time?"

Keeper could feel anxiety building in his chest. Drive-bys and break-ins? What the . . . ? "Eleven thirty?"

"Perfect." Y opened the car door and slid out. "It's a date."

Keeper and Toby watched Y put on her helmet, roll her scooter off the center stand, and straddle the seat.

"Wow," Toby said, watching Y speed away. "I've never been on a date before."

Keeper closed his eyes briefly, hoping for a moment of serenity. "It's not a date. I'm pretty certain that any kind of activity with this girl will end in emotional suffering and imminent doom."

Toby put the car in reverse and backed out of the parking space. "My mom thinks she's delightful."

CHAPTER 12

TOBY'S bedroom was also his parents' basement. Keeper would have sworn he had stepped through a time warp if it hadn't been for the large flat-screen television and PlayStation. The walls were lined with fake wood paneling, the carpet was orange shag, and the sofa pea green. There was a door leading to a small bathroom and another door leading to a small bedroom. The bedroom barely held Toby's full-size bed and a nightstand. The clothes that weren't neatly folded and stacked in a laundry basket were in a pile on the floor. There was a partial fake wall separating the living space from a washer, dryer, and boxes of holiday decorations.

At 11:20 p.m. Toby closed his laptop. "I think there's more to uncover about the Cookie Maven, but we're out of time."

Keeper stood and stretched his back. "It's fine. We have

enough information for tonight's exploratory debacle."

Keeper followed Toby over to a long, high transom window with a folding chair underneath it. "We need to use my secret exit," Toby said. "I have an eleven o'clock curfew, and my dad is a light sleeper. My mom would cover for us, but if she tells my dad we're going for food, we'll never get rid of him." Toby made a sweeping gesture toward the chair. "After you."

Keeper climbed onto the chair, opened the window, and hauled himself up. He was about halfway through when he came face-to-face with a pair of black Vans high-tops. His eyes moved upward, following the pair of athletic but definitely feminine legs to their owner.

"Looking for something?" Y asked. She had a full-on smile. It reminded Keeper of the wolf in "Little Red Riding Hood." It was white and perfect and offered promises of semi-legal and entirely illegal fun.

"What I'm looking for is a basement door," Keeper said, standing and brushing off his shirt. "Help me pull Toby out."

Toby managed to get himself up to the window and his top half out. Keeper and Y each grabbed him under an armpit and pulled him the rest of the way, lifting him onto his feet.

"Thanks," Toby said. He felt around in his pants pocket and pulled out a car key. "We can take the Kia. We just need to fill it up when we're done. My mom gave me gas money."

Y's smile was back. "You told your mom you were going out to do some B&Es? And she gave you gas money?"

Toby unlocked the Kia, and everyone piled in, Y in the back. "Very funny. I told her Keeper and I might want to go to the twenty-four-hour diner for grilled cheese, because that's what all the cool kids do. I don't want her worrying about me any more than she already does."

Keeper patted Toby on the shoulder. "You're a good son, Toby."

"I do my best." Toby drove the Kia out of his neighborhood. "Joanne Larbole, sometimes JoJo to her friends, worked for a number of caterers before opening the Cookie Maven ten years ago. The store expanded three years ago. She's been divorced for eleven years, has no children, and lives in the town of Parsimmon. Thirty-year mortgage, decent rate, never been late on a payment until recently," Toby said.

"Let's go to her home first," Y said. "We can check the mail, make sure she's home, see if there is anything odd about her house or the neighborhood. Do you have any info on home security just in case we need to search her house?"

Toby shook his head. "No. Didn't have time, but I can do it tomorrow if necessary."

Keeper turned a bit to look back at Y. "Chaos said the Cookie Maven's shop was closed. Joanne Larbole hasn't been making cookies. That makes me wonder if she's being threatened and not blackmailed. She might be scared to leave her home."

Y's mouth turned down into a slight frown, thinking. "Or maybe she's not home at all. Maybe she's missing."

Keeper hadn't thought of that. The sinking feeling was back in his stomach. "Blackmail doesn't seem so bad anymore."

Fifteen minutes later Toby turned off the car's headlights and slowly crept down Joanne Larbole's street. It was a quaint suburban neighborhood of newer houses. There seemed to have been three models of homes to choose from when the development had originally been planned. Joanne's was a modest two-story. A sidewalk and three steps leading up to a small covered porch were all that separated the house from the street. There was an attached one-car garage and a high privacy fence surrounding the backyard.

Most cars seemed to be in garages or parked in their home's driveway, so Toby left the Kia farther down the street to avoid being noticed. There were decorative streetlights lining the road, but they were yellow and dim.

Y checked the mailbox for the Cookie Maven's house. "Empty," she said. "Hopefully that means she's home." She pointed to the interior of the mailbox. "There's a sticker inside that says Larbole, so we know we have the right house."

They stood in silence for a few minutes, watching the dark windows.

"Let's check out the back," Y said, walking toward the house. She wedged herself between a row of hedges and Joanne's privacy fence and shuffled sideways down the length of it. Keeper and Toby followed.

There was a break in the hedges at the back of Joanne's

property. About three feet separated Joanne's fence from more privacy hedges, hiding the view of the house that backed up to hers.

Y put a hand on Keeper's shoulder from behind and kicked him in the back of his leg.

Keeper's legs buckled, and he dropped to his knees. "Fffudge!"

"You kiss your nana with that mouth?" Y swung her legs over his shoulders and wrapped her calves under his arms. "Okay. Pick me up so I can see over the fence."

Keeper sucked in air. "A, I would never even think of kissing my nana. B, my nana's skill is knowing when I swear. I could be halfway around the world, and she'd know." Keeper grabbed on to Y's knees, bracing her legs against him, and rose onto his feet. "You could have just asked for a lift up."

"I didn't want you to think I couldn't do things on my own and get the wrong impression," Y said, weaving her fingers through Keeper's unruly hair to steady herself.

"Yeah. We wouldn't want to have any wrong impressions. See anything?" Keeper asked.

"There's a light on and a figure in the kitchen. Looks female. Frantic. Seems to be picking things up or looking for something. She just disappeared."

A minute later, there was the sound of a garage door rising from the front of the house. Y used Keeper's head as a brace. She held herself up, swung her legs free, and slid down Keeper's back. "Go, go, go! She's leaving. We need to follow."

Keeper stood frozen. His eyes shifted to Toby.

Toby shrugged. "My mom also described her as fiery."

Keeper rolled his eyes and took off after Y. He raced down the side fence and slammed into her at the end. She braced her hand against his chest, signaling for him to hold, while she peered around to the front of the property.

"There she goes," Y said, taking off at a sprint. "She's heading in the direction of the Kia. Silver SUV. Hurry."

Keeper stretched his arm behind him, palm up, and Toby passed the car key to him. There was no way Toby's legs were going to be able to keep up with Keeper's and Y's.

Y reached the car first, her strides silent and effortless. Keeper wasn't far behind. He unlocked the car with the key as soon as he was within range. Y was closing the passenger door as Keeper was opening the driver's side. He started the car and put it into gear. Toby threw himself into the back seat, pulling the door closed behind him. Toby was sucking in air and panting.

"Sorry. I'm not designed for speed," Toby said, resting his head back and closing his eyes.

Keeper took off down the street in the same direction as Joanne Larbole. "You did great," he said. "Keep an eye on the side streets. She can't be far. Luckily, there aren't many cars at this hour."

"For crying out loud," Y said. "You drive like an old lady. We're never going to catch up."

"There's this thing called the speed limit," Keeper said. "Maybe you've heard of it? If I get a ticket, my nana will kill me."

"There!" Y said, pointing. "Take a right. That has to be her."

Keeper turned off the car's headlights, convinced himself that he could cry and beg himself out of a ticket if he was caught, took a right, and followed the silver SUV in front of him. They wound through various neighborhoods and cruised down a highway lined with traffic lights and strip malls. The car finally pulled into a small gravel parking lot for Marble Park. It wasn't a good neighborhood, and it wasn't a bad neighborhood. It definitely wasn't any place for a decent person to be at midnight.

Keeper rolled past the lot and pulled to the side of the street, where they were hidden by a grove of trees. They exited the car, and Toby sniffed the air. He looked worried.

"I don't like it, Keeper," Toby said.

Keeper handed the car key to Toby. "I agree. You stay here. Keep the car running and an eye out for us. Just in case."

Toby nodded. "Be careful."

Keeper smiled. "Don't worry. I'll let Y finish any fights that start." He turned, jogged over to Y at the edge of the lot, and disappeared with her into the park.

The dirt path was lined with trees and very dark, making it difficult to see. They stumbled over roots and stubbed their toes on exposed rocks, stopping occasionally to listen. All they could hear was rustling, hopefully from woodland creatures. The tree canopy opened slightly when the trail they were following split.

Y took out her phone, bent down, and put on the flashlight mode. She studied the dirt, looking for a sign showing which way Joanne might have gone. "Let's try to the left." She turned the light off and stood, taking Keeper's hand, and pulling him forward.

They continued for another three hundred feet before the trees parted ways again. This time there was a clearing in front of them. A large pond was in the distance. Wooden picnic tables were scattered around its perimeter. Two silhouettes could be seen on the right side of the pond.

Keeper and Y snuck behind a grouping of boulders that flanked the path's opening. They watched the figures, straining to hear.

"Any idea what they're talking about?" Y whispered to Keeper.

"No. Hold on." Keeper pulled a single AirPod out of his pocket, placed it in his ear, and slid his finger down it. "I tinkered with this a bit to make it more like a hearing aid. It's not as good as Toby's hearing, but it's good enough to know when my nana is approaching. Hopefully I can make out something."

Y stared at Keeper. He was a genius. He was an inventor. Was that his skill in some way? Was that why her father wanted him in the dojo? Keeper's hair was pushed back from his ear, curling around it. Thick black eyelashes framed the darkest blue eyes Y had ever seen.

Keeper caught Y staring. "What?"

Y shook her head. "Nothing. Hear anything?"

"It's pretty garbled. The other figure is male. His voice is low. Joanne's not so much. She's kind of hysterical. I swear she's saying she doesn't have any more money for peanuts."

The figure of Joanne put her hands to her face, turned, and ran back toward the path entrance. Keeper and Y crouched down, hiding until she passed.

"I'm going after the mysterious male figure," Keeper said. "You stay with the Cookie Maven. Make sure she gets back to her car safely." Keeper turned to leave, and Y grabbed his arm.

"Wait," she said. "Take this." Y removed an expandable baton that had been hidden in a pocket of her tights as if it were a magic wand. "Pay attention. Down to open and you'll be prepared to strike. Knees, groin, elbow, you'll take the person down." Y demonstrated strikes with fluid and precise moves. "Head, heart, and lower back only if it's a matter of life or death. Got it?"

Keeper stared at Y with a mixture of awe and horror. Who was this girl? "What? No . . ."

Y collapsed the baton and shoved it into Keeper's hand. "Good. Go." Y gave Keeper a push toward the pond and took off in the opposite direction, following Joanne.

Keeper ran out into the open space of the pond area. The

figure had already disappeared. Keeper slowed as he got closer to where the meeting point had been, moving into a crouch. Looking and listening. He could see an entrance to another path, leading away. That had to be where the figure had gone. Keeper slowly entered and crept down the path until it came to a split. He chose the left, following it for what seemed like forever. The figure must have gone the other way. Keeper backtracked, came to the split, and wasn't sure which path to take. Why did he have to have such a bad sense of direction? He went to the left until the path split again. He went right, crossed a wooden bridge over a stream, and heard voices.

Keeper followed the voices until he saw the people they belonged to. There were three of them. None of them looked like the man who had met Joanne Larbole. Hardened criminals? Probably. Gang members? Definitely. The park was a well-known hideout for such types at night. They were throwing rocks at someone who was backed into a small alcove of a rock formation.

Turn around, the voice in Keeper's head said. *Save yourself.* But Keeper had already stepped out into the light, Y's baton expanded.

CHAPTER 13

KEEPER'S shoulders were back, his posture perfect, but his eyes were narrow, and his teeth were clenched. He silently moved in on the trio of degenerates, trying to piece together the situation and see if any of them were armed.

"Homeless, ungrateful, runaway sack of garbage. I'll teach you to bite the hand that feeds you." The middle delinquent threw a rock into the alcove. There was the sound of contact and a yelp of pain. "Not so tough now, are you?" he called out. "When I'm done stoning you, I'm going to . . ."

WHACK! Keeper brought the baton up between loser number one's legs with a strength he had no idea was within him. Loser number two tried to pull a gun out of his waistband, but Keeper brought the baton up, hitting number two in the elbow. His elbow bent in the entirely wrong direction, and he dropped the gun. In one swift motion, Keeper swept the gun away with his foot, went into a crouch, and swung around to get loser number three in the knees. Three had a low pain threshold and went down screaming profanities and begging for help.

Keeper stood and turned toward the dark alcove. He couldn't see who was in there and started to have doubts about what he'd just done. For all he knew it was a rival gang member, possibly getting what he deserved.

"They won't be down long," Keeper called into the darkness. "I suggest you leave while you can."

There was no reply, but Keeper could hear shuffling. He turned and walked back toward the bridge, hoping to make better directional decisions this time around.

The shuffling sound was getting closer. Following him.

Keeper turned to see an enormous animal, neck down, head out, limping toward him. As it got closer, Keeper could see its fangs bared, a low growl rumbling through them. Keeper put his hands up and slowly backed away. The injured animal, possibly a werewolf, let out a monstrous howl and charged . . . right past Keeper and slammed his head into the person who had just emerged from the wooded path behind him.

Y went flying backward and skidded down the dirt path until a mess of exposed roots stopped her. She sucked in some air and clasped her chest. "That pony just headbutted me!"

Keeper ran to her side and helped her up. "I think it's a dog."

They looked back at the giant beast. It was sitting watching them, tail wagging, tongue flopped out of the side of its mouth. It was mostly legs, and its gray coat was wiry and matted.

Y got to her feet and brushed the dirt off. "Did you find the mystery man or just the freak-of-nature dog?"

"Just the dog. I couldn't catch up to the man. I got lost trying and found a group of horrible human beings being horrible. Turns out they were being horrible to this dog."

Y looked past Keeper at the three figures struggling to right themselves and regroup. Two of them were almost standing and were seriously ticked off. "You did that? To save a dog?"

Keeper looked down at his sneakers, then up, and found Y's eyes. "Yes."

Y was staring at him again. Her mouth grew into a smile. Keeper thought he saw hints of amusement and something else. Something he couldn't quite put a finger on but was definitely trouble.

Y turned on her heel and headed back down the path. "As much as I'd like to see you in action, we need to get going. Joanne Larbole left, and Toby is waiting. This way."

Keeper followed Y, the dog followed Keeper, and Y followed the path back to the small gravel parking area. Toby emerged from the Kia when he saw them.

"Whoa," Toby said, approaching the dog, hand out for it to smell, then moving into full-on behind-the-ear scratches. "This is the biggest dog I've ever seen. It is a dog, isn't it? It smells like a dog."

Y opened the back door. "It smells like it's been rolling in garbage."

The dog didn't waste any time deciding what to do. It took off for the open door, climbed in, and made itself comfortable, sprawling across the back seat.

"Garbage if we're lucky," Toby said. "The dog is coming with us?"

Keeper opened the passenger-side door. "Are you going to tell it to get out?"

"Good point." Toby jogged around to the driver's side.

"Wait. What? Seriously?" Y raised her eyes to the sky, hoping for a miracle, like chivalry, to happen and for one of the boys to offer to sit in the back with the dog. When it was clearly a lost cause, Y reached into the car and tried to shove the behemoth over to one side of the bench seat. It was a futile effort. Y squeezed herself underneath the back end of the dog. She closed her door, buckled her seat belt, and waited for Toby and Keeper to finish laughing. "In light of the current situation," Y said, "I think it would be best if we skip the Cookie Maven shop tonight, but I still want a grilled cheese."

An hour later Keeper, Toby, Y, and the dog were full of grilled cheese and french fries, courtesy of Toby's mom, and the car was full of gas. Toby parked in the driveway, and everyone piled out.

"Same time tomorrow?" Y asked.

"No can do," Keeper said. "Emergency chapter meeting called over the closing of the Cookie Maven shop."

"That's a shame. Guess I'm on my own." Y turned to leave. "Well, it's been fun, boys."

Keeper stepped in front of her, hands up. "What about the dog?" he asked.

"He who saves it bathes it."

Keeper watched Y brush past him and cross the street to her Vespa.

"Crud." Keeper turned his attention to Toby. "Any ideas on how we're going to get this dog into the house?"

Toby shrugged. "Same way we're getting in?"

They walked over to the ground-level window and tried to size up the opening and the dog. Seemed only reasonable that if Keeper and Toby could fit through it, so could a dog.

"One of us needs to go in first and catch the dog," Keeper said. "And one of us needs to stay out here and push him through."

"This is one of those no-win situations, isn't it?" Toby asked.

Keeper was starting to think his life was a no-win situation. "I'll go in and catch. There's a good chance this dog weighs more than you."

Keeper slid through the window, feet first, and pushed the folding chair to the side. "Okay. I'm ready."

Keeper waited for a minute. He could hear Toby huffing and puffing, and there might have been some swear words. Finally, two enormous front paws appeared at the edge of the window. They were spread apart and bracing against the window's ledge. There was some growling. Keeper couldn't tell if it was the dog or Toby.

Keeper moved the folding chair back into place and stood on it to look out. Toby was straddling the dog, trying to lift it up under the armpits and drag it forward. The dog was winning. Keeper took hold of the dog's paws and picked them up over the ledge. He reached forward, helping Toby push the dog's head down so it could fit through the window.

Toby moved toward the back of the dog. He put his shoulder into its backside, dug his toes into his father's perfectly mowed and fertilized grass, and put everything he had into pushing the dog. The dog went through the window before Keeper was ready. The chair went out from underneath him, and Keeper went down on his back, knocking all the air out of him, cushioning the fall for the dog. At least Keeper thought it was the dog who knocked all the air out. It could have been Toby, who fell through the window after the giant beast.

Keeper, Toby, and the dog lay on the floor for a moment, stunned, trying to clear their heads. There was the sound of the basement door opening and footsteps coming down the bare, wooden plank stairs.

Keeper angled his head backward a bit and stared up at an upside-down Toby's mom. She had on a matching shorts and short-sleeved-shirt pajama set, covered in gnomes and declaring that Toby's mom was HANGING WITH HER GNOMIES.

Great, I'm going to get kicked out and have to go home to Nana, Keeper thought.

"Oh, Toby," Toby's mom said, looking down at the four-arm, eight-leg pile. "You know you can't keep him. Remember what your father said about the last animal your brother brought home?"

All Toby could squeak out was a pathetic "Yeah."

Toby's mom knelt, stroked the dog's head, and kissed Toby's. "I'll make him some chicken soup tomorrow. Poor dog looks like he could use a warm meal."

She stood, went back up the stairs, and turned before she closed the door. "Don't stay up too much later, boys. You'll be tired tomorrow."

They waited until the door was closed, and they were sure Toby's mom wasn't going to reappear with pizza bagels or cups of hot cocoa. When the coast seemed clear, they dragged themselves to their feet and over to the couch.

"What did your dad say about the last animal?" Keeper asked Toby.

"He said if anyone brought another animal into the house, he was getting rid of the animal and the person who brought it."

"What kind of animal did your brother bring home?"

"Squirrel." Toby looked over at Keeper. "My brother thought it was sick, but in hindsight, it was probably just in some sort of hibernation. In the middle of the night the squirrel woke up.

Chewed through all the wires in the house, took a leak wherever it pleased, and tried to attack my dad. It was terrifying. We had to evacuate the house and call a professional to come in, get the squirrel, and return it to the wild."

Keeper slouched onto the couch and closed his eyes. Exhaustion setting in. "That's a shame."

"Yeah." Toby stood, rubbed his eyes, and ran his hands through his hair. "It was a cute squirrel. Red. Bushy tail. Gave my brother fleas. I'm going to bed. My mom left a pillow and sleeping bag at the bottom of the stairs for you."

"Thanks, Toby."

"Anytime, Keeper."

CHAPTER 14

IT was well past noon by the time Keeper and Toby woke up, and it was coming up on midnight by the time they had bathed the dog, brushed the dog, cleaned its wounds, fed the dog countless bowls of chicken soup, and named it Gandalf. Gandalf was asleep on Toby's bed, snoring, when Keeper and Toby snuck out the basement window and borrowed the Kia.

Toby parked on the second level of a small parking garage built for the Forsham Theater, where the emergency meeting had been called. There were a few other cars scattered about in the garage. Keeper suspected most of them belonged, in one way or another, to members of Chapter 626. They crossed the street to the theater, walked past it, and turned the corner. Sticking to the shadows as best they could, they made their way across the street to a five-and-dime that hadn't been open since the seventies. Following Showboater's instructions, they entered the abandoned store through a cracked plexiglass panel and found a trapdoor located behind the old soda fountain counter.

Toby went first and Keeper closed the trapdoor behind them, making sure it clicked into place. They followed the tunnel, lit with hanging work lights, back under the street to the theater. At the end of the tunnel stood Frog. He was tall and thin and dressed in a green spandex suit with a glittery green eye mask. Frog seemed to be all legs and arms until Keeper noticed the enormous narrow green feet.

"Keeper Chance and Toby Boggs?" Frog asked.

Keeper and Toby nodded.

"Up the stairs and through the next trapdoor. The villains are expecting you."

They squeezed past Frog and took the stairs leading up. The open trapdoor was an entrance to Showboater's private lair. It was a large room that, in a previous life, was a speakeasy. The bar now served as a kitchen counter and was currently covered in late-night snack food. The shelves behind the bar held boxes of cereal, cans of SpaghettiOs, bottled water, and a complete set of dishes for four. Reams of flashy fabrics and a sewing machine were stacked against a wall.

Two large round wooden tables that looked as if they had stories to tell sat near the bar. Each table had four chairs placed halfway around, facing out at a scattering of folding chairs.

Showboater noticed Keeper and Toby and left the circle of villains standing in the middle of the room. "Ah, you made it. Any trouble finding your way in?"

"No," Keeper said, still taking in the space. "It was exactly as your instructions said."

"Good, good." Showboater put his arms around the boys' shoulders, guiding them farther into the room toward the villains. "I apologize for the unconventional meeting. Sudden change of plans. This evening's theater performance went later than usual. There are still a few actors and the cleaning crew next door, so we need to keep it quiet. Normally sidekicks and high-level henchmen would be included in this meeting. Let me introduce you to the other villains while we wait for Chaos to arrive."

Showboater moved into the center of the circle and motioned toward the woman standing to Toby's right. "Villainy does not preclude proper manners, so ladies first. This is Dr. Spot."

Dr. Spot looked to be in her early twenties. Her long highlighted brown hair was clipped up with strands falling about the sides of her face. She had eyes the color of chocolate and a mouth the color of strawberries. She wore black leggings and a tailored type of lab coat over a tight red tank top.

Before Showboater could stop him, Toby reached out his hand to shake Dr. Spot's. Dr. Spot took Toby's offer and dropped him like a sack of wet cement. Toby was on his knees, his arm hanging limp, tears welling up in his eyes. "F-f-f-f-f . . ." was all Toby could get out.

"Yes," Showboater said. "You should probably refrain from handshaking. Dr. Spot has the amazing ability to hit nerve spots."

Toby dragged himself back onto his feet. "Pleased to meet you," he said, his arm still useless. Dr. Spot was clearly happy with her handiwork.

"Next to Dr. Spot," Showboater continued, "is Joy Sucker."

Joy was in her early twenties, as well. She was petite with long brown hair. She would have been attractive except she wore an outfit of brown, mustard brown, and everyone's least favorite color, burnt sienna. Joy opened her mouth, but Showboater was faster.

He waved his hands in a stop motion. "Aaaahhhh."

Joy snapped her mouth closed and put her palms together to say *Thank you*.

Showboater gave her a genuine smile. "Always happy to help." Showboater turned back toward Keeper and Toby. "Joy hasn't figured out how to control her skill yet. She has the phenomenal ability to suck the fun out of any situation by simply speaking."

Joy raised her arms and pointed two fingers at her head. "Ultimate party pooper."

"No need to brag," Showboater said. "But yes, it's true. Next to Joy is Staticanator and her husband, Barricade. You might want to put your hands in your pockets, Toby. Shaking hands with Staticanator can be a bit of a shock."

"Yeah," Barricade said, his white teeth shining in the midst of his trimmed black beard. "I like it." He held out an enormous hand that would have given the Hulk a run for his money. It matched the rest of Barricade. He was at least six foot five and three hundred pounds of solid muscle.

Toby's arm still wasn't fully functioning, so Keeper shook Barricade's hand. "It's a pleasure to meet you, sir."

"Sir. Ha! Barricade is fine, or Barry. You boys like football?"

Keeper and Toby weren't sure how to answer. They were terrified he was going to challenge them to a game.

"My nana won't let me watch football," Keeper said. "According to her, teamwork only encourages and supports the delusions of the weak. She also said she found the tight pants disgraceful."

Barricade's smile was gone. He smashed a giant fist into the palm of his other hand. "Your nana sounds like she could use a good pounding."

Staticanator put a hand on Barricade's shoulder, sending off a spark. Staticanator was, in some ways, the complete opposite of Barricade. She had shoulder-length blond hair and blue eyes and wore a stunning outfit of white and yellow. Gold thread was woven through the fabric of her pants and the sleeves of her jacket in the shape of small lightning bolts. As she moved, one bolt would catch your eye and then disappear, and another one would briefly pop up.

Barricade didn't even flinch at the shock. "Sorry. Sorry," he said to Keeper. "I would never pound your nana."

"It's all right," Keeper said. "You aren't the first person to have the thought. Nana has the personality of a hobgoblin."

"Barricade used to play pro football," Showboater said. "Then he met Staticanator and they joined E.V.I.L. Barricade has the skill to create an impenetrable barrier around himself. Up to three feet. Made him unstoppable as an offensive tackle." Showboater continued down the line of introductions. "You, of course, know Slasher, and last but not least is Tsunami."

Tsunami was in his mid to late forties. His hairline was starting to recede, his arms were crossed over his chest, and he wore blue-gray cargo pants with black reinforced fabric in the pattern of a wave over his knees and shins. His jacket was black with multiple pockets and an underlying silver thread that made it look like rain when Tsunami moved. A short, dark gray cape was draped over his shoulders.

"Tsunami, you and Keeper should get along famously," Showboater said. "It turns out Keeper is a bit of an engineering genius."

Tsunami's arms stayed crossed, his eyes becoming slits as he focused on Keeper. "I have two degrees, an MS and a PhD from MIT. What do you have?" he asked.

"I'm in high school. I only have real-life experience." Keeper wasn't sure why he had said it and immediately felt a sense of regret. Normally it took a lot to get under Keeper's skin, but there was something about this guy that instantly pushed Keeper's buttons.

There was an audible intake of air from the rest of the villains, except Barricade, whose smile kept getting wider. The air in the room became humid, and Keeper was almost certain he felt a drop in the barometric pressure.

Showboater stepped forward and jabbed his finger into Tsunami's chest. "I swear by the name of Electro that if you didn't bring a mop with you, you'd better think twice about what you're about to do. And I remind you, if I get ousted out of my lair because of your doing, I'm moving in with you."

It was hard to read Tsunami's face. He was either weighing his options or trying to decide if Showboater was all talk.

A forced half smile appeared on Tsunami's face, and the air quality returned to normal. "Hya, hya, hya." It was like a hyena had been released into the room. "I was just testing the kid."

Showboater didn't look like he believed Tsunami, but before anything could be said, Chaos emerged from the open trapdoor. He went straight to the bar, removed a tray of miniature pretzel dogs from the spread of snack food, and passed it down the trapdoor to Frog.

"I officially call this emergency meeting of Chapter 626 of E.V.I.L. to order," Chaos said, approaching the circle. "I see all villains and soon-to-be-villains are accounted for. Showboater, have proper introductions been made?"

"All villains have been introduced. I saved the introduction of the soon-to-be villains for you."

"Very well." Chaos took a step forward and gestured with an outstretched hand. "Keeper. Toby." He stepped back into the circle. "On to the next order of business. Showboater, you called this meeting. The floor is yours."

Showboater strutted into the center of the circle, raised his arms over his head, and began turning in a circle. "Esteemed villains of Chapter 626 . . ."

"For the love of . . ." Chaos closed his eyes and rubbed his temples. "Frog is getting impatient in the tunnel, and some of us have evil plans for this evening. Get on with it."

"Yes, yes. Of course." Showboater grabbed the hem of his cape and swung it around to hang over his opposite shoulder. Glitter sprayed out, covering Barricade, Slasher, and Tsunami. "Cookies! The cookie world is being invaded by a sinister force, bent on destruction of the most delicious and perfect confection, whether alone, with coffee, or in a lunch box. I don't mean to alarm the present company, but Cookie Maven has been targeted by this abomination."

"Good gumdrops!" Tsunami said, eyes wide in horror. "Are you talking about poisonous cookies?"

"Worse! No cookies!"

Tsunami's face was losing color at an alarming rate. He bent over, hands on his knees, and started deep breathing. "Oh, man. I need to sit down. When did this happen? I used to steal some poor sap's Cookie Maven cookies once a week. I had to take the month off. The real butter and fine French chocolate were starting to make the costume a bit tight."

Slasher placed a hand on Tsunami's shoulder in understanding. "It happens to the best of us."

Keeper had never had a Cookie Maven cookie, but judging from everyone's reaction, they were clearly a bucket list item. The desire to bask in the gloriousness of a chocolate toffee coffee chip cookie was becoming overwhelming. For crying out loud, at this point Keeper would settle for oatmeal raisin.

Chaos stepped forward again and motioned for Showboater to withdraw, back into the circle. "In the interest of time management, let me lay out the situation. Keeper and Toby stole the obligatory box of Cookie Maven cookies for their initiation ceremony. When we opened the box, it was full of money. The box was returned to the warehouse and tracked to a plumbing showroom in the designer district. In the meantime, the Cookie Maven store appears closed. No lights, no people, no cookies."

"Who would go after the Cookie Maven?" Staticanator asked. "And why?"

Joy started counting off people on her fingers. "Cookie haters, vegans, psychopaths." Her eyes focused on Chaos. "Someone with a recent gluten issue who has become insane with anger and rage over the lack of edible food and wants to take it out on the world. I noticed you gave away the pretzel dogs and left the hummus and corn chips, Chaos."

Chaos rolled his eyes. "Thank you for that insight, Joy, but

I did not shut down the Cookie Maven, and I am not full of anger and rage."

Joy nodded. "Just full of gas? Probably from the hummus."

Showboater stepped out of the circle and planted himself directly in front of Joy. She closed her mouth, did the worldwide locking-of-the-lips motion, and gave Showboater the imaginary key. Showboater pretended to put it in his pocket, patted Joy reassuringly on her shoulder, and returned to his spot.

Chaos rubbed his face. "For crying out loud. I have no idea what I was even talking about. Honestly, Joy, it's an honor to have someone as skilled as you in Chapter 626. Please don't talk for the rest of the meeting."

"Cookies and the Cookie Maven," Slasher offered.

"Ah, yes." Chaos pulled his shoulders back a bit and resumed the role of chapter head. "Showboater feels that the closing down of the Cookie Maven falls under the contingency of an evil emergency and warrants further investigation. I need not remind everyone that award-winning cookies are required for an E.V.I.L. initiation ceremony, and there are none more award-winning than the Cookie Maven's. Furthermore, as E.V.I.L. villains, it is our job to dish the panda poo out, not to have it thrown at us by some second-rate crime monkey, whether knowingly or not. All in favor of looking into the Cookie Maven drama, raise your hand."

There was a unanimous raising of hands.

"Very well. It's official. Someone will need to research the owner and . . ." Chaos looked at Keeper. His hand was raised. "Keeper?"

"Um, sir," Keeper said. "Toby and I have already done a little investigating into the Cookie Maven. Her name is Joanne Larbole. Toby and I went by her house last night."

The room was silent. It was possible Keeper and Toby had blundered.

"Just the *two* of you?" Chaos asked.

Keeper made a point of looking Chaos directly in the eyes. "Yes." Keeper could have sworn he saw a smile twitch at the corner of Chaos's mouth.

"What did you find?" Chaos asked.

"She was home," Keeper said. "Then she left and met someone in Marble Park."

Chaos raised an eyebrow. Waiting for more.

"I couldn't get close enough to see who it was or hear what was being said. The Cookie Maven left upset."

Chaos was quiet for a moment, thinking. "The cookie money box was found at the Porcelain Palace. Let's assume the stranger in the park was the store's owner. You and Toby have twenty-four hours to gather as much information as you can on Larbole and the Porcelain Palace store owner. I remind you, this isn't English 101 or some creative writing course. Keep it simple and straightforward. I don't need to know Joanne Larbole skinned her knee when she was eight."

"Yes, sir," Keeper said.

"Once I look over Keeper's and Toby's findings, I'll send out a text with the next plan of action. Meeting adjourned. Pizza pockets and hummus for anyone feeling the need to partake in midnight snacking and insincere chitchat."

CHAPTER 15

Y sat on a bench watching the old Forsham Theater. She had secretly followed the boys from Toby's house to the theater district. She still wanted to search the Cookie Maven shop, but it would be way more fun with Keeper and Toby, and villains weren't known for long get-togethers. She could wait. She was also insanely curious why Chapter 626 was interested in the Cookie Maven's problems. She thought villains took pleasure in ruining lives, not saving them. Not to mention, for all Chapter 626 knew, the problem could be the handiwork of a villain from a different chapter.

"What a surprise to find you sitting, alone, on a bench, in the middle of the night." Sensei Love silently slid next to Y. He leaned backward, spread his arms across the back of the bench, and casually crossed his legs. "Is there a reason for it?"

"Just thinking." Y kept her eyes forward.

"About how to get E.V.I.L. to offer you an invitation to join? You'd make a lovely sidekick."

"Why would I have any interest in joining E.V.I.L.?" Y said, keeping her tone as even as possible.

"I don't know. Maybe you're only interested in helping them?"

"I'm not helping E.V.I.L."

Sensei Love frowned and fixed his eyes on Y. "Despite what you say, you aren't helping me, either. You've always been a bit, shall we say, independent? But I can't help feeling that something has changed."

Y was used to her father's method of trying to get her riled so she'd say something she shouldn't and reveal her cards. Y would like to be able to say it never worked, but it did, sometimes. "Is there a reason we're having this conversation?" Y asked.

"I'm just here to let you know you are being relieved of your position on this mission. Seemed only proper to tell you face-to-face."

Crud. Y had hoped it would take longer to be fired. "I can do this. I just need more time."

"There will be other missions. After you've grown up a bit more, maybe you'll be ready to try again." Sensei Love patted Y's leg. "After all, you are my child." The latter sentiment was followed by a smile that Y assumed was supposed to be paternal.

Sensei Love stood and looked down at Y. She averted her eyes and focused on her shoes.

"I'll let your mother know you will be returning to the dojo," he said. "I've arranged for a car to pick you up in the morning and drive you back upstate." He turned silently on his heel and slowly made his way down the street, arms behind his back as if out for an evening stroll.

Y watched him disappear into the darkness, knowing full well he wasn't going anywhere. He was going to follow her and hope she led him to Keeper. Y turned her gaze back down to her shoes, planning on how she was going to draw her father away from the area and then lose him.

She finally rose from the bench and walked in the opposite direction Sensei Love had gone. She reached the end of the block, crossed the street, walked another block, and turned left. Y went about a hundred yards before she stopped and stared at the empty spot where her Vespa had been parked.

Y clenched her teeth. "You tight-pantsed, bald-headed, pompous . . ." She closed her eyes and took a deep breath. It was bound to happen sooner or later. Sensei Love had commandeered his company vehicle. It was the equivalent of no television for a week or dojo janitorial duty. Y was well versed in both.

It was a smart move on her father's part. Y was pretty sure she could lose him on the Vespa. On foot, he had the advantage. It was okay. Challenge accepted.

Y took out her phone and called an Uber to pick her up three blocks away at a skeezy bar near an underpass and take her to a dance club in the city. Once the pickup was confirmed, Y began walking at a hurried pace. Hoping to give the appearance that she was nervous or upset.

As she got closer to the pickup spot, a few questionable night dwellers emerged to ask for money and make offensive comments. Y broke into a jog, being sure to stay as much in the streetlights as possible, in case her father was close behind. The vagrants didn't worry her. She wasn't as good at martial arts as her father. It was his skill. But she was highly trained and could beat the best of them.

The Uber arrived at the bar as Y was approaching. She hopped into the back seat of the car and powered off her phone. Y had blocked the tracking on her cell phone weeks ago. At least she hoped she had. She wasn't bad with technology, but she wasn't some super genius, either. Better safe than sorry.

The Uber went under the underpass and took an immediate right and then a left. Y looked behind to make sure there were no headlights yet.

"Stop here, please," Y said to the driver. "This is my apartment, and I'm not feeling well. My friend Becky is waiting for me at the dance club on Broad. Please go get her and take her home. I'll pay for the extra trip once I'm inside."

The driver pulled to the curb. "Whatever. You paid for me to drive to Broad. That's where I'm going."

Y opened the door and bolted out. "Thank you. Please hurry."

The driver took off toward Broad as soon as the door closed. Y guessed he was used to weird requests.

The street was lined with brick apartment buildings and trash cans waiting out front for morning pickup. Y jumped a railing that led to a basement-level apartment and hunkered down. The Uber account belonged to Sensei Love, so he would know where the car was heading. After a few minutes there was the sound of a car passing by. Y poked her head up, to look between the railing's bars, and saw the back end of the white sedan. When the glow of taillights faded away, she climbed the stairs and took off at a sprint, backtracking through the underpass and past the questionable bar. She went two more blocks, then crossed to the alley that ran behind the old theater. She went through the alley to the next street. There was a parking garage nearby. She hoped if she headed to the top, she'd have a bird's-eye view and be able to see when the villains emerged from their meeting.

She took two stairs at a time, quickly glanced behind to be sure no one was following, and slammed into Keeper on the second landing. Keeper grabbed Y's arms to steady her.

"Oh, Keeper. There you are." Y was breathing heavily. "I was passing through when I saw Toby turn into the garage. Figured the meeting was around here somewhere and decided to wait for you guys. It would be more fun if we broke into the cookie shop together."

Keeper looked down at Y. "Why are you so sweaty and out of breath? Are you being chased?"

"What? No." Y took a step back, releasing herself from Keeper. She placed her hands on her hips and tried to regain some composure. "Just thought I'd get in some exercise."

Keeper stared at her for a few seconds. Taking it all in. "Okay. Toby and I can't go to the shop tonight. We need to get home to the dog. Where did you park your scooter? We can give you a ride back to it."

Y shook her head. "That's okay. No need. The scooter is gone."

"Gone? As in someone stole your scooter?" Keeper asked.

"Stole. Repossessed. Returned to its owner." Y waved it off. "Po-tay-to. Po-tah-to. How is the dog?"

The dull yellow bare bulb illuminating the cement landing exploded.

"What's this about a dog?" Chaos asked, coming up behind Y.

"Oh, sir, it's nothing," Keeper said, not sure he wanted to go into detail and reveal Y was at Marble Park with them. "I found a lost dog—"

"He saved it," Toby said from behind Keeper. Toby looked at Chaos, then Keeper, and then back to Chaos.

Chaos stared at Toby for a moment, then raised an eyebrow. "Really?"

Keeper put his hands up in defense. "No, no, I didn't. . . ."

"It's okay," Chaos said. "Nothing wrong with saving a dog. After all, you know the first rule of E.V.I.L. We don't harm people or animals."

"I hurt some people saving the dog," Keeper said. "I mean seriously hurt."

Chaos shrugged. "More of a guideline than a rule. I'm sure they deserved it. What's important is that you saved the dog." Chaos's hand shot out to the side and grabbed hold of Tsunami's neck as he tried to sneak by. "Ah, just the villain we need."

Tsunami attempted to shrink his head into his shoulders like a turtle. "Lucky me."

"It seems our young villains, and their friend, have found a lost dog. I suspect they can use some help finding the owner," Chaos said.

Tsunami didn't look impressed. "Put up a poster."

"We can't do that," Keeper said. "The people I rescued the dog from might use it to come after us. And kill us."

Tsunami let out a groan of annoyance. "I don't know. Then see if the dog has a chip. Everyone chips their dogs these days."

Keeper and Toby exchanged a look. "How do we find out if the dog has a chip?" Keeper asked.

"What am I? Google? Two options. One, you can buy a reader online. Cost you about three hundred dollars for one that's reliable or thirty dollars if you're a gambling man. Two, you can sneak into a vet's office and either steal the device or just read the chip, get the number, and beat it before you get caught. I'd help you out—"

"Excellent idea, Tsunami!" Chaos said. "Nothing better

than learning on the job. When and where should Keeper and Toby meet you tomorrow?"

Tsunami waved his hands in protest. "What? No! I'm not a babysitter. I have way better things to do."

"No, you don't," Chaos said. "Besides, no one loves animals more than you. When and where?"

"Aaahhhhh!" Tsunami had his eyes closed tight and there was the distant rumble of thunder. "Fine! Paws and Claws off Stonebriar. Eleven forty-five a.m. Park on the side of the building. Bring the dog. Don't be late. Timing is everything. All of you can bite me. I'm going home."

Tsunami pushed his way past Keeper and Toby, being sure to give Keeper an elbow jab. They watched Tsunami stomp his way to a blue Bronco, climb inside, and peel out of the garage, tires screeching.

"That went well," Chaos said, smiling. "Now, I'm sure you kids would like to be out all night, getting into trouble, but I think it would be best if you take Y home and then return to Toby's. The dog is probably scared and lonely, and there's no sleeping in tomorrow. You don't want to be late for your playdate."

Keeper hadn't missed that Chaos knew who Y was. He also hadn't missed that Chaos was splitting them up. At least for tonight.

CHAPTER 16

KEEPER, Toby, and Gandalf the dog arrived at Paws and Claws around 11:40 in the morning. At 11:44, Tsunami approached the car on foot. Keeper and Toby exited the car and stood next to Tsunami. Tsunami had on scrubs and a plastic name tag that read FRED DRAPER.

"Okay, listen, babies," Tsunami said. "Since this is supposed to be a lesson in villainy, pay attention. I parked my car at the Taco Town down the street. If we need to make a fast getaway, one car, not two. Let's see this dog."

Toby opened the door to the back seat, and Keeper dragged the monstrous animal out. Tsunami's eyes were unblinking, taking it all in. From the look on Tsunami's face Keeper suspected Tsunami was expecting something more like a Chihuahua or a Maltipoo.

"His name's Gandalf," Toby said. "At least that's what we call him."

Tsunami continued to stare.

"You know, like the wizard," Toby said, closing the car door. "He's tall, gray, and has a beard."

"I'm not some nitwit loser," Tsunami said, letting the dog smell his hand. "I've read all of Tolkien's work and seen the movies a bazillion times."

Toby nodded. "I missed Tom Bombadil in the movies."

"Duh, who didn't?" Tsunami was now into full-on pets and ear scratches. He stepped back and looked over the dog one more time. "Gandalf is a good name for an Irish Wolfhound. You're okay, Toby."

"Now, listen up. This is how it's going to go down." Tsunami looked at Keeper. "If you need me to talk slower, let me know."

"I'm going to pick the lock to the back pen, where they take the dogs to do their business, and enter through the back door. You two, and Gandalf, are going to enter through the front at noon. That's when a new person will take over the front desk. Wait until there is someone checking in with the new staff member before you enter. Go directly to the seats on the left and park yourselves. I'm going to call you into a visitation room. We're going to scan the number and take a picture of it. You leave through the front. I'll leave through the back. We get in Toby's car and drive to Taco Town. You can look the chip number up online. There are a bunch of sites. Got it?"

Keeper and Toby nodded.

"Good. Go walk Gandalf around where you can see the front door."

Keeper and Toby took Gandalf around to the front and began circling in a patch of grass. A woman came and took the place of the young man at the front desk. As soon as she was busy checking in some sort of doodle, Keeper and Toby went to the door. Toby opened it, and Keeper went in first. Gandalf's front legs braced at the door's threshold. Toby picked up one paw and then the other while Keeper pulled. There was a lot of toenail-on-tile noise, some lady's cat in a carrier started to growl, and the doodle was cowering in fear behind his owner.

The woman at the front desk was staring. "Checking in?" she asked.

Keeper dragged Gandalf while Toby pushed him toward the seats on the left of the lobby. "No, we're good," Keeper said. "Already checked in. Just needed a bathroom break." Keeper sat down and Gandalf backed up to sit on Keeper's lap. Gandalf's tongue was practically to the floor. A small puddle of Irish Wolfhound drool was forming at Keeper's feet.

One of the exam room doors opened, and Tsunami's voice called out, "Gandalf."

Keeper stood up, and the dragging of the dog began again. No one had the courtesy to pretend to look elsewhere. All eyes were on the spectacle and the battle between man and beast. Beast was winning.

Tsunami pulled a dog biscuit out of his pocket, and Gandalf decided the vet wasn't so bad. Once they had the dog in the room, Tsunami closed the door and locked it.

"Okay, I found a scanner," Tsunami said, holding a gray device that looked like a magnifying glass without the lens. "Let's see if Gandalf has a chip. Get a phone out and be ready to take a picture."

Tsunami passed the device between Gandalf's shoulder blades, and a fifteen-digit number came up. Toby took a picture of the device's screen.

"Always cover your tracks," Tsunami said as he pressed the reset button and shut the scanner off. He threw the scanner into a drawer filled with cotton swabs, an otoscope, and various other veterinary things.

"Hello?" A voice came from the lobby side of the door, followed by a knock. "I couldn't find where Gandalf was checked in. What's his last name?" There was the sound of the locked doorknob trying to turn.

"Hinky dinks!" Tsunami said. "The jig's up. Out the back door."

Toby opened the door to the back hallway, lined with counters and minilabs. Gandalf put on the brakes. He obviously didn't have the same sense of urgency as the rest of the team.

Keeper looked at Toby. "You run blocker."

Toby gave him a thumbs-up.

Keeper looked at Tsunami. "Take the front. I've got the rear."

Tsunami picked up the front half of the dog and Keeper lifted the back as if the giant animal were a battering ram. Toby rushed through the door and down the hallway, shoving techs against walls, and running toward the exit on the far end.

"Everyone out of the way," Tsunami yelled. "This dog needs to get to grass, stat."

Most people plastered themselves against counters and walls, looks of confusion and horror on their faces. A side door opened near the exit, and a woman stepped out, a folder in her hand and a cranky look on her face. She was clearly the office pencil pusher, all about order and control.

"What's going on here?" the woman demanded. "And who . . . ?"

Before she could finish her sentence, a gustnado formed inside her office. Files, paperwork, and photographs of loved ones took to the air, circling and raining down like confetti. The paperwork was clearly more important than the three people running with a dog, because the woman turned and started grabbing at whatever was within arm's reach. "Not the payroll! Not the payroll!"

Keeper and Tsunami rushed past with Gandalf and out the exit leading to the grass enclosure. Keeper kicked the door closed behind him. Toby had left the gate leading to the parking lot and the back door of the Kia open.

They shoved Gandalf into the car, Tsunami following. Toby peeled out of the parking lot as Keeper jumped into the passenger's seat.

"Hya, hya, hya." Tsunami leaned forward, between the two front seats. "Did you see the look on that desk jockey's face?" He put up his hands and raised his voice a couple of octaves. "Not the payroll. Not the payroll. Hya, hya, hya." Tsunami leaned back, resting his arms across the top of the back seat, sticking his chest out. "That's how it's done. Gonna take her all day to get those papers back in order."

Keeper's heart was pounding so loud in his ears, he could barely hear Tsunami. It was becoming apparent that being an evil villain equated to one disastrous event after another.

"That went smoothly, huh?" Tsunami said, taking out his phone. "Like taking candy from a baby. I'm feeling generous. Let's see that chip number. I'll look it up for you."

Toby handed his phone to Keeper, and Keeper read the number off. Tsunami typed into his phone and tapped some buttons.

"Found him. His name is Peanut. Get this—he belongs to . . ."

"Joanne Josephine Larbole," finished Keeper. He stared straight ahead, eyes unblinking. There was an emotion swirling around him and rising in his throat, but he couldn't figure out what it was. What were the odds? She really had been saying she didn't have enough money to get Peanut in the park. Was the cookie money a dognapping ransom?

"You know," Tsunami said. "This is why no one likes you, kid. You interrupt people and make it all about you. You should break that bad habit."

Keeper snapped out of the fog. "What? I do not. And people like me."

Tsunami rolled his eyes. "Who?"

Keeper's mind went blank. He needed a name. "Toby. Toby likes me."

Toby turned into the Taco Town parking lot and parked next to Tsunami's SUV. "It's true," Toby said, nodding. "I do like him."

Tsunami scratched the dog behind the ears. "Doesn't count. You're young and naive and don't know any better. You'll grow out of it eventually."

Toby looked at Keeper, unsure if he had just been insulted or complimented. Keeper shrugged, unsure himself.

Tsunami turned his attention back to Keeper. "What now, genius?"

"We return the dog to Joanne Larbole. It's her dog."

Tsunami threw his head back. "For the love of Skeletor! Seriously? And you want to be an E.V.I.L. villain."

Keeper was thoroughly confused. "We don't return the dog?"

"Gah!" Tsunami rubbed his temples. "Of course we return

the dog. Larbole is probably worried sick over her missing baby. However, there's no reason to not get something out of it. Something you need?" Tsunami waited for a response from Keeper or Toby. "Something Larbole can give you?"

Keeper was completely lost. "Money?"

"What? Money?" Tsunami officially hit the fed-up mark. "What in the world do you need money for? Cookies, moron. Cookies. You need cookies."

Toby looked at Keeper. "That's true. We do."

Tsunami reached behind himself and pulled the seat belt forward, locking it into place. "Okay, let's go. I don't have all day."

Keeper could now definitely identify the emotion as panic. "Oh. No. That's not necessary. You don't have to come with us. We'll be fine."

"Pbbblt." Tsunami didn't buy it. "Right. I let you two babies go off on your own and you come back with no cookies and who do you think will have to deal with the wrath of Chaos? Me. That's who. It's not happening. Put this bad boy in drive, and crack the windows. The dog breath is getting to be a bit much back here."

Keeper and Toby exchanged a look of agreement. The dog's breath was a bit overwhelming, and there was no way they were getting out of this one. Tsunami tagging along was totally cringeworthy. Best to just get it over with.

Toby backed out of the parking spot and headed in the

direction of the Cookie Maven's home. "On the plus side, once we return the dog and get the cookies, were done, right? Problem solved."

"Solved?" Tsunami said. "What world are you living in? Some colossal dung beetle stole a dog. We're going to hunt this loser down, and I am going to rain on his parade at a monsoon level."

Keeper looked back at Tsunami. "Let me get this straight. It's okay for you to demand cookies in exchange for the return of someone's lost dog, but it's not okay to dognap a dog and demand money for its return?"

"Yeah, that's right, genius," Tsunami said. "Look, if you stole the dog and gave him a fluffy bed, his favorite dog food, brushed him, and played with him, and all that stuff, while you waited for the ransom, that's a different deal. It's like a doggy vacation. However, according to Toby, here, you saved the dog. And not from the dognapper. The dognapper is such an epic loser that he either lost the dog or handed him over to the people you had to save him from. People so horrible you couldn't put up a found poster. Not okay. Totally irresponsible dognapping. I should also point out that demanding a ransom so high that it puts a person with an important business, like cookies, out of business is also a big no-no. Capiche?"

Keeper thought about it for a moment. In a weird villainous way, it did make sense. "Yeah. Capiche."

"Besides," Tsunami said, looking out the window. "I'm not

going to demand cookies. I'm going to emphatically appeal to her sense of gratitude. If that doesn't work, we'll let you do your thing to her."

Keeper pivoted in his seat to look at Tsunami. "My thing?"

"Yeah. Your skill. Charming people. That's what you do, right?"

Once again Keeper couldn't tell if Tsunami was trying to be complimentary or insulting. "That is not my skill. I don't charm people. Besides, you just said people hate me."

"Yeah, and then you charm them. Doesn't work on me, though, because I'm wise to your game and mentally unyielding."

"What you are," Keeper said, "is loudmouthed and narcissistic. I don't have a skill."

Tsunami's eyes narrowed, and he sucked on his teeth for a couple of seconds. "First of all, thank you. Are you sure your skill isn't charming? And second of all"—Tsunami leaned forward toward Keeper—"that's total claptrap. Chaos wouldn't want you if you didn't have a skill. According to him, everyone has a skill."

Keeper turned back, to face forward. "Well, mine isn't charming people."

Tsunami leaned back in his seat, studying Keeper. "Maybe not, but it's something. Something big. Or at least Chaos thinks it is. And since he clearly hasn't bored you with his skill theory, allow me to do his dirty work. As I said, Chaos thinks everyone has a skill. Some people ignore it or squash it down or choose to play blind to it, living in denial. Others simply can't recognize their skill. Might be that their skill is seemingly small, like they always hit green traffic lights, or maybe red. Some people have their skill since birth. Other people might not have their skill show itself until they're ninety-eight and on their deathbed. There's no rhyme or reason other than that everyone can do something special. Sometimes those special things are frowned upon by conventional society or can't be controlled. That's when E.V.I.L. shows up."

Toby pulled to the curb in front of the Cookie Maven's house. He looked at Tsunami in the rearview mirror. "How was it for you?" Toby asked.

"Started in my late twenties, at least I think it did. I tried to keep squashing down my skill until it couldn't be squashed anymore. Ruined my career with NASA. Destroyed everything I knew and had worked for."

Keeper and Toby had turned in their seats and were looking at Tsunami.

"Keep your lame, sorry sentiment to yourselves," Tsunami said, unbuckling his seat belt. "It didn't destroy my life. It gave me a new one. And don't go asking other E.V.I.L. villains about their past. In general, villains don't like to talk about it or be judged by it. It's the past. We live in the present."

Keeper found himself feeling oddly relieved by Tsunami's final statement. Keeper had absolutely no desire to talk about any moment of his life between birth and sitting in the car outside the Cookie Maven's house with Toby, an E.V.I.L. villain, and a stolen Irish Wolfhound.

Tsunami pushed his door open and took hold of the dog's leash. "I'm tired of talking about this garbage. Let's return the dog, get some cookies, make some dognapper's life a living nightmare, and have an initiation ceremony so I hopefully won't have to see either one of you again until the holiday party."

CHAPTER 17

KEEPER, Toby, Tsunami, and Peanut the dog, formerly known as Gandalf, stood on the front porch of Joanne Larbole's home, waiting. Keeper rang the doorbell three times. No answer. He went to ring it a fourth time and Tsunami pushed him out of the way.

"For crying out loud," Tsunami said, and started hammering on the door with his fist. The door popped open, as if it hadn't been fully latched closed.

Keeper, Toby, and Tsunami exchanged looks. Something was definitely not right.

"Babies first," Tsunami said, motioning with his hand.

Keeper looked at Toby and rolled his eyes. Tsunami wasn't just obnoxious. He was also a coward.

Keeper raised the leg on his jeans and pulled out the telescopic baton from his sock. He moved forward, pushed the door open the rest of the way, and stepped inside with Toby on his heels. The entryway seemed clear. There were stairs, and a hallway leading to the kitchen, in front of them. To the right was a living room and to the left a dining room. Neither room was overly furnished, making it relatively easy to see there was nothing nefarious lurking.

"Smell anything?" Keeper asked Toby.

"Cookies."

"Anything else?"

"Yeah, and I don't like it," Toby said. "Sort of a mix of smells. None of them good. They don't belong in a house that smells like cookies."

"Stay behind me," Keeper said. "If you hear or smell anything, tug on my shirt and point me in the right direction."

"I'll stay here with the dog," Tsunami said. "We don't want him to get dognapped again."

Keeper crept forward, toward the kitchen. "Yeah, no, we wouldn't want that," he said under his breath.

Keeper moved slowly and quietly, waiting for the tug on his shirt. All he felt was Toby stepping on his heels and breathing down his neck. He carefully leaned forward to see inside a room that spanned the length of the house. There was a kitchen on one side with a door that Keeper suspected led to the garage. On the other side of the room was an area for eating breakfast.

There was a door to the backyard and windows that let in plenty of light. The room looked clear, but there was always the garage, and Keeper had noticed another door. He went toward the breakfast nook first and slowly opened the mystery door to find a half bath. He moved back across the kitchen and found a short hallway leading to a large walk-in pantry, filled mostly with flour, sugar, and a variety of things to put in cookies.

Keeper turned to Toby. Toby had a death grip on his own shirt. He looked like Keeper felt. *Anything?* Keeper mouthed.

Toby shook his head.

Keeper pointed toward the garage door and slowly made his way to it. Part of him hoped he would open the door and a bad guy would be there. Then they could just get it over with.

The garage door had a weather seal around its frame and made some noise as it was opening. Joanne Larbole's car was parked in the garage. There was light coming in from a high window on the garage door, but not enough to see clearly.

Keeper looked at Toby and motioned with his head at the garage. Toby stood still listening and then sniffed the air. He shook his head and silently mouthed, *Nothing.*

Keeper went down two stairs into the garage and felt the car's hood. It was cold. He circled the SUV, looked inside its windows, and returned to Toby.

"Car hasn't run recently," Keeper whispered. "Let's check the upstairs."

"Maybe she went for a walk and didn't close the door all the way," Toby offered, following after Keeper.

"We can only hope," Keeper said.

He made his way back to the front door. Tsunami was still standing there, holding tight to Peanut's leash. Peanut was panting and looking almost as anxious as Tsunami.

"Downstairs seems clear," Keeper said. "We're going up."

"Well, stop lollygagging," Tsunami said, his eyes darting about as if he was hearing noises. "Poor Peanut is getting nervous."

Keeper noticed a strange fog on the ground, circling around Tsunami's and Peanut's feet. "Yeah. I can see that."

Keeper climbed the stairs with Toby following. There were three bedrooms upstairs. One had been converted into a home office. Keeper couldn't find anyone lurking under beds or in closets.

Toby seemed a bit more relaxed. "The smell isn't up here. It was only downstairs."

Keeper frowned. "That means the giver of the bad smell was here and gone by the time we arrived. The question that remains is the whereabouts of the Cookie Maven. Did she leave with the bad smell willingly or by force? Did she leave to follow the bad smell? Or, maybe she's somewhere else, like you said, out for a walk."

"If she went for a walk, she would have returned by now," Toby said. "My instinct says she left with the giver of the bad smell."

Keeper nodded. "Mine too. And it doesn't really matter if it was willingly or by force...."

Toby's eyes went wide, and he held up his hand for Keeper to stop talking. "Did you hear that?" he whispered.

Keeper shook his head.

"Like a thump. Downstairs."

Keeper and Toby hurried down the stairs to the entryway. The door was still open, but Tsunami wasn't there. Instead, there was a small puddle of water on the floor. At least Keeper hoped it was water.

Keeper turned and looked down the hallway toward the kitchen. Peanut was on the floor, lying on his side. Keeper rushed over and felt the dog's chest. He was breathing and snoring. Keeper pulled a tranquilizer dart from Peanut's hip and turned to show Toby.

Toby was in a full-on freak-out. "Omigosh! Omigosh! Omigosh!"

Keeper stood up. "It's okay. Peanut is fine. Just sleeping."

"That's not it," Toby said, wringing his shirt. "The smell. It's stronger now. It took Tsunami. I know it."

"The smell's funeral. Why would anyone want Tsunami? The dog I get. The dog is awesome. Tsunami . . . not so much."

Toby was pacing. "You don't understand. This is bad. REALLY bad. We just got a villain kidnapped. Kidnapped! And what if Slasher was right, and you're bad luck, and this was your fault? And I'm an accomplice. If Chaos finds out, we'll never get into Chapter 626. The only other organization that will maybe take me is the army. I'm not designed for push-ups, Keeper! Look at me! PUSH-UPS!"

"Get it together!" Keeper ran his hand through his hair, thinking, the pressure mounting. "Chaos doesn't need to know anything. At least not yet. We have one lead. The Porcelain Palace guy. Let's get the dog back to your house and plan what will hopefully be a rescue mission."

Toby nodded, but he looked like he was going to pass out.

Polyp parked his beat-up Bonneville in the Porcelain Palace's back loading zone. He retrieved a lopsided and well-used two-wheel hand truck that was sitting next to the back door and rolled it to his car's trunk. He popped the trunk open, stared inside for a few seconds, then did his best to remove the sinister smile from his face and replace it with a look that was all business.

Polyp reached inside the trunk and pulled out a roll of duct tape. He loosened a length of it and put the end of the tape in his mouth, then reached into the trunk and tried to pull Tsunami out by the armpits. It took some doing, but eventually Polyp had the unconscious E.V.I.L. villain duct-taped to the hand truck, his head hanging down.

Polyp jogged over to the back door, opened it, and put the doorstop down. He jogged back over to the car and rolled

Tsunami, who he knew for a fact was not Keeper Chance, into the back room.

"Here you go," Polyp said to the man sitting patiently, meditating, on top of a crate. "I am delivering Keeper Chance."

Sensei Love opened his eyes but didn't move. He didn't smile, and he didn't speak. Polyp thought it was pretty impressive that Love could look so calm while he was trying to compose himself. Must be part of the martial arts thing.

Polyp wasn't about to give himself up, either. He stood, looking as proud as he could possibly look, and gestured toward the body on the hand truck.

Sensei Love unfolded his legs, effortlessly hopped down from the crate, and walked over to them. He removed the tranquilizer dart from the body's shoulder and dropped it on the floor. "Our deal was for you to deliver Keeper Chance. This is not Keeper Chance," Love said. "Not even close."

Polyp had detected a slight quiver to Sensei Love's voice. Things were going even better than planned. "Are you sure?" Polyp asked, doing his best to sound confused and horrified.

"Yes, I'm sure!"

"But this is definitely a villain, and with Chapter 626."

Sensei Love was working overtime to keep his composure. All those years of Whylene working him over had to be the heavens' way of preparing him for this moment in his life. He reminded himself that it would all be worth it to have Keeper Chance in his dojo. One had to expect things like this to happen when one hired exiled villains to do one's dirty work. "This is Tsunami. Keeper Chance is younger, taller, and has dark hair."

"Ohhhhh. My bad. You probably should have supplied those details up front. I can try again. No biggie." Polyp hooked a thumb at Tsunami. "What do you want to do with him?"

Sensei Love stood staring at Tsunami. Polyp knew the wheels were turning in Love's head, and more likely than not, they weren't turning toward good. The slope toward villainy was slippery, especially when one had delusions of righteousness.

"Wheel him out to your car," Love said. "We'll have to hold him someplace until I have my meeting with Keeper. Once Keeper and I are gone, drive him out to a field somewhere and let him go. He'll have plenty of time to rethink his life while he finds his way home."

Polyp went to the hand truck. "Will do. I know the perfect holding spot. There's an old abandoned factory on the edge of the industrial district, just outside of Parsimmon. It shouldn't take me long."

Sensei Love followed Polyp and the hand truck out of the Palace. "I'm sure I can find it," Love said. "You are staying here. I guarantee Keeper Chance will be showing up at your place of business within twenty-four hours, looking for the missing member of 626. It's inevitable. Get me Keeper."

Polyp bowed slightly. "As you wish, Sensei. Would you like this villain attached or detached from the hand truck?"

"Detached, but give me the duct tape."

Polyp rolled Tsunami back outside and cut him free. Sensei Love put him into the trunk of Polyp's car.

"When you get Keeper, you can use my car. Keys are in the center console," Love said. "Don't mess up again. I'm a busy man."

Polyp smiled. "Of course. Apologies." He watched Sensei Love drive off in the Bonneville before turning to go back inside. "What a pretentious peacock. I'll give you Keeper Chance when I'm good and ready." Polyp was also going to demand a new and improved scepter with his Vogue costume. Sensei Love could consider it a smugness surcharge. But there wasn't time to daydream about the happy days ahead. This was only the first stage of Polyp's master plan, which meant he had to continue leveling the playing field with the legendary 626. There was work to do before the two boys arrived. At least now Polyp had an idea of which one was Keeper.

CHAPTER 18

KEEPER and Toby had been sitting in the Kia, watching the Porcelain Palace, for five hours. It was now ten at night, and they were parked down the street. They had circled the block countless times. Toby had listened at both the front and back doors to the store, but there were never any sounds. The dumpster in the back loading dock area made it hard to smell anything other than expired Chinese takeout and urine.

"There hasn't been any activity since we got here," Keeper said. "No lights on, no car parked in the lot or by the back door."

"I don't think Tsunami is in there," Toby said, polishing off a cracker snack pack. He had his laptop open on his lap. "I just sent off everything I could find on this porcelain guy and Larbole to Chaos."

"Did you find anything interesting?"

Toby shook his head. "I don't think so. Owner is Todd Jones. No other employees, so that had to be the guy we talked to. Business has been open for a couple of years. Nothing outstandingly interesting about Todd Jones. To be honest, hardly any info at all. No social media accounts with pics of him. Just some basic, boring paperwork trails. For some reason, that kind of bothers me. If I'm pulling information on the correct Todd Jones, the guy we met, the store, even the dognapping, seem, well . . ."

Keeper raised an eyebrow. "Out of character?"

"Yeah." Toby closed the laptop. "Or maybe off in some way. But I'm just looking at stats on a screen. And I'm pretty freaked out by the whole losing Tsunami thing today. I'm not sure I trust myself."

Keeper looked at Toby. He trusted Toby. If the trail seemed off or wrong, it probably was.

Keeper placed the night-vision goggles Chaos had given him on his head. "I'm going in. Want to pick the lock for me?"

"Yeah." Toby put his laptop in the back seat and opened the driver's door. "And I'm coming with you."

"You don't have to do that," Keeper said.

"Yes, I do. I have your back. I'll know if trouble is coming before it's too late."

Keeper and Toby made their way down the deserted sidewalk to the back of the Palace. Toby took out his lockpick set and went to work on the back door. Keeper removed the screwdriver from his back pocket. His eyes scanned over the back lot, looking for shadows moving or signs of being watched. He glanced down and noticed a piece of paper sticking out from under Toby's sneaker.

"I owe you one, Toby," Keeper said, bending down to pick it up. It was soggy, smeared, and crumpled, but looked to be a receipt for an exorbitant amount of Chinese food. He flipped the paper over and saw what was at one time a crude stick-figure doodle with *Xs* for eyes, 626 written on its stick-figure chest, and what might be cookies around it. "I need to learn how to open locks."

"After we find Tsunami and you get me into Chapter 626," Toby said. "Get ready. I think I have it."

Keeper shoved the troublesome receipt into his pocket, so he could get a better look at it later, then lowered his goggles and switched them on. Toby turned the door's handle and pulled it open. Keeper stepped inside and looked to the right and then the left. He used his screwdriver to pop the casing off the alarm panel, now blinking red, and then ripped the entire motherboard out with it.

"Let's keep this search around five to ten minutes," Keeper said, and snapped the case back onto the alarm panel. "Five would be best."

Toby started making his way systematically around the exterior of the room. Keeper went to the desk first. Bills, invoices, junk mail, all addressed to Todd Jones or Porcelain Palace. He opened the laptop on the desk and pressed an arrow button to wake it up. Nothing. He pressed the button to power it on. A red battery symbol appeared briefly, and then the screen went blank. Keeper closed the laptop and pushed the chair to the side so he could access the drawers. He looked down, and a glint of something caught his eye. He picked it up and turned it over. It was Tsunami's Fred Draper name tag. Keeper put it in his pocket and continued searching.

The drawers were far less interesting. Mostly brochures from manufacturers regarding sinks, tubs, and towel bars.

"Find anything?" Keeper asked Toby.

"There are definitely smells that were also in the Cookie Maven's house. I'm thinking burnt microwave popcorn and Chinese food," Toby said. "The sleeping bag and cot smell like everything else here. Maybe add in some body odor and drool."

Toby bent to look under the cot, and there was a crunching sound under his sneaker. Keeper crossed the room to Toby and knelt down. Toby picked his foot up, and Keeper retrieved a small object, now bent.

"Looks like an earring," Toby said.

"I don't remember Todd Jones wearing earrings. Especially ones that are diamond *J*s. But I bet Joanne Larbole does." Keeper glanced at the door and put the earring in his pocket. "Time to go."

He led Toby to the door, picked the motherboard up off the floor as he exited, and threw it in the parking lot's dumpster.

"Todd Jones is going to know someone was in the back room," Toby said, powerwalking alongside Keeper to the Kia.

"We have bigger problems. Todd Jones is definitely responsible for the dognapping ransom in one way or another." Keeper slid into the passenger seat of the Kia and waited for Toby to turn the engine over and pull away from the curb. He moved the goggles back to the top of his head and pulled the name tag out of his pocket. "I found this over by the desk." He turned one of the front lights on and held the plastic badge under it. "It's the name tag Tsunami was wearing."

"Crud," Toby said. "Do you think we should go back? What if Tsunami is being held in the showroom?"

Keeper shook his head. "Tsunami is wherever Todd Jones is right now, and we've been waiting for over five hours for him to appear. I don't think Jones is going to show tonight. The real problem is we didn't find any clues telling us where he would have taken Tsunami and Joanne Larbole."

"Let's not forget the other big question," Toby said. "Why? Why would he kidnap Tsunami? Why leave the dog this time? Why kidnap the Cookie Maven, assuming that's what happened to her."

Keeper removed the goggles and stared forward, thinking. "Let's prioritize. We need to get Tsunami back and Larbole if she's with him. If we can find them, they might be able to shed some light on things. I say we return tomorrow, during business hours. If Todd Jones leaves, we follow."

"I'll have my mom make us sandwiches for the stakeout," Toby said. "She'll like that."

Polyp waited until it was late at night, well past what he assumed was bedtime for villainous teenage boys, before returning to the Porcelain Palace. He opened the back door and looked at the keypad. It was dark. Fantastic. The stupid thing blinked red all the time, keeping him up at night. It wasn't connected to a security service. That service had been shut off once the bill wasn't paid. No biggie. There wasn't a whole lot of point alarming a building filled with toilets and tubs that, if you wanted to get technical, were already stolen.

Polyp immediately went to his desk and looked underneath. The name tag was gone. Excellent. He went to a metal file cabinet, pushed against a wall in a corner, and opened the bottom drawer. The dog's collar was still there.

Polyp closed the drawer and rolled his eyes. "How could those two pubescent dunderheads have missed the collar? It was sooooo easy." Polyp stood for a moment, thinking. Bad enough the rotten dog had pulled his head out of his collar and run away two days after he had dognapped it. He should never have brought the beast along while he was scouting for a meeting spot at Marble Park, but he was tired of picking up the dog's poop in the back parking lot. Let the Cookie Maven's precious puppy do its business in the woods for once and make it someone else's problem.

Polyp had thought for sure the dog had found its way home. A stroke of luck that the hound hadn't. The box of money had arrived as planned, but since he didn't have Peanut to turn over, he'd sent a message to Larbole demanding more money. Polyp had made sure the second asking price was so exorbitant he wouldn't have to return the dog at their next meeting. There was no way she'd be able to pay. Who knew she'd be so distraught she would shut down her store?

Polyp had intended to use the illicit funds to buy some plastic tubs and a thousand rats. He would release the rats in the Cookie Maven store's kitchen, call the health inspector, and then watch the shop be closed down. No more cookies. No initiation ceremony for 626.

Instead, he used some of the money for a night of gorging himself on Chinese takeout.

"Yes, sir, the wheel of fortune is definitely spinning toward my peg," Polyp mumbled to himself. "Saved me three steps, a couple of days, and I had a meal that didn't consist of expired microwave popcorn."

The dog was a mystery, though. How did the villains get the dog? And how did they know it was the Cookie Maven's?

Polyp waved off the question as if it were a fly buzzing about his face. "Dumb luck. Just dumb luck. The world is surprisingly small. Focus, Polyp, focus."

He walked over to the cot and looked underneath. The earring was gone. Two out of three clues had been found, not so bad. It had to be enough to pique the villains' interest. Doubtful enough interest for Chaos himself to show up at the dome, but someone would come.

Polyp stepped on the heels of his shoes, pulling them off and kicking them to the side. He stretched out on his cot and sleeping bag, put his hands behind his head, and stared up at the yellowing ceiling panels. Yes, yes, good fortune indeed. He was starting to feel like his old self again. And once he destroyed Chapter 626 and Chaos, he would start his own army of disgruntled villains to take over E.V.I.L. worldwide, and there would be none of the ridiculous rules. "No villainy on other villains. *Pbbblt.*" Polyp blew a raspberry at that idea. His followers would *only* do villainy on villains.

Polyp burst into peals of laughter over his own brilliance. "Genius. Pure genius. Who wouldn't want to join?"

He might even destroy Sensei Love and his dojo of doom . . . No. *Careful, Polyp. You're good, but not that good. You don't have what it takes to bring Love down,* he said to himself. Doing something like that would require someone special. Someone with an extraordinary skill.

Polyp sat up, thinking. Keeper Chance maybe? Why did

Love want him so badly? What was the kid's skill? "This is something you'll have to find out," Polyp said to himself, lying back down. "Tomorrow, revise the master plan to get Chance, just like Sensei Love wants. Then keep the boy for yourself."

He closed his eyes, a smile on his face, and drifted off into a well-deserved sleep. Dreaming of evil deeds and going down in E.V.I.L. history for becoming its supreme leader and revolutionizing E.V.I.L. rules and regulations.

CHAPTER 19

KEEPER and Toby were sitting in Carpet Castle's parking lot, watching the Porcelain Palace, when a silver SUV pulled into the spot next to them. Y opened the driver's door, dropped out, closed and locked the vehicle, and jumped into the Kia's back seat.

"I thought I'd find you two here," she said, sitting forward, resting her elbows on the backs of the two front seats. "Before you fill me in on the dog, listen to this. . . ."

Keeper was still staring out his side window at the silver SUV. He turned to look at Y. "What the fudge? Is that Joanne Larbole's SUV? You stole her car?"

"Borrowed, Keeper. Borrowed," Y said. "I'll return it. Eventually."

"Did you 'borrow' Joanne Larbole, too? I bet you have all her spoons stuffed in your pockets."

Y let out a gasp. "I knew it! The Cookie Maven is missing! Last night I got tired of waiting outside Toby's house for you guys, so I decided to search the shop and her house on my own. I went to her house first. Door was unlocked, no one home, and get this." Y paused for effect. "There was a puddle of water on the floor by the front door."

"That was from Tsunami," Toby said. "Good to know it was water. We weren't a hundred percent."

"Whoa, whoa, whoa!" Y held up her hands and inched a bit closer to the edge of her seat. "Why were you in the Cookie Maven's house with Tsunami? I thought *we* were a team."

Keeper really wanted to roll his eyes, but he used every last bit of his energy to refrain. "Look, to make an unbelievably ridiculous story short, the dog we found is named Peanut and belongs to Joanne Larbole. We went to return Peanut, and Tsunami got kidnapped."

Y stared at Keeper. Looking directly into his dark blue eyes. Keeper's level of discomfort was growing tenfold every second. The corner of Y's mouth began to twitch, and she finally gave in, collapsing back into the seat with laughter to the point of tears.

"So awful!" Y said through gasps, trying to catch her breath. "Someone has to help the poor kidnapper."

"It's not funny," Keeper said. "If Chaos finds out we got

Tsunami kidnapped, we'll never get into Chapter 626. This is worse than no cookies."

"Or you'll get medals of E.V.I.L. honor," Y said, laughing even harder.

Keeper turned back to watching the Palace and slouched down in his seat.

"Okay, okay," Y said, wiping away tears. "You need to get Tsunami back. How hard can it be? You think this Porcelain Palace guy did it?"

"We know he did," Toby said. "Last night we broke in and found Tsunami's fake name tag and a diamond earring in the shape of a *J* in the back storage room."

Y's brow furrowed slightly as she thought. She leaned forward again. "Did it take you a long time to find these things?"

Keeper was sitting up straighter now. He turned to look at Y. "No. How fast we found the name tag and earring didn't seem weird until just now. When Toby said it out loud."

Y shook her head. "Why would the kidnapper want you to know he has Larbole and Tsunami?"

Keeper shrugged. "Maybe the name tag and earring were supposed to be for someone else to find?"

Y wasn't smiling anymore. "Maybe they weren't."

"Ohhhhh no! Oh no. Oh no." Toby was bouncing in his seat, and nervous sweat seemed imminent. He was staring at the front door of the Palace. "Look who's going into the Palace. It's Dr. Spot. This isn't good. What do we do?"

Dr. Spot, Chapter 626's master of nerve damage, had appeared out of nowhere. She was wearing skinny jeans, a pink tunic type of top with embroidered flowers and low heels. Her hair was up in a messy bun. A medium-size tote hung on her shoulder.

"Are you sure?" Keeper asked. He had only met Dr. Spot the other night, and this person looked . . . ordinary. Your typical bathroom renovation shopper.

"Yes. Yes, I'm sure. My fingers are still pins and needles from shaking her hand. One doesn't forget that easily." Toby covered his eyes with his hands. "What is she doing here, and why is she going inside?"

"I suspect Chaos sent her to investigate," Keeper said to Toby. "Let's not panic. She certainly doesn't look like a villain, and she's a lot more experienced than us. I'm sure she can handle herself."

They sat, waiting, watching the front door. Ten minutes passed and then twenty.

"I don't like it," Toby said. "Something's not right."

"I agree," Keeper said. "But we could be wrong, and I don't want to ruin Dr. Spot's cover, or interrupt a situation where she's getting information. That would be another one-way ticket out of Chapter 626."

"I'll go in," Y said. "Neither Dr. Spot nor the Porcelain Palace guy . . ."

"Todd Jones," Toby offered. "The owner's name is Todd Jones."

"Neither Dr. Spot nor Todd Jones knows me. I'll just pretend I came in to ask for directions to Burger Boy." Y took a new burner phone out of her pocket. "Give me your number, Toby. If there's an issue, I'll text."

Toby took out his phone and exchanged a text with Y. Y put her phone back in her pocket, exited the Kia, and crossed the street to the store.

Five minutes later Toby's phone buzzed with a message to join Y in the Palace.

They jogged across the street and slipped through the front door. The showroom seemed empty, except for Y.

"No one is here," Y said. "I searched the entire floor. The door to the back is locked. I couldn't see anyone through the grimy window. Maybe you can take a listen, Toby?"

They walked toward the storage room, and Toby put his ear near the door. "Nope. Nothing," he said.

Toby punched in the code he had used the last time, and the lock clicked open. Keeper went in first, followed by Y and then Toby.

Keeper was confident in Toby's skills. If someone was there, he would have heard something . . . unless the person was dead. Keeper really didn't want to find a dead person. Especially if the dead person was Dr. Spot or Tsunami or the Cookie Maven. Fortunately, there were no dead people in the back room. Unfortunately, there were no live people there, either.

"I don't get it," Toby said. "I was watching. No one came out the front door, and I never saw that beat-up embarrassment of a car—not that I'm judging—that's always parked out back pass by any of the side streets. I chose that parking spot at the Carpet Castle for a reason."

Keeper opened the door that led to the back lot. It was empty. "There's no car," Keeper said. "Either we missed the getaway, Jones was parked elsewhere, or . . . I don't know."

There was a moment of silence as everyone digested the situation. Things had gone from bad to worse to abominable.

"What do we do now?" Toby asked.

Keeper ran his hands through his hair and closed his eyes, thinking. "Showboater," Keeper said. He opened his eyes to find Toby and Y staring at him in disbelief.

"I'm afraid to ask," Y said, "but what about him?"

"Toby is going to text him that we need to talk privately. We find a safe meeting spot, explain the situation, and pray for a miracle. He might know what to do."

Y shook her head. "What he's going to do is rat you out to Chaos. He's a senior member."

"I don't think so," Keeper said. "Slasher would go to Chaos for sure. Showboater . . ." Keeper bit on his lower lip, trying to find the right words.

"Is the kooky uncle," Toby said, smiling. "The one who is always encouraging—and bailing you out of—bad ideas."

"Exactly," Keeper said. "If he thinks there is no other option, he'll go to Chaos. Otherwise, Showboater is our only hope."

KEEPER CHANCE AND THE CONUNDRUM OF CHAOS

◎◎◎

Polyp drove Sensei Love's sedan into the abandoned warehouse through a crumbling wall that left just enough space for a car to enter. Once inside, he parked next to his Bonneville and unceremoniously dragged the unconscious body of Dr. Spot from the back seat. He threw her over his shoulder and made his way to the chosen meeting spot, a small office with a metal door.

Polyp kicked at the office door with his dilapidated shoe. It swung open slightly and slammed shut from the hydraulics. The only thing still working in the deathtrap of a building.

"Hello!" Polyp called out. "Sensei Love? A little help here. My hands are full."

A few seconds later the door opened to show Love silhouetted by the light of several battery-powered camping lanterns. It didn't look like he was going to help any further, or move, so Polyp plowed forward with his load, through the door.

"I've brought you Keeper," Polyp said, knowing full well the villain he had was Dr. Spot. He dumped her body on an old metal desk and stepped back so Sensei Love could properly lament the ill-done handiwork.

Sensei calmly walked over to the desk and towered above Dr. Spot. "That's not Keeper."

Polyp's jaw fell open in surprise. It was a move he had been practicing all afternoon. "Villain, younger, taller, dark hair. Came into my shop, just like you said. Are you sure this isn't Keeper?"

"Yes, I'm sure. It's a girl! A girl!" Sensei Love's voice was approaching a volume it seldom experienced.

"Yes, I know this is a girl." Polyp was highly impressed with himself. Word on the street was that nothing riled Sensei Love. He was a pillar of self-control.

Sensei Love closed his eyes, took a deep breath, and slowly exhaled, internally chanting a mantra of serenity. When he was done, he opened his eyes. "Keeper is male."

Polyp preferred Love's loud voice to the eerily calm one, but it didn't matter. Polyp had the upper hand. He was certain. "Oooohhh. Well, why didn't you say so? I mean, with a name like Keeper, how am I supposed to know?"

Sensei Love looked calm, but there was an almost imperceptible twitch in his jaw. "I apologize. Let me be clear. Keeper Chance is male. Dark hair. Lately he's been seen with a sidekick who is also male and the same age. Do you understand?"

"Yes, yes, I totally know who you're talking about now. So sorry about the mess up. Do you want the sidekick as well?"

"What I want," Love said slowly, "is Keeper Chance. I don't care one way or the other about the sidekick. Get. Me. Keeper."

This Keeper kid must have a serious skill for Love to be putting up with so much ineptitude, Polyp thought. *What skill would a dojo master want this bad? Maybe Keeper can use the Force! Play it cool, Polyp!*

Polyp clasped his hands in front of his chest and looked

down at Dr. Spot. "Don't get your knickers in a bunch, Sensei. I made a few mistakes. It happens. What would you like me to do with this one?"

"Grab the roll of duct tape and help me carry her to where I'm holding the other villain."

CHAPTER 20

IT was late afternoon when Toby dropped Keeper off at the meeting spot chosen by Showboater and went to find a parking space at least two or three blocks away. Showboater had chosen a large antiques store in the town of Parsimmon, if by antiques you meant old, rusty, partially broken, and way overpriced. There was rarely anyone in the store. How it managed to stay open was a mystery, but the villains would be able to get lost easily in one of the back rooms for a private conversation.

Toby had texted Y the meeting time and location once he'd heard back from Showboater. She was already at the store, waiting for them, when Keeper arrived. He stood next to her, in front of a large-pane window, while she pretended to have interest in a set of "vintage" hammers.

Keeper glanced toward the man sitting at the cash register to make sure he wasn't overly interested in them. It was hard to tell since the merchant was hidden behind old tin signs and beaded table lamps, but there was a lot of coughing and throat clearing, so Keeper assumed it was okay to talk in hushed tones.

"Hey," Keeper said to Y. "Toby is going to park a few blocks down. Showboater has a meeting with the senior members not far from here. He'll come over when he's done."

Y looked up at Keeper. "No doubt that meeting is about the disappearance of Dr. Spot."

Keeper shrugged. "Not sure if they know yet. But I think it's safe to say the meeting is about Todd Jones, the Porcelain Palace, cookies, and possibly us." Keeper dug into his pocket and pulled out the receipt from the back lot. "Take a look at this. I found it near the Porcelain Palace's back door."

Y turned the scrap of paper over to see the doodle. "Who do you think this is supposed to be?"

"Doesn't have long hair. I think we can eliminate Dr. Spot, Joy, and Staticanator."

Y studied the drawing. "No beard, so not Barricade. If it was you, it would probably have curly hair."

"Agreed," Keeper said. "And let's be honest. If it were Tsunami, it would probably have stink lines."

Y studied the paper. "I'll give you that one with a twenty-five percent chance you're wrong."

"That leaves Showboater, Slasher, Chaos, and Toby," Keeper

said, taking the scrap back from Y and returning it to his pocket.

"Has Toby seen the doodle?" Y asked.

"No. Toby's my best friend and has some super-impressive skills, but I'm not sure he could handle this. Until we can figure it out, I need your help keeping him safe."

Y's arm wrapped around Keeper's, and she took his hand in hers. Keeper froze for a moment, torn between panic and full-blown freaking out.

"Can I help you?" The voice came from behind Keeper. It was full of phlegm and followed by coughing. It was the man from the counter.

"No, thank you," Y said, smiling. "We're just waiting for my uncle and cousin. My uncle is all about antique tools."

The shop merchant looked Y and Keeper over. He was short and round and had a weepy eye. "Don't steal anything."

"We'll try not to," Y said.

Keeper had a feeling that ideas had just been put into Y's head.

Y watched the man turn and wobble back to his position behind the tin signs. Keeper looked out the front window, desperate for any sign of Toby or Showboater. He leaned forward a couple of inches and squinted over Y's head. "Is that . . . Todd Jones?"

Y looked out the window and saw a middle-aged man in maroon sweatpants and a ratty gray T-shirt doing a weird strut down the sidewalk.

"Come on." Keeper pulled Y out of the store and down the street after Jones.

They made sure to follow at a distance. Jones strutted two blocks and took a left. Keeper and Y jogged across the street, doing their best to hide behind parked cars and the occasional tree. After another couple of blocks, the beat-up Bonneville came into view.

"That's his junker," Keeper said. "We're going to lose him."

Y pulled her hand from Keeper's. "I don't think so," she said.

Keeper watched Y round the car they were next to and go to the driver's door. Keeper's heart began to beat faster, and his mouth went dry. He knew this car. He walked to the back and glanced at the license plate. SLASHR. What were the chances?

"No, no, no, no, no. We can't take this car."

"Of course we can," Y said, putting her lockpick set back into her pocket and pulling out a small screwdriver. "I can hot-wire anything. Get in."

Keeper stood with his mouth hanging open as he heard the car roar to life. He ran back to the passenger's side and jumped in as Y pulled away from the curb.

"You don't understand," Keeper said, settling into the blue and black luxury seat. "This isn't just any car."

"I know," Y said, following the Bonneville, keeping two to three cars back. "It's a Rolls-Royce Wraith, and I swear it drives even better than it looks. Must have cost a small fortune."

Keeper clicked his seat belt into place. "I doubt it. This car belongs to Slasher. He talks everything down to rock-bottom prices. He told Toby and me that we weren't allowed to do so much as breathe on this car. He loves it!"

"Holy moly," Y said. "It drives like butter. You have to try driving it. I feel so classy. Look at all the little lights on the roof, like stars. After this, we should totally park someplace dark and get the sound system pumped up."

Keeper stared at Y. "No. Just no. There are these things called rules. Perhaps you've heard of them? Doing villainy on another villain is a major no-no. It's like you're purposefully trying to keep me out of E.V.I.L."

"Honestly. I don't know how you aren't enjoying this car. Stop worrying. We'll see where Todd Jones is going and then head back. Slasher will never be the wiser."

"Except for all of the wires hanging out," Keeper said.

"Slasher doesn't know it was us. Hang on." Y sped up and raced through a light that had turned red. She had to weave around a Honda in front of her to make it. "Handles like a dream. Didn't even feel that pothole."

Keeper yanked at his seat belt, making sure it was at its optimal tightness. How had he managed to get so tangled up with this girl? She was a disaster. She was going to ruin his life. He'd never get into E.V.I.L. if Slasher found out about his car, and Keeper's career options after that were dismal to downright depressing. Maybe he could live in Toby's basement for the rest of his life.

"Hold on," Y said. "I think we've been spotted."

There was a slight lag, but then the Bonneville took off at a surprising speed, billowing smoke behind it as it burned oil. The Rolls didn't have any lag at all and shot off like a rocket when Y pressed her foot down.

The Bonneville took a tight turn down a narrow, single-lane road lined with parked cars. Y slammed on the brakes and drifted around the corner after Jones, taking out a couple of trash cans.

Keeper's head whipped back toward the rear of the car, as if he'd be able to see the damage. "What the barf? You just ran a stop sign to take out those cans. It's like you never took driver's ed."

"I didn't. Don't worry. I'm sure we can buff any dings out."

The Bonneville jumped the curb at the end of the block, plowing into the front of one car and the back of another. Both cars were pushed out of the way, and Jones cut off the corner as he took a left. Obviously, Todd Jones wasn't as concerned about damage to his rust-bucket Bonneville as Keeper was to Slasher's pristine Rolls-Royce. Y also didn't seem overly concerned about the Rolls. Her only thought was Todd Jones. There was the sound of metal scraping and a spray of sparks flying as she squeezed the Wraith through the parked cars after the Bonneville.

"For the love of Godzilla! What are you doing?" Keeper yelled, his eyes glued to the street in front.

"Chasing Todd Jones."

"And then what?" Keeper asked, his voice hysterical. "What are we going to do if we catch him?"

"I don't know." Y was running high on adrenaline. She couldn't remember the last time she'd had this much fun. "Kidnap him. Make him tell us where the others are."

"You're out of your mind."

"Hold on. I'm cutting him off at the pass."

"The what? Gaaaaaahhhhh!"

Y plowed through a bunch of orange construction cones. It sounded and smelled like one was caught underneath the car. She sped up and used a pile of dirt and broken asphalt as a ramp, launching the Rolls-Royce into the air. They came down hard. A cautionary wooden workhorse shattered the windshield, and the Rolls landed in front of the Bonneville. The Bonneville slammed into the back corner of the Rolls, sending it spinning. By the time Y had turned the Wraith in the right direction, the Bonneville had already limped off and disappeared.

Keeper turned and glared at Y.

Y forced a smile. "Good news. I don't think the cone is underneath us anymore."

"Fantastic."

Y turned the car in the direction of the antiques shop. One of the axles must have been bent because there was a lopsided wobble to the car, or maybe it just needed a realignment. By the time they made it back, there was also the smell of something burning and the check engine light was on.

Toby was standing on the sidewalk watching. Even from a hundred yards away, Keeper could see the recognition and panic in Toby's eyes. Color was draining from his face at an alarming rate.

Y pulled to the curb, and Keeper turned toward her. "You take care of Toby and stall Showboater. I'll get rid of the car."

Y shook her head. "You were never here. It was all me. You don't need to be a part of this."

"It's okay," Keeper said. "I have an idea of what to do with the car. Slasher will never know. We will never speak of it again. Understand?"

Y searched Keeper's eyes. "Are you sure?"

"Yes, but you'll need to buy me some time and make an excuse for my absence."

Y shoved the driver's door open and got out as Keeper straddled the center console and moved over to drive. Before she closed the door, she bent down and brushed her lips against Keeper's ear. Her breath was warm and soft on his neck. Keeper stopped breathing.

"FYI," Y whispered, "it doesn't drive like butter anymore."

Keeper felt his eyes narrow. "I'm aware."

Y closed the door and joined Toby on the sidewalk. They watched the Rolls hobble down the road and turn the corner, never to be seen again.

"Was it fun?" Toby asked after a few minutes of silence.

"Oh yeah."

◎◎◎

Ten minutes later, Frog appeared at the end of the street. His giant feet slapped against the sidewalk as he walked past Y and Toby, into the antiques store, without acknowledgment.

Y and Toby exchanged a glance and tried to see Frog through the store's overcrowded front window. After five minutes, Frog emerged from the store, stood next to Toby, and croaked. Loudly. Signifying that the coast was clear.

"Gunk! Gunk-gunk-gunk-gunk."

Showboater came around the corner of a building on the far side and crossed the street. He stood in front of Toby and Y and looked around. "I have to admit, Toby, when I got your message, I assumed it would be you and Keeper in trouble, not you and a girl."

"Keeper's parking the car," Y said.

Toby nodded. "My mom said we had to walk the dog before we went out, so we're running a little late."

Showboater's eyes went from Toby to Y and back to Toby. "Sure. We'll go with that."

Frog gunked and jerked his head down the street.

"Ah," Showboater said. "Here comes Keeper now. Perfect timing. Shall we go inside? Frog will keep watch outside."

Keeper was now at a slow jog. He had sprinted as far as he could before it felt like his heart was going to explode. He made a mental note to get in better shape if he ever made it into E.V.I.L.

Keeper did his best to walk calmly past Frog and through the front door. He stopped when he was next to Toby and Y, but he was still breathing heavily and was soaked with sweat. Everyone was staring at him.

"Trouble finding a spot for the Kia?" Toby offered.

"Yeah. Yeah." Keeper tried to take a calming breath and used the bottom of his T-shirt to wipe the sweat from his face.

The shopkeeper's good eye and weepy eye appeared over the tin signs. Showboater raised a hand in acknowledgment. "Just browsing." The smile faded, and he looked back at the young villains. "Let's head to a back room, shall we?"

Showboater led the way through a maze of old junk. There were a number of side rooms, filled to bursting. Showboater picked one that was more the size of a large closet and filled with old metal oil and gasoline cans, as well as a collection of extremely used shoes.

"I can only assume that you three are in a heap of trouble," Showboater said. "I'm appointing Keeper as the spokesperson. I encourage you, Keeper, to avoid any stretching of the truth. After all, I'm here to help you out of whatever disastrous situation you've gotten yourselves into."

Keeper took a deep breath. "Well, it seems Tsunami and Dr. Spot have been kidnapped trying to help us get cookies. We think the kidnapper is Todd Jones from the Porcelain Palace. We have no idea where he is holding them . . . and the Cookie

Maven. We think he has also kidnapped the Cookie Maven."

There was silence.

Keeper waited for a response. "That's all, sir."

"Great Caesar's ghost," Showboater said. "I didn't see any of that coming."

"It seems to be a bit of a snowball effect," Keeper added.

Showboater took a long breath and ran his hands down his chest, taking it all in. "Time frame. I need a time frame. When did this all happen?"

"Not sure about the Cookie Maven," Keeper said. "Tsunami was taken late yesterday afternoon, and Dr. Spot went into the Porcelain Palace sometime before noon. Never came out."

Showboater's brow furrowed. "She went in on Chaos's orders. We looked over the information you sent us, Toby, and there were a number of warning signs that Todd Jones is not Todd Jones. You have to understand that identity theft isn't uncommon among villains, for any number of reasons. We sent Dr. Spot in to see if Todd Jones was a villain. It's not wrong for a villain to move outside his or her chapter's jurisdiction, but it is unusual. If something goes wrong, there's no immediate backup. It was our hope that this was the case, and there was a simple misunderstanding in targeting the Cookie Maven."

"With all due respect, sir," Keeper said. "I don't think Todd Jones has made any mistakes. I think he knows what he's doing."

"My dear boy, Todd Jones has made the biggest mistake of all. Nobody messes with Chapter 626." Showboater broke into a dance that involved a lot of arm waving and hip shaking, sending glitter everywhere. Most of it stuck to Keeper since he was still damp with sweat. "I'm going to talk to Chaos." Showboater held up his hands to stop any naysayers. "It will be fine, I assure you. In the meantime, the three of you should stay together. I don't want anyone else getting snatched. Wait for my phone call."

CHAPTER 21

KEEPER, Toby, and Y closed the doors to the Kia and sat in silence. The idea of sticking together, with Y, until they heard from Showboater was daunting to Keeper, a sign from above to Y, and problematic to Toby, who really didn't want to bring Y back into his parents' house for fear of complete and total humiliation.

"Now what?" Toby asked. "How long do you think we have to wait?"

"I wouldn't think too long," Keeper said. "I suspect Showboater's on the phone now."

"Let's go shopping," Y said.

Keeper and Toby turned in their seats to stare at Y, unsure if they had heard her correctly.

"What?" Y said, buckling in. "We have to do something, and Keeper desperately needs new shoes. I give the ones he's wearing two more days, max, before they disintegrate off his feet."

"An excellent and worthy observation," Keeper said. "Sadly, you failed to observe that I have no money to buy shoes."

Y unbuckled her seat belt and came forward, closer to Keeper. "Why would you need money for shoes? I thought you were a villain. I hate to say it. . . ."

Keeper raised a finger at Y. "Don't. Don't you dare. I know exactly what—"

"You're a bit of a Goody Two-shoes." Y sat back and crossed her arms, triumphant.

Keeper felt his jaw clench. His eyes locked with Y's in a silent battle.

"Toby," Keeper finally managed. "Take me to the Shoe Châteaux. I'm getting new shoes. And there won't be anything *goody* about them."

"Okey dokey," Toby said, pulling away from the curb and heading toward the strip malls in the more suburban area of a neighboring town.

It took Keeper a minute before he managed to end the stare down with Y and move his stare forward, to what was outside the car's windshield. Truth was, it was possible Y was right about him, and the worst part of that realization was not that he was good but that Y would be right and win.

Over my evil body, Keeper thought. He sat fuming and rationalizing his need for shoes for twenty minutes while Toby fought his way through lights and traffic to get to the Shoe Châteaux.

They piled out of the car and approached the store's double doors. The Shoe Châteaux was a discount warehouse type of operation, selling last season's styles for less. Keeper was hoping he could find something at least three seasons old that the store would be more than happy to have someone steal so they wouldn't have to shelve them anymore.

Keeper held the door open for Y. "I've been informed that villainy is no excuse for bad manners."

"So true," Y said, walking past Keeper. "What type of shoes are you looking for? Running? High-tops? Maybe you're a gentleman villain and need some wing tips?"

"Maybe you'd like . . ."

Y turned and looked at Keeper. Raising an eyebrow.

"To be more helpful," Keeper said, trying to rein in his emotions. "I want a pair of boots. Black, flexible sole, nonslip, and let's not forget comfort."

"Done and done." Y smiled, turned, and made her way down aisles lined with stacks of boxes and people trying to find their size in the bedlam of other people putting boxes back wherever they pleased.

Over an hour later, and what seemed like at least forty pairs of shoes, Keeper had on new socks and boots. He had to admit that neither he, nor his feet, had ever felt so good. Problem was that for being last season's style, they were not at last season's prices. Keeper couldn't help but feel guilty about walking out in the boots, but the idea of Y winning the battle was even worse.

"Here's the plan," Keeper said to Y. "You go to the front and pretend to look at the sandals near the door. Toby and I will join you. After a few minutes, you decide there is nothing you want, and we walk out."

Y went to the front, and Keeper and Toby held back for a bit before making their way toward Y. The line at checkout was getting unusually long. People were desperate to make their purchases before the store closed.

"I'm so sorry," the girl at the counter was saying. "The computer has been on the fritz for a couple of days now. It seems to be getting worse and worse."

Another woman, looking managerial, was standing next to the girl. She kept hitting the credit card device on its side and then poking the payment screen with her finger as if she were trying to jab out someone's eye.

Keeper looked down at his feet and then at the line of customers growing more impatient by the second.

"I might be able to help," Keeper said to the women behind the counter. "My mother is a software engineer, and my father is a senior engineer in microchip technology. I've spent my entire life taking computers apart, putting them together, and learning how to program."

"Well, you certainly can't make things worse," the manager said, stepping aside and allowing Keeper behind the counter.

Keeper took the case off the card reader, tinkered with the machine a bit, and put the case back into place. Then he went to the tablet computer and rebooted. The manager put in her security code, and Keeper began tapping icons and looking through internal code. Finally, he restarted the machine again.

"Should be fine now," Keeper said.

The manager put in her security code again and rang up the customer, no problem.

"Amazing," she said. "You're my hero. I can't thank you enough."

"No big deal," Keeper said. "Happy to help." He turned, and in the commotion of the register finally working, walked out the front door wearing his new boots, Toby and Y right behind him.

"You know," Y said. "You didn't have to help."

Keeper pivoted on his heel and came at Y, his eyes fixed on hers. He forced Y to take steps backward until she was up against a brick pillar. "No?" Keeper placed his hands against the brick on either side of Y's head. He leaned in tighter, his head tilted slightly. "FYI, it was just a loose wire on the card reader. I went into the computer and made it so every transaction has a two percent tax for foot odor."

Y tried to stay focused, but Keeper was getting closer and closer.

His voice became softer. "When they try to fix the tax, it will change to a five percent donation for the Ingrown Toenail Federation."

Keeper's mouth was now an inch from Y's and not moving. Y forced her eyes up to meet Keeper's.

"Evil enough for you, Y?" Keeper asked.

"It's pretty evil."

"You know it." Keeper pulled back, dropped his arms, and turned to head back to the Kia. "Let's go. I'm starving. What time is it?"

Toby looked at his phone. "It's five of seven."

"If we can get to Reggie's on Apple Blossom in Peachmont before seven thirty, we can heist a pizza, easy," Keeper said.

Toby unlocked the Kia. "I might have to run some yellows, but I think it's possible."

They piled into the car, and Toby backed up. Y leaned forward a bit. "How do you know about easy pizza heists?" she asked Keeper.

"Look, I'm only human, and I'm not as good as you think. All the kids at school talked about eating pizza. I asked Nana for some, and she gave me whole grain toast with tomato paste and mushrooms."

Toby gasped. "Did she at least cut off the crust?"

"No. No, she didn't. I was desperate to try real pizza," Keeper continued. "Reggie's is super popular. One day I noticed that the delivery guy leaves his car door open while he goes back for more pizzas. It's easy pickings if you don't care what you get."

Y was smiling. "How often do you steal pizza?"

"Don't judge me. Turns out pizza is addictive."

Toby nodded and ran a yellow. "And delicious."

Y leaned back in her seat. "I'll second that, and since Keeper impressed us with his villainy at Shoe Châteaux and Toby has the getaway car, pizza theft is on me."

By 9:30 p.m., Keeper, Toby, and Y were sitting in the back of a grocery store parking lot, twiddling their thumbs. The pizza was gone, three of the six root beers Keeper had stolen from a shopping cart were gone, and Toby had moved from checking his phone every ten minutes to five minutes to thirty seconds.

"Text him," Keeper finally said. "Just say something like, *making sure everything is okay.*"

Toby sent the text to Showboater and the waiting continued. Five minutes, ten minutes, twenty.

"Someone needs to call Chaos," Y said from the back.

Keeper looked at Toby.

"What? Why me? You call him, Keeper."

"I don't have a phone. You do."

"If I have to call Chaos, I guarantee that we'll never be allowed into E.V.I.L." Toby held his phone out to Keeper. "There is no way I'm not going to say all the wrong things. I'm terrible on the phone."

Keeper took the phone from Toby. "Fine. Anything to get out of this car."

Keeper pressed the favorite icon for Chaos's alias, Eddie Farlow, and waited. Chaos picked up on the first ring.

"Um, hello, sir. It's Keeper. Keeper Chance."

"Thank the Doofenshmirtz," Chaos said. "I was afraid I was going to have to talk to Toby. Have you ever talked to Toby on the phone? It's horrible."

"Yes, well, I haven't personally had the displeasure yet, but I have heard that about him. We were wondering if you had been in touch with Showboater lately."

"There was a senior meeting this afternoon. Showboater was present. Why?"

"It would be after that, sir. We ran into Showboater and told him we were concerned Dr. Spot had been kidnapped. Showboater was going to get in touch with you and then back in touch with us, but we haven't heard from him."

"Where are you now?"

"The Food Jester parking lot in Peachmont."

"There is a gas station a block away, on the corner of Honeycrisp and Macintosh," Chaos said. "Meet me in back where the air machines are. Fifteen minutes."

Keeper hung up. They waited ten minutes before driving to the gas station.

"Drop me off in front," Y said. "I'll wait for you guys in the store."

"I don't think so," Keeper said. "It was your idea to call Chaos. You're in this up to your armpits, just like we are."

"Not this time. This meeting is E.V.I.L., and I'm not a part of E.V.I.L. I've made my position clear with you and Chaos."

Keeper couldn't believe what he was hearing. "If you don't want to be in E.V.I.L., then why are you always showing up and going on car chases and encouraging us to break into people's houses?"

"I know why," Toby said.

Y kicked the back of Toby's chair, hard.

"Hey! This is my mom's Kia. Have a little respect."

Y opened her door and climbed out. "You need to mind your own business. Come get me when you're done."

Keeper and Toby watched Y close her door and head into the gas station market before driving around to the back of the building. Chaos was already there, standing outside a Range Rover, next to the air pump.

Keeper and Toby got out of the car and approached Chaos. Chaos stood staring at them, saying nothing. Waiting for something.

Finally, Keeper couldn't take it anymore. "Sir . . ."

Chaos held up a hand for Keeper to stop. "I have a strong suspicion that whatever escapades you have been up to, there were three of you involved. Where's the third?"

"With all due respect, sir," Keeper said. "The third party has only been involved in some of the escapades. Said party has made it abundantly clear that it will not be involved in E.V.I.L. business."

Chaos smiled, clearly amused. "Very well. Before I make a decision about the third party, tell me the details. All of them, and don't candy-coat it. If an E.V.I.L. member truly has been kidnapped, time is of the essence."

Keeper retold Chaos everything, from the dog belonging to Larbole up to not being able to get in touch with Showboater. After he was done, Chaos held up a finger for Keeper and Toby to wait a moment. The minute of what would have been silence seemed to go on forever, except that it was broken up by the sound of crashing and screaming and people running from the market. Then Y appeared.

She had the remains of a red frozen drink down the front of her and what looked like nacho cheese in her hair. "You called?" she said to Chaos.

"Ah," Chaos said, admiring his handiwork. "The third party. How are you, Y?"

"Shirt is ruined. Cherry Frozee doesn't come out. Other than that, I'm fine. Thank you."

"Ah, yes, unfortunate things happen sometimes. Soak it in OxiClean. Should do the trick," Chaos replied. "The missing members of Chapter 626 are also unfortunate. Wouldn't you say so?"

Y smiled slightly, accepting the game of wits. "It is. Sadly, it's my understanding that E.V.I.L. business is E.V.I.L. business, and I thought I was clear that I didn't want to join."

"Hmm, yes, yes," Chaos said, thinking about his next move. "Except I would beg to differ on this being strictly E.V.I.L. business. It seems to center on two young men who are not members of E.V.I.L., and . . . how shall I put this . . . ? Are a bit wet behind the ears. Someone, a friend perhaps, who clearly already has training and skill would be highly welcome and appreciated."

Y wasn't smiling anymore. It sounded like Chaos was hinting that he knew she was the child of Vogue and Sensei Love. "I don't know what you're talking about."

Chaos didn't seem to be fazed. "You have my word as a villain and head of Chapter 626 that if anyone should ask, or accuse, I will irrevocably stand at your defense, declaring that all your actions were entirely yours and yours alone, done for nothing more than selfish reasons."

This seemed to appease Y a bit. "And when it's all done, promise you won't hound me relentlessly to join E.V.I.L."

Chaos's eyes softened. "Y, Chapter 626 is happy to have you, but only if you want to have us. All I ask is that you follow your heart."

Keeper watched Y. Chaos's final comment seemed to have unnerved her a bit, not that she fully showed it. It was a simple flick of her eyes toward Keeper's, then down to the ground.

"Fine," Y said. "I'll help Keeper and Toby, and if my path should cross 626's, in a common goal, it's purely coincidental."

"Excellent!" Chaos clapped his hands together. "I'm calling a meeting at my place, tonight, midnight, for remaining villains, soon-to-be-villains, and friends of soon-to-be-villains. Why don't you three follow me? Y, you can take a shower and feel free to pick out a new outfit from whatever you can find in the house."

CHAPTER 22

POLYP paced the abandoned factory's bunker floor, thinking and waiting. Showboater and Frog were tied up, complete with obligatory duct tape over their mouths. They sat in chairs next to a large metal table. Tsunami and Dr. Spot sat tied in chairs across from them.

"Not long now, not long now," Polyp said mostly to himself. "Chaos is definitely coming. Speaking of which"—Polyp stopped, put his hands on his hips in annoyance, and looked at the door—"that sanctimonious Sensei is late."

As if on cue a shadow of a figure appeared behind the door's small, filthy window, and Sensei Love silently entered the room. He looked around, briefly, then settled his gaze on Polyp. "Where is he?"

Polyp put on his largest, most proud smile and gestured with both hands to Showboater. "Ta-da!"

Sensei Love held up a finger, turned, and left the room, closing the door behind him.

Polyp smiled an evil smile and glanced over at Showboater. "He just needs a moment to regroup so he doesn't embarrass himself by gushing all over me with gratitude."

Showboater answered by raising his eyebrows and rolling his head.

Sensei Love reentered the room and placed his palms together, the tips of his fingers touching his lower lip. He closed his eyes and drew in a deep breath. "That is not Keeper Chance."

"You know," Polyp said, "I think you're messing with me. I'm following your description to a T, every time. Male. Taller than this loser." Polyp hooked a thumb in Tsunami's direction. "Dark hair. Hanging out with a male buddy."

"Keeper is sixteen. SIXTEEN! And this so-called *buddy* looks like a frog. Keeper's friend is short. More of a . . . I don't know . . . a beagle."

"Wait a minute. Are you telling me Keeper Chance is a kid?" Polyp said as incredulously as he could muster.

"He's of age to join the dojo," Love said, taking a wide stance and crossing his arms over his chest.

"Of course, of course. I guess when you get to be my age,

everyone is a kid." Polyp slapped Showboater on the back. "Am I right or am I right?"

Showboater shrugged slightly and nodded in agreement.

"Look," Polyp said. "Let's just cut to the chase. Do you have a picture? An address? Anything that will assure I bring you the right person? I'm getting tired of wandering all over Chapter 626's jurisdiction, looking for villains. I have a store to run."

"No, no, and no," Love said. "Nothing to give, other than my utmost faith in you."

"Very touching but not especially helpful."

"Why don't you go back to the Palace and wait," Love suggested, his voice back to being eerily calm. "No need to traipse all over town. The boy will show up. I guarantee it. You know what they say: patience is a virtue."

"Hmm, yes. I've heard that," Polyp said, then thought that Love should know all about patience since Polyp had been working him over for days now. However, if Sensei was correct and Keeper showed up, it would indeed be most fortuitous. Polyp could move step three of his plan to step one. "Very well. If you need me, you know where to find me."

Sensei Love watched the door close and stood, staring motionless for a few minutes. "So," Love said. "This is taking a bit longer than I expected." His eyes shifted to Showboater. "How many more villains are there in 626 before Polyp doesn't have any choice but to bring me Keeper Chance?"

"Mmmph," Showboater said.

Love's eyes went back to the door. "Yes, indeed. Patience is a virtue."

Keeper, Toby, Y, Chaos, Slasher, and Joy were huddled together at midnight, in the kitchen of Chaos's current lair. At ten after midnight, Barricade and Staticanator were the last to arrive.

"Sorry we're late," Staticanator said. "The youngest one has some sort of weird rash. What that kid rolled in, or the others spread on him, is anyone's guess."

Barricade slapped Slasher on the back with a meaty hand, causing a brief buckling of his knees. "Hey, Slasher, how's it hanging? Wasn't sure you were here. Didn't see your car out front."

"Probably for the best that we don't discuss that," Chaos said.

"Someone stole it," Joy offered.

Barricade's eyes grew large in disbelief. "No! That's terrible. What is this world coming to? Who would do something like that?"

Joy looked up at the ceiling in thought and began counting off on fingers. "Hooligans, scofflaws, carjackers. Car is probably in a thousand pieces by now, being sold on the black market. Or eBay."

"Valid observations, Joy, thank you," Chaos said. "However, let's try to not suck any more fun out of this already not fun meeting until the meeting is done. Agreed?"

Joy gave him a thumbs-up, pressed her lips together and sucked them in a bit.

Chaos pushed his cape behind his shoulders and stood a bit taller. "Before I start this meeting, I would like to introduce YinYang, who goes by Y. She operates outside E.V.I.L., but she is a friend of our newest recruits. We are down a few villains, and she has agreed to help as she sees fit. Until this disaster is over, Y is to be thought of as family. Understood?"

There was a collective nodding of heads.

"Excellent. Then let's move on to business." Chaos repeated everything Keeper had told him with surprising precision. When he was done, he looked over at Keeper and Toby. "Have I missed anything or misinterpreted?"

Keeper and Toby shook their heads. "No, sir."

"Very well, then, if we were to boil it down, we have three priorities. Who is Todd Jones really? Why is he kidnapping villains and the Cookie Maven? And where is he holding the kidnappees?" Chaos paused for a moment. "Obviously, where our members currently are is the most important of the three, but it's likely we need the answers to one or both of the first two questions to get that answer."

"We need to stay in teams," Barricade said. "Staticanator and I can go into the Palace...."

Chaos shook his head. "No. This Todd Jones seems to know the members of 626. You two have children depending on you. I don't want to risk your disappearance if it's not utterly necessary." Hints of evil sparkled in Chaos's eyes. "We're going to send in Joy and Y." Chaos turned his head to address Y. "Don't go in together. Joy will go in as the decoy. Todd Jones will want to kidnap her, but he won't be able to do it with a civilian watching. While Joy is doing her worst, Keeper and Toby will go through the back door to do a thorough search." Chaos's eyes moved to Keeper. "You should have time and light. Get that computer running enough to know if you should take it with you. Go through drawers, boxes, dirty laundry baskets. Leave no roll of toilet paper unturned."

Keeper gave a nod of understanding. "Yes, sir."

"Before you leave tonight, see Slasher. He has official E.V.I.L. burner phones for the three of you. Take pictures, even of things that don't seem like anything. When you are done, check in with me. You'll find all the members of 626 in the contacts, under their proper pseudonyms, of course."

"Are you sure there isn't anything Staticanator and I can do?" Barricade asked. "I feel bad sitting out in a situation like this."

Chaos smiled at Barricade. "Don't worry. I can almost guarantee your unique skill will be needed before this is over. Rest up and be ready. Speaking of which, this meeting is over. I apologize for the lack of midnight munchies, but things were a bit last minute. Frozen hors d'oeuvres are in the oven, probably done. I think they're crab puffs, but who knows. Sodas are out and up for the taking."

Toby went to collect sodas and crab puffs for the ride home. Keeper and Y went to Slasher to collect the phones.

Slasher didn't seem overly pleased about handing them out. "These are not toys. They are not normally given to nonmembers, but Chaos feels circumstances are extenuating. When this is all over, if you are not a member, you will return the phone."

Keeper was pretty sure Slasher was talking about Y, but Slasher's eyes kept shifting to him. It could only mean Keeper and Toby were on thin ice. They better not mess this one up, and they definitely better not lose Joy.

CHAPTER
23

IT was coming up on 11:00 a.m. when Toby did a lap around the Porcelain Palace in the Kia. Keeper was next to him, and Y and Joy were in the back seat. The beat-up Bonneville was parked in the back.

Y leaned forward a bit. "Hey, Toby, before we do this, drop me off on the west side."

Keeper turned in his seat. "Did you see something?"

"There's no real traffic or activity on the west side. I can scale the building and look down through the skylights, assuming they aren't too filthy," Y said. "Might be helpful to see what Todd Jones does when he thinks no one is watching."

Keeper raised an eyebrow. "You know how to scale buildings?"

Joy leaned forward to join them. "I know how to weave back

hair into a friendship bracelet." She gave Keeper an overexaggerated wink.

Keeper resisted the urge to bolt from the moving car. "Drive faster, Toby. For the love of monkey ninjas, drive faster."

Toby took the corner at Mach speed, causing everyone to slide, and slammed on his brakes near the curb. Y jumped out and looked back at the car. It was still sitting there. Everyone was watching, waiting to see Y scale the building.

Y rolled her eyes and signaled for Toby to move on. She watched as he reluctantly pulled away from the curb and headed to the Carpet Castle parking lot. Once she was alone, Y looked over the building's surface.

It would have been easier at night. She could have used a grapple, but no matter. The building had small decorative ledges on one side, staggering their way up. It really wasn't much different from the bouldering walls at the dojo, except this one didn't have a mat underneath if she fell.

Y took a deep breath and jumped up to hang by her fingers from the highest ledge she could reach. Then she pulled herself up a bit and released one hand to grab at the ledge above. Once she felt solid, she pulled up a bit and brought her other hand up to meet the first. She inched down the ledge, moving her fingers on one hand and then the other, until she could repeat for the next ledge. On the plus side, she could now place her toes on the ledge below to help support herself. Her knees had to bend to the sides slightly, and Y was pretty sure she looked super lame. Nevertheless, it was working. It was easier as the curve of the building grew, but by the time she reached the windows at the top of the domed roof, her fingers were cramped and shaking, and her arms felt like noodles. She didn't want to think about how she was going to get down.

Y moved across the top of the Porcelain Palace to the front and looked for the Kia. Once it was in view, she raised herself up a bit and waved. She was pretty sure she saw motion in the Kia and assumed it was waving back. She flattened herself down, again, crept up to the windows, and peered through. Todd Jones was sitting on his throne, on the fake pile of gold, jiggling his crossed leg in rapid fashion and tapping his golden plunger on his head.

"Jeez louise," Y said to herself. "Is this seriously what this guy does all day? I climbed all the way up here for this?"

She waited for a few more minutes, hoping something—anything—would happen. There was the sound of wheels on gravel toward the back of the Palace. Y slowly inched her way until she could look over the side. All she could see was the front bumper of a car parked next to the Bonneville. She had missed the car's occupant. The person must have access to the back door. She crawled back toward the center of the domed building and carefully looked down, into the windows.

The person who had entered was hidden under a canopy of string lights and fake palms for an outdoor shower display. Todd Jones seemed agitated on his throne, and the conversation seemed heated. Jones rose from his seat and pointed his golden plunger scepter at the mystery person, then took a step forward, stopped, then another step and stopped. With the third step, the mystery figure took a step back, exposing himself.

Y jerked away from the window. It was like her heart had stopped beating and then started up again in a fury. She was shaking. She must be confused. It couldn't be. She tried to swallow even though her mouth had gone dry and eased herself back toward the window to peek through. She hadn't been confused. The mystery man was her father.

"There's no way. No way," Y whispered to herself. She watched as her father continued retreating. He was calm and unhurried. He didn't seem threatened, but he never showed fear or any emotion for that matter.

Her father's arms dropped out of their usual crossed, judging position, and he opened them, challenging Todd Jones. Was he offering Jones a match of skill against skill? That would mean Jones was definitely a villain. Todd Jones stopped his advance, some more words were exchanged, and Jones returned to his throne.

Y's father turned and walked to the door leading to the back room, appearing to be the victor. Y waited until she heard a car start up and pull out of the lot. She continued watching Jones. He wasn't nervous anymore. Now that her father was gone, Jones was also giving off the appearance of someone who had been victorious.

Y rolled over onto her back and absently stared up at the

blue sky. "Pull it together, Y," she said to herself. "Stay calm and think this one out. Sensei is all about stopping villainy. Kidnapping, even if it's villains, is wrong. And the Cookie Maven isn't a villain, and she's missing."

Y closed her eyes tightly and willed the tears to stop. "If Keeper finds out my father . . ." Y opened her eyes. "Keeper." Her father was looking for Keeper. Keeper's trail undoubtedly led to Todd Jones. "Dad probably doesn't know Jones has been kidnapping villains and the Cookie Maven," Y said to herself. "He just wants Keeper." But even as she said it, she had to will away the doubts of the small internal voice of instinct.

Y rolled over again, crawled to the side of the dome, and began the arduous task of descending. It was far more difficult than ascending, but Y's mind was too busy to care.

"Take a lesson from Chaos," she said, her toes finding footing on a ledge. "Figure out what's essential and then prioritize. Essential, keep Keeper out of the dojo." If her father talked him into going to the dojo, Keeper might change, and he was already perfect the way he was. "Essential, rescue the villains and the Cookie Maven and get Keeper into Chapter 626, if that's what he wants. To do that, I need to make sure my father doesn't come in contact with Keeper. That means we need to find the kidnappees and obtain Cookie Maven cookies as quickly as possible so the initiation ceremony can happen." Once Keeper was officially a villain, her father would back off and return to their home upstate.

Y's fingers couldn't hold on much longer. She looked down and decided the drop was a bit farther than she wanted but doable. She pushed off from the wall and tried to absorb the landing on the sidewalk below with the balls of her feet and deep into her knees. She stood up, smoothed out her T-shirt and skirt, brushed the dust from crawling around the dome off her tights, and looked around to make sure no one had seen her.

She used the walk to the Carpet Castle parking lot to take some deep breaths and refocus. As far as she was concerned, there had been nothing to see other than Todd Jones sitting on his throne, looking anxious.

Y came around the corner and crossed the street to see Keeper and Toby standing outside the Kia, their backs to the car. As she got closer, she could see Joy locked inside the car, pressed against the window. Joy waved hello. Y raised an eyebrow at Keeper. "Problems?"

"It was like a mental apocalypse of verbal grenades," Keeper said. "She's fine. We cracked the windows . . . on the other side of the car."

Y frowned in mock sympathy. "They're just words, Keeper. Ignore them. They can't hurt you."

Keeper's eyes met Y's. "You wouldn't have lasted two minutes."

"Seriously," Toby said. "You had the easy job."

Y's eyes shifted back to see the ecstatic face of Joy, nodding in agreement, and suspected Toby was right.

"Did you see anything?" Keeper asked.

"Not really." Y looked back across the street at the Porcelain Palace to avoid eye contact with Keeper. "Just Todd Jones sitting on his throne, jiggling his leg. It's like he's waiting for something."

"If Chaos is right, he's waiting for another villain." Keeper jerked his head in the direction of Joy. "I say it's time to give him this one. He doesn't stand a chance."

There was a knocking on the car window, and everyone turned to look at Joy. She held her hand up in oath position, pressed her lips tight together, then tried to open the car door.

"I put on the child locks," Toby said, opening the door from the outside.

Joy slid out of the Kia, pressed her palms together, and did a slight bow of silent thanks. She pointed to herself, then at the Palace, then held up one finger for a moment, and then pointed the finger at Y.

Y suspected the one finger was for one minute. "I think leaving you alone in the Palace for one minute is too long," she said. "We don't know how villains are being taken down. I'll give you twenty to thirty seconds. Stay to the right of the store so I can find you quickly."

Keeper checked his phone for the time. "One minute after Y enters the store, Toby and I will head to the back of the building to search." He turned toward Y. "Y, have a text at the ready to send me. If we need to stop the search and get out, or if you need help, let us know. Joy, are you ready?"

Joy gave two thumbs up and headed toward the Porcelain Palace, waiting briefly for traffic to pass before crossing the road. She opened the front door and entered as if she didn't have a care in the world. Have mercy on Todd Jones.

Y waited twenty seconds and followed Joy. Even though Y walked quickly and with confidence, Keeper thought she seemed a bit tense. He couldn't blame her. The situation of one bad thing after another was beginning to get out of control.

"Okay, Toby, we're up," Keeper said. "Let's keep in mind there could be planted clues. We should focus on who this guy is if he isn't really Todd Jones. Anything that might tell us something about this Porcelain Palace guy's psyche, other than shady, would probably be helpful. If he's not holding his victims in the Palace, then where?"

"Got it," Toby said.

They walked to the end of the block before crossing the street and circling around to the back of the Porcelain Palace. Toby picked the back door's lock, and they slipped into the empty storeroom.

Y entered the Palace and looked toward the golden throne that rose above its porcelain fiefdom like the sun over Mount Fuji. The throne was empty of its occupant. Y moved toward the right side of the store until she found Joy. Joy seemed to be alone, browsing an elegant and over-the-top gold-themed room. Todd Jones had to be somewhere, hiding. The bathroom hardware and fixture displays were like a maze at ground level. Y eyed a heavy iron toilet-side magazine rack in a rustic, blacksmith-themed display. She approached the rack, pretended to be reaching for the price tag, and knocked it over. The crash echoed through the Palace, and Jones magically appeared from behind a wall of showerheads. He didn't look pleased.

"Oh my gosh. I'm so sorry!" Y said.

Jones's mouth was thin. "It's quite all right. Happens all the time."

"Really?"

"No. Is there something I can help you with?" Jones said, holding his ground between Y and Joy.

"Hey!" Joy yelled. "I was here first, toilet-man. That's no way to be number one in the number two business. I demand you help me with my toilet crisis first."

"It's fine," Y said. "I can wait."

Jones half rolled his eyes. "If you don't have a 'toilet crisis,' just something I can help you with quickly . . ."

"Oh, no," Y said emphatically. "I'm here on behalf of the company I'm interning with for a week. They're opening a new office and need lots of stuff. LOTS. I'm not at liberty to buy, but they sent me with an insanely long list of questions and requirements. I can wait."

Todd Jones's shoulders slumped slightly, and he sighed. "Wonderful. Thank you. I appreciate your patience."

"That didn't sound very sincere," Joy said.

Jones turned toward Joy. "I assure you it was. What is the crisis that I can help you with today?"

"What's my crisis?" Joy asked incredulously. "My crisis is my toilet's doody!" Joy threw her head back and broke into peals of laughter interspersed with loud snorting noises.

Jones looked like he wanted to run out of the building and never come back.

Joy wiped tears from her eyes. "Oh my goodness. Don't worry. I have a *butt*load of toilet jokes to crack. *But*, seriously, I need a new toilet." Joy started snorting again.

Jones's eye began to visibly twitch. "The one you are looking at is a very nice piece. Has nonstick coating and a cyclone flush."

"How dare you!" Joy put her hands on her hips and glared at Jones. "I demand to speak to the manager! I find your implications about what I do in the bathroom insulting!"

"I am the manager."

"Then I want to speak to the owner."

Both of Jones's eyes were now twitching, and he was starting to shake as he fought against the natural survival instinct of flight. "Once again, that would be me."

"Hmph," Joy said. "I suspect you don't even have any employees for me to work with, either, since people clearly hate you and you smell like fish. Fine! Let's keep this relationship professional. Stop looking at me as if you *like*-like me! I'm not interested in a date."

Jones went from looking like he was holding back tears to looking like he was holding back throw up.

Y had planned on pretending to browse and mind her own business, but her feet were frozen to the floor in horror. Her mouth hung open, her eyes large and unblinking, unable to look away from the verbal slaughterfest Joy had now launched on Todd Jones, thanks to Jones claiming he'd rather look at gangrene toes than Joy's face across a candlelit table for two.

For the love of Rita Repulsa, Y thought, *Keeper and Toby better hurry up. This could quite possibly be Todd Jones's worst day ever, and I suspect that's saying something.*

Suddenly, there was a change in Jones's face. It was brief, like a flash of willpower found in his deepest and darkest reserve. Jones willed his feet forward, toward Joy. One step. Then another. He was about ten feet away when Joy suddenly stopped talking. Her face scrunched up in pain, and her hands went to her stomach. Then the unthinkable happened. Joy farted. It was far from silent, and it took deadly to a whole new level.

Jones appeared to be enjoying himself until the cloud of malodorousness hit him. He backtracked, choking, and tried to cover his mouth and nose with his grimy shirtsleeve, but there was no relief to be had.

"Wooooooo!" Joy said. "That came out of nowhere. Smells like a burnt crab."

Jones had now backed up so much, he was closer to Y than Joy. "I think it would be best if we took our conversation about your plumbing needs to a more private location," Jones said to Joy through gasps. "There's no need to subject this poor young woman"—he motioned toward Y—"to any more unpleasantness."

Y was suddenly overcome with chills. An all-too-familiar pressure growing in her lower intestines.

"Are you saying my flatulence is unpleasant? Is that what you're saying?" Joy demanded.

Jones did his best to pull back his sloping shoulders. "Yes. Yes, I am."

Y started looking around the room. Desperate. Bathrooms as far as the eye could see, but where in the world was one with working plumbing? This was about to be a four-alarm, 911 emergency.

Joy waggled a finger at Jones. "Compliments will get you nowhere. It's too late."

"Wait. What? I would never compliment you." Jones was back to losing the battle. He took a few steps forward in Joy's direction.

Y was taking steps backward, trying to see past displays for a glimpse of a restroom sign. Things were about to get uglier than they already were. Must have been Chaos's crab puffs. They were wreaking havoc on her's and Joy's bowels. He'd poisoned what was left of Chapter 626 with his late-night snacks.

Jones was now back to within ten feet of Joy. Joy was looking pale again, and her upper lip was sweating.

"You don't look well," Jones said sympathetically. He didn't seem to be put off by the situation. "Maybe you'd like to 'freshen up'? Let me show you to the employee bathroom. Much more private."

Y felt her phone buzz in her hand. She looked at it. Keeper and Toby were back in the car. Time to go. Hallelujah!

Joy pointed an accusatory finger at Jones. "You! This is all your fault! You've upset my delicate constitution with your disgustingly long nose hair."

Jones looked temporarily horror-struck. He stopped his advance, and his hands shot up to his nose to examine the length of the hair growing out of it.

Y made eye contact with Joy and jerked her thumb toward the door, signaling it was time to leave. "Um, sir?" Y said. "I see you have your hands full. I'll come back later."

Jones barely heard her. He had all but forgotten she was even there. "Yes, yes. You do that."

"No need!" Joy declared. "I know inferior porcelain products and second-rate service when I see it! I'm taking my business elsewhere!" Joy bolted for the front door as fast as she could, clutching at her stomach.

Y and Jones watched Joy barrel through the door and take off at a run down the sidewalk. It appeared as if she was heading to the Porcelain Palace's parking lot, but Y knew Joy was going to run two blocks past it before taking a left and meeting Keeper and Toby in the Tower of Tile's fifteen-minute loading zone. Y was supposed to keep Jones busy for a couple of minutes and then retreat to the Carpet Castle. She would wait five minutes, making sure she wasn't followed, then exit and cross the street on the far side to Bard's Hardwood Floors. Bard's had a side-door exit Y would use. Toby, Keeper, and Joy would pick her up in the Kia.

Jones turned to Y. He looked exhausted and like he wanted to crawl under a rock. "You had questions, miss?" he asked with less-than-lackluster enthusiasm.

"Um, yeah, I don't know," Y said. "Was she right about the quality and your customer service? I mean, she was right about your nose hair."

Jones's shoulders slumped a bit more, and his eyelids became heavy. "Get out."

"Omigosh, thank you," Y said. She all but ran to the door. "I'll tell my boss you were closed, and he can handle the acquirement of toilets, sinks, and bathroom fixtures," Y called over her shoulder as she exited.

CHAPTER 24

TOBY picked Y up on the far side of Bard's Hardwood Floors. Y settled into the back seat with Joy.

"How did it go?" Y asked Keeper. "Find anything?"

"Maybe. We had to take the computer," Keeper said, holding it up. "Couldn't find a cord to get it charged and running, but we did find a box filled with electronics for recycling. As luck would have it, there was an old laptop. It had been opened and its motherboard removed, but I doubt Jones will notice the switch. Toby says he has a cord that should work on this computer."

Toby stopped at a red light and dug into his pants pocket. He pulled out a piece of paper and handed it to Keeper. "Show her this."

Keeper took the paper and handed it back to Y. "Oh yeah. We also found Todd Jones's wallet. It had a fortune from a fortune cookie about the wheel of fortune and how it turns incessantly, soon in his favor. There was also what we think was a mummified raisin and three dollars. No forms of ID, but Toby noticed that something had been in it and caused an imprint in the faux leather interior. We tried to use the old pencil and paper trick to get the imprint, but I'm not sure it's worth anything."

Y looked at the rubbing, turning the paper to the side and upside down, trying to make something out. Nothing.

Joy took the paper from Y, looked it over, then handed it back to Keeper. "Chaos," she said.

Keeper looked at the rubbing and then back at Joy. "You think he'll know what this is?"

Joy shrugged and gave a little smile.

Keeper folded the paper back up. "How did things go for you guys?"

"Let's just say that there isn't enough Häagen-Dazs within a one-hundred-mile radius to bring happiness back to Todd Jones's day," Y said.

Joy broke out into an enormous, victorious smile. She held her hand up, demanding a high five from Y, Keeper, and then Toby.

"We had a moment where it was a little touch-and-go, though," Y said. "I think Chaos's crab puffs were bad."

Joy reached out and touched Y's arm, then shook her head. "Skill," Joy said.

"Seriously?" Keeper said. "The guy gives people food poisoning? I mean, I've heard the expression that being around somebody makes one's bowels cramp, but I didn't know it could literally happen."

"A skill can be anything," Y said. She thought about her father backing up. She thought about Todd Jones advancing and retreating on Joy. When Jones advanced, Joy seemed to feel the effects of gastric disarray. When Jones retreated, Joy seemed to rally. However, at the same time Jones retreated, he came closer to Y, and that's when she felt the effects of intestinal peril. Y realized the feeling of imminent intestinal doom had left as fast as it had come on and hadn't returned since she'd left the store. "Distance," Y said. "He has to be within a certain distance of his target."

Joy pointed a finger at Y and touched her nose with her other index finger.

Keeper looked back at Joy. "Did you recognize him? Is he an E.V.I.L. villain?"

Joy did a combo shrug and shake of the head. She didn't know.

"Okay." Keeper paused, thinking. "Here's the plan. Toby will drop Y and Joy off at Y's borrowed SUV. Y, you take Joy home. Make sure she's safe before you leave. Then you can join me and Toby back at his parents' place. Toby will get the computer running and see if there is anything on there that tells us something about Todd Jones. I'll get in touch with Chaos and see when he wants to meet."

"I'm going to have to pass on meeting back up at Toby's," Y said.

Keeper turned and looked at her. There was an overly long silence.

"I said I'd help, and I will," Y said. "But I have a few personal things I need to take care of, sooner than later."

Keeper's eyes continued to hold hers. He couldn't help feeling something was off. Hopefully it was just the inevitable side effect of Joy sucking all the fun out of the afternoon. "Understood."

Keeper sat across from Toby at a folding table in the basement. Toby was searching through Todd Jones's computer, and Keeper had odd parts from various electronics spread around them. Peanut, the dog, was sound asleep on Toby's bed. He'd had an exhausting day of eating through a box of Christmas decorations, shedding all over the couch, and rolling in the dirty laundry.

"We need to figure this out and find the Cookie Maven fast," Toby said. "My mom has the patience of an angel, but I can tell she's almost at the end of her rope taking care of Peanut for us and hiding him from my dad."

"I caught Peanut dragging your mom down the street on his leash," Keeper said. "She made me promise to never speak of the incident. So, you know nothing."

Toby nodded. "I know nothing. Have you heard back from Chaos yet?" Toby slid his computer next to Jones's, opened it, and began typing away. "I wouldn't say I found anything concrete, but I'm feeling fairly certain Chaos was right. The Todd Jones we know is not the real Todd Jones."

Keeper moved his chair over to Toby's side of the table so he could see the computer screens. "Last I heard from Chaos, he was going to get in touch with Slasher, then pick a meeting spot for the four of us. What did you find?" he asked.

"Everything on Jones's computer is all business," Toby said. "Documents and e-mails for purchases and sales. Detailed Excel files for bills and income. But it all seems to stop about two months ago. Jones's calendar is all business, too, except for one thing." Toby pulled up the calendar. "Here. At around the same time sales stopped, he blocked a week out with one word, *Honduras*."

Keeper frowned, looking at the calendar. "Vacation? There are a few appointments after the blocked week, but they seem to dissipate. They could have been added before he left for Honduras."

Toby turned to Keeper. "What if Todd Jones never came back from Honduras?"

"Let's hope it was because of his own will. If he traveled out of the country, he has a passport. Can you pull up passport pictures for all the Todd Joneses from Durian and surrounding towns?" asked Keeper.

Toby shook his head. "Passports and driver's licenses are tricky business. With time I think I could hack in, but I wouldn't do it from my parents' house just in case I mess up. That kind of trouble would have to come down on someone else."

Keeper's phone buzzed on the table. He picked it up and read the incoming text. "Chaos says to meet at Valentino's on Marcel Street in half an hour. Back booth."

Toby closed both computers and placed the one belonging to Todd Jones in a messenger bag. "We should head out now," Toby said, standing and swinging the messenger bag's strap over his head. "Chaos hates late."

CHAPTER 25

VALENTINO'S was one of at least twenty-five Italian restaurants lining the streets of a four-block section in the West End of Durian. The outside of the restaurant had a green, white, and red striped awning and a few tables for two on the sidewalk. The inside was dark with redbrick walls and tables covered with white linen tablecloths and a flickering faux candle. A large brick pizza oven was heating behind a counter. The restaurant was relatively empty, the lull between lunch and dinner. Keeper and Toby wove their way through the tables to the back of the room and slid into the booth Chaos and Slasher were occupying.

A waiter approached, put waters down in front of Keeper and Toby, and asked if there was anything else they would like to drink. Keeper and Toby declined. Chaos and Slasher already had espressos. Once the waiter was gone, Toby removed the computer from his bag.

Chaos leaned forward, elbows on the table, his voice low. "I'm assuming everyone came out unscathed?"

"Everyone except Todd Jones," Keeper said. "My understanding is he's going to need an emotional support animal."

A smile twitched at the corners of Chaos's mouth. "That's a pity," he said, clearly not owning the sentiment. "Did you find anything?"

"The computer is all legit business files," Toby said. "But the business stops about two months ago. Around that time a week is blocked out on the calendar for Honduras. I don't think this computer has been touched since that trip."

"We also found Jones's wallet. Pretty much empty, but something had been in it," Keeper said, sliding the piece of paper across the table to Chaos. "Joy thought you might be able to figure it out."

Chaos squinted at the paper in the dark room and held it at a distance before removing his phone and shining its flashlight mode on it. He turned the paper a couple of times. Slasher was looking over his shoulder. They exchanged a glance, and Slasher gave a nod.

Chaos turned off the flashlight and placed his phone down on the paper. He stared at them for a moment, tapping his index fingers together, thinking. When he was done, he placed his elbows back on the table and leaned in toward Keeper and

Toby. "There is more to the initiation ceremony than a hearty handshake and cookies. An E.V.I.L. villain also receives a medallion. It is made specifically for that individual. It's like a form of identification. It should be carried at all times and carefully guarded. Hopefully you'll never have use for it, but should you ever be outside your chapter's jurisdiction and need help or a place to hide, it will assure you get what you need from any E.V.I.L. villains nearby."

"And you think that's what Todd Jones had in his wallet? An E.V.I.L. medallion? He's an E.V.I.L. villain?" Keeper asked.

"I'm ninety percent sure it was an E.V.I.L. medallion, but I can't read it well enough to see the chapter number or the villain's name. The question that prevails is, where is the medallion? If it had been in his wallet long enough to cause an imprint, why wasn't it there anymore?"

Keeper shrugged, thinking. "You said it's supposed to be carefully guarded. Maybe he had it on him?"

"Hmmm. Maybe." Chaos turned his head slightly toward Slasher without completely looking at him. "Heard any good gossip down the E.V.I.L. line in say, the past six months?"

Slasher was leaning back in his seat with his arms crossed. His head dipped slightly as he thought. "Word is that 902 dismantled completely."

"Yes, but there were only three members, and they lived in the middle of nowhere," Chaos said. "Not much villainy to happen other than cow tipping, and they owned the cows they were tipping. The head of the chapter stayed, trying for a normal life. The other two moved away and were taken in by other chapters."

Slasher furrowed his brow, trying to think harder. "What about Repeat and 787? I heard he got arrested again."

Chaos rolled his eyes. "Honestly. Repeat is a disgrace. He doesn't even get arrested for using his skill. Nevertheless, his chapter is devoted to him, and he was back on the streets within thirty minutes. So, no, I don't think it's him."

Keeper raised his hand.

Chaos's gaze moved to Keeper. "Yes?"

Keeper lowered his hand. "Um, sir, Joy thinks Todd Jones has the skill of giving people food poisoning when he gets too close. Or something like that."

Chaos's eyebrows rose, and his head turned back toward Slasher. "Interesting. My understanding is there was some sort of a big brouhaha in Chapter 403 a while back. Don't know any details. They kept things pretty quiet. Do you know any of the members in 403, Slasher?"

Slasher shook his head. "No, but 403's area is northeast of the city. It's not unreasonable to think one of their members might have ventured over this way."

A smile grew on Chaos's face. It had hints of evil. "It would be rather distasteful for a member of E.V.I.L., much less the head of a chapter, to pry into another chapter's files within the E.V.I.L. database." Chaos unwove his fingers and pushed

Jones's laptop toward Toby. "However, if someone who isn't in E.V.I.L. should do that . . ."

Toby looked a bit nervous. "I don't . . ."

"Cut the Thomas Crapper, Toby," Chaos said. "I know you've hacked into the E.V.I.L. database already and have been through 626's records. You probably know more about the chapter than I do. Wi-Fi password here is *lasagna*."

Toby opened the laptop, connected to the Wi-Fi, and did some typing. "Okay, I have the roster for 403 up. Just based on the names, I don't see anyone who might have a skill like food poisoning."

"Go to past members," Chaos said. "Most recent first."

Toby clicked the mouse a few more times. "First one up is a villain named Polyp."

"Well, now," Chaos said. "Looks like we're getting somewhere. If you click on the small E.V.I.L. icon on the top right, you'll get a pop-up for chapter heads to sign in. Password is always the chapter head's username plus . . ."

"I'm in," Toby said.

Chaos and Slasher exchanged quick evil smiles. Toby was definitely going to be an asset to Chapter 626.

"See if you can find Polyp's file," Chaos instructed. "It should have his real name, skill, information on why he is no longer with 403, and when he left."

Toby squinted at the screen, searching for pertinent information. "Real name is Raymond Ark-am-boo. I'm not sure I'm pronouncing that right. Skill is intestinal cramping within ten feet. He quit the chapter about four months ago. A chapter vote to remove him was scheduled but canceled."

"Reason for the vote?" Chaos asked.

Toby looked up from the screen. "He committed an act of villainy on another E.V.I.L. villain. No details."

Everyone was silent, watching Chaos. Waiting while he sat motionless, thinking.

"Our main objective remains the same," Chaos finally said. "We need to find the missing members of 626 and the Cookie Maven. Toby, I need you to go home and see what kind of information you can find on Raymond Arkamboo. More than likely, he was already living in Chapter 403's jurisdiction before joining. We need some sort of insight into his personality, his past. Something that might tip us off on where he's hiding his kidnappees. Scour 403's files. Maybe there's something repetitious logged about him? I'm going to alert Barricade and Staticanator about Polyp and his limited-distance skill. Keeper, I have a very special job for you."

"Yes, sir?"

"I need you to go car shopping with Slasher."

Out of the corner of Keeper's eye, he could see the look of panic on Slasher's face and that he was minutely, but rapidly, shaking his head back and forth in silent protest.

"Sir? Wouldn't it be better if I went home with Toby . . . ?"

"No. You see, Slasher has a theory about your skill."

Keeper could now see Slasher's hand moving back and forth, silently begging Chaos to cut off his statement at the neck.

"He believes," Chaos continued, ignoring Slasher, "your skill is bad luck. Wherever you go, bad things happen."

Slasher closed his eyes and slapped the palm of his hand to his forehead.

Keeper felt all the blood drain from his face. "That's awful!"

Chaos shrugged. "Not really. There are no bad skills. Truth is, it could be a great skill. We'd just have to figure out how to aim the effect in the correct direction. That being said, I don't think it's your skill."

"What do you think my skill is?" Keeper asked.

"I'm not sure, but it doesn't really matter. Best for you to figure it out and come to terms with your skill on your own, in your own time." Chaos finished off his espresso. "Builds character. Plus, it really isn't anyone else's business to tell you who you are."

Keeper looked at Toby. "Do you think I'm bad luck?"

"No." Toby's eyes went from Keeper to Chaos. "Are you going to eat that biscotti?"

Chaos slid his biscotti across the table to Toby. "If I can think of a good lie," Chaos said, "I'll try to get in touch with the head of chapter 403. See if I can pry out any information about Polyp. Now, if we are all adequately full of caffeine and carbohydrates, let's get a move on. I remind you time is of the essence."

CHAPTER 26

CHAOS dropped Keeper and Slasher off at the Porsche dealership. It had been an uncomfortable and awkwardly silent car trip, and now that Keeper and Slasher were standing in the dealer's parking lot, it wasn't any better.

Slasher was looking over cars and reading window stickers. Keeper had never shopped for a car before, much less a Porsche. "Um, sir?" Keeper said. "What can I do to help?"

Slasher straightened and sighed. "For starters, you could not cause trouble."

"I understand, sir. I'll do my best."

Slasher's brow furrowed and then softened. He patted Keeper on the back. "It's all right. Sorry about that. It's like Chaos said.

No bad skills. If you do attract bad luck, best we know sooner than later."

Keeper tried to manage a smile.

"Let's go inside the showroom," Slasher said. "That's where they keep the good stuff. Follow my lead, and let me do the talking."

They pushed through the double glass doors into the showroom, and a salesman in shiny pants and pointy-toed shoes came out of nowhere. He swept down on Keeper and Slasher like a vulture on newly discovered roadkill. Keeper suspected the salesman's skill was selling, and he was going to put Slasher, and his skill of slashing prices, to the test.

Slasher took a few moments to observe the showroom floor. Keeper wasn't sure if he was sizing up all the visible salesmen or the cars on display, but he was clearly in Slasher mode.

"Welcome, welcome," said the salesman with a smile that was unnaturally white. "How can I help you today? We have a wonderful selection of used cars in the back, as well as some base models out front."

This was the salesman's first mistake. Never judge a man by the paper clip he's using as a zipper pull.

Slasher sucked on his teeth as if completely insulted by the comment. "Perhaps you can help by directing me to a salesman who actually wants to sell a car and not dish out judgmental insults."

The salesman went a bit white but recovered quickly with a lie of equal aptitude. "I'm so sorry. I thought perhaps you were here to buy a car for your young son," he said, gesturing to Keeper. "I usually recommend newer drivers in something used or with less muscle under the hood. For safety reasons."

"Well, you thought wrong. I'm looking for a car he's not allowed within six feet of, much less behind the wheel."

The salesman's eyes twinkled with dollar signs. "I would be more than happy to help you with that. Do you have a trade-in?"

"No. My Rolls was stolen."

The salesman gasped in polite horror. "My sincerest condolences. Civilized society is going the way of the dodo."

Slasher eyed up the salesman, as if the thought that the salesman had stolen the Rolls had come into Slasher's mind. Keeper suspected that when one was an E.V.I.L. villain, it was best to not trust anyone, especially salesmen in shiny pants.

"I blame the internet," Slasher finally said.

The salesman nodded as if sympathetic to Slasher's borderline conspiracy theory belief. "I couldn't agree more. Come look at this fully loaded 911 Targa. Do you like convertibles?"

Slasher and the salesman walked off to look at the flashy red sports car. Keeper examined the showroom and wandered off in the opposite direction. There were seven cars on display inside, various models that all gleamed under the showroom lights and screamed fast. Even the SUVs and the electric sedan. To Keeper's far right, a row of cubicles lined the floor. They had direct access to a service porte cochere and a door leading back to the service bays. Next to service, there was a waiting area with drinks and snacks. Past that was a long alcove filled with Porsche merchandise like T-shirts, hats, mugs, and key tags.

Keeper looked back at Slasher. He didn't seem impressed with the convertible.

"It's no Rolls," Keeper could hear Slasher saying. "Why doesn't it go faster? Maybe I need a better Porsche dealership. One with offensively high-priced cars that are barely street legal for upper-crusters with exorbitant taste. I'm taking my kid and business elsewhere." Slasher motioned for Keeper to join him.

Keeper reluctantly meandered over, as instructed. Just in case his skill really was bad luck, he had hoped to keep some distance from Slasher during negotiations.

The salesman was waving his hands in protest. "No, no, no. Please, forgive me. I . . . I . . . I might have a car you would like. It was special ordered for a client, but we haven't been able to get in touch with him. It's in the service bay being prepped. Please, come look. I think it's exactly the type of ostentatiousness you're looking for."

Slasher let out an exasperated sigh. "Fine. Let's go. But this is your last chance."

Keeper trailed after Slasher and the salesman. They entered the service bay, and the salesman took Slasher over to a python-green GT3 with a carbon fiber roof.

"No expense was spared," Keeper heard the salesman say,

but Keeper was more interested in the work being done on a Taycan. Someone was having a Burmester 3D High-End Sound System installed, and all the parts were laid out on a worktable. It was exactly what Keeper needed for a project idea he had been thinking about. Better than what he needed.

Keeper's eyes went from Slasher and the salesman to the sound system, back to Slasher, and then back to the sound system.

"Don't do it," Keeper's inner voice said. "It's wrong. This isn't a pair of boots. It's a seven-thousand-dollar sound system."

"But I need it." Keeper internally argued with the voice. "I can't afford it, and if my invention works, it might just help Chapter 626. And if I help 626, it might not matter that I'm bad luck."

"Keeper . . . ," the voice warned.

Keeper squeezed his eyes shut and struggled to make a decision. "Hey, Dad," Keeper called out, opening his eyes. "I need to use the bathroom. I'll be right back."

Slasher waved at Keeper to go without looking at him. Slasher and the salesman were both in deep negotiations, trying to work the other over. Clearly enjoying the challenge.

Keeper walked out into the showroom, passed by the bathroom, and went straight to merchandising. He took some time browsing, holding up T-shirts and trying on sunglasses. He looked around and didn't see any cameras, but that didn't mean there weren't some pointed in the direction of the alcove from the far side of the room. Keeper finally picked up a Porsche backpack. He chose one that was a top loader, unzipped it, and swung it over his shoulder. He pretended to try it out and look at his reflection in some of the glass displays. It was all black. Nothing extraordinary other than its price tag. Keeper turned and headed back to Slasher, stopping to use the fancy coffee machine to make a hot chocolate. He didn't really want the drink, but for some reason he felt compelled to use the machine. When the steaming drink was ready, Keeper grabbed the paper cup and continued on to the service bay, drink in hand, bag on back. A woman from service eyed Keeper as he approached the door, and her mouth opened as if she was going to say something.

"My dad is inside, looking at the GT3," Keeper said.

The woman closed her mouth, relaxed, and smiled.

Keeper pushed through the door and slowly headed toward the Taycan. He took his time studying the room to see how many people were in the back. How busy they were. Who might be watching him. Keeper thought carefully about which pieces of the sound system he actually needed. He was almost at the worktable when he stopped. Not because he was having second thoughts. It was something else. A sound maybe? Or something he saw out of the corner of his eye?

Slasher was looking up at the GT3, now raised on a lift. The salesman was underneath the car, pointing up, and talking about a front axle lift system.

Before Keeper knew it, his fingers were burning from the

hot cup. He let go of the cup, dropping it and its contents. Hot chocolate covered the immaculate floor.

The salesman's head snapped forward, in the direction of the commotion. "Hey! No food or beverages in the service bay!" He took two steps toward Keeper, and the GT3 came crashing down, missing him by inches.

It wasn't long before everyone in the service bay and showroom were huddled around the salesman and GT3. The salesman was in a state of shock and kept repeating "I almost died." The rest of the crowd was in a state of frenzied confusion and excitement. No one seemed to notice Keeper or the spill, except Slasher.

Slasher looked completely calm and unfazed. He met Keeper's eyes and signaled with his head that Keeper should leave.

Keeper nodded and waited for Slasher to return his attention to the salesman. Everyone was huddled around him. The salesman had their full attention with his overly dramatic relaying of what had just happened. Keeper quietly walked over to the worktable and slid the woofers, amplifier, center speaker, and as many tweeters as he could into the backpack. He zipped it closed, swung it over his shoulder, and exited the building.

Forty-five minutes later Slasher texted Keeper for his location. Keeper was sitting on the grass in front of the dealership, hidden from view by the base model cars.

Slasher pulled up to the curb on the main street in a black

Panamera. Keeper climbed into the passenger's seat and placed the backpack between his legs.

"This is nice," Keeper said, buckling in. "Not as nice as the GT3, but I like it." Keeper's head tilted down slightly as he stared at his hands. "Sorry about the bad luck."

"What bad luck?" Slasher asked. "What happened that was bad? Did someone get hurt?"

Keeper thought about it for a moment. "No. Just the Porsche."

Slasher shrugged. "It can and will be fixed, and then it's mine for $56.13. One of my best price slashes ever. This is just a loaner." Slasher cast a glance at Keeper. "Turns out that lift broke yesterday, and it's not the first time. The tech forgot to send out a company-wide memo. You didn't cause it to break."

"That's a relief," Keeper said. He paused. "So, you don't think I'm bad luck?"

Slasher shook his head. "No. If anything, it was lucky you were there." He looked down at Keeper's feet. "I don't remember you having a backpack. Where did that come from?"

Keeper gave him a sheepish smile. "The merchandise alcove."

"Heh, heh, heh. Good for you," Slasher said. "However, I don't think you really care about having a Porsche backpack. What's in it?"

Keeper couldn't help but feel a bit guilty. "A Burmester High-End Surround System."

Slasher burst out into a full-on laugh. "You crazy kids and your music! I tell you, I'm feeling good for the first time in a while. We're going to find our chapter members, find the Cookie Maven, and get our cookies. Everything's going to be all right. Then you and Toby can have your ceremony and rock out to whatever kind of music you kids listen to these days."

"Yes, sir," Keeper said. "Sounds like a plan."

CHAPTER 27

Y patiently followed the mom pushing a stroller through the park. Y recognized a person who takes way too many pictures when she saw one, and she hadn't been disappointed. There had already been fifteen photos taken of adorable spit bubbles and the eating of animal crackers. It was a given that when they got to the pond, the baby would have to come out of the stroller for a photo shoot with the bronze bee statues.

Sure enough, the young mother parked the stroller, absent-mindedly put her phone down on a bench, and began unbuckling the baby while she talked about who was cuter—the baby or the bronze bumblebees. The baby seemed to be winning, but Y didn't have time to wait for the outcome. She quickly grabbed the phone and made sure to keep touching the screen so it wouldn't lock while she backtracked to a clump of trees.

Y hid behind a tree, touched the phone icon, and dialed her father. There was no answer. Y wasn't surprised. She was calling from an unrecognized number.

"Hey," Y said after the voicemail tone. "It's Y. It's five o'clock. We need to talk. Meet me in Schimel Park by the bees. Don't call back. This isn't my phone. I stole it."

Y hung up, deleted the call from the recent list, and locked the phone. She left the clump of trees and quickly walked down the path to the mother and bees.

The mom was still busy propping up the baby and getting his bucket hat just right. She hadn't even noticed her phone missing.

"Excuse me," Y said to the mom. "You dropped your phone back on the path."

The mom's head whipped around. The inevitable shock of one realizing she had lost, or almost lost, her phone on her face. "Oh no! Thank you! Thank you so much!"

Y handed her the phone. "No big deal. Have a good afternoon." Y didn't want to spend time with niceties. She hoped if she simply moved on, the mother would hurry up the pictures. Thanks to the *I stole it* comment, Y suspected her father would show in fifteen to thirty minutes.

Ten minutes and a gazillion pictures later, the mom packed up her baby and left. Y came out of hiding and sat on the bench.

She crossed her legs, put her hands in her lap, and kept her eyes forward. Another ten minutes later, Sensei Love slid onto the opposite side of the bench.

"I should never have let you stay. You haven't been off the dojo's grounds for more than a month and you have already been more influenced by villains than by my years of teachings," Love said.

Y kept her focus forward, her posture relaxed. "You've taught me a lot of things. I'm having a hard time telling what's the truth and what isn't."

"Huh." Love let out a breath of amusement. A half smile appeared on his face. "Despite what you think, you are not grown up, and you have no true understanding of the ways of the world. When you are eighteen you may do as you please, but until then you will do as I say. It's for your own good."

Y turned her head toward her father. "I saw you in the Porcelain Palace, talking to the king of commodes."

"That doesn't concern you. However, your sneaking out at night does concern me. I assume you are still trying to make contact with Keeper Chance. Hoping to prove yourself to me. There's no need. Chance is also not your concern anymore. I thought I made that clear."

"Did you know the Porcelain Palace guy has been kidnapping E.V.I.L. villains?"

"Of course."

Y stared for a few moments, waiting for more. "And?"

"And what?" Love replied.

"And what are you doing about it?"

"Nothing. They haven't been harmed, and Polyp, or as you like to call him, the king of commodes, has agreed to release them in a location away from their jurisdiction. You have no idea what you're getting yourself involved in, Y. You are not prepared or skilled enough to deal with Polyp."

"So, he's an E.V.I.L. villain?" Y asked. "And he's committing evil acts against his own kind?"

"Not exactly. He's not in E.V.I.L. anymore," Love said.

"Did you know he's also kidnapped the Cookie Maven?"

Love became more rigid than usual. He turned his head to look at Y. "Who's the Cookie Maven?"

"Her real name's Joanne Larbole. She makes cookies. Owns a store called the Cookie Maven. She's a civilian."

Sensei Love studied Y. As always, it was hard to get a read on Love's thoughts and emotions, but Y knew when her father was unhappy. She had plenty of experience in making Sensei Love unhappy. The Cookie Maven was a curveball. He hadn't known about her, and Sensei Love didn't like surprises.

"Do you have proof?" Love asked.

"For complete proof, I would need to be able to locate the Cookie Maven," Y said, "but there is enough evidence to strongly support the suspicion."

"And what is this evidence?"

Y faltered. There was no good way to tell him without getting into all the nefarious details about stealing, breaking and entering, and other various villainous and highly frowned upon things she had been doing. "I'm not at liberty to say. As you like to put it, it's not my business."

A thin smile drew across Sensei Love's face. "Protecting E.V.I.L. villains, are we?"

Y did her best to not show her hand. "No." It wasn't a total lie. Mostly she was protecting herself and Keeper, and Keeper wasn't in E.V.I.L. yet. "Are you?"

Love's gray eyes stared at Y. He didn't like it when she challenged him. He liked it even less when people tried to play him. "The kidnapping of anyone outside of 626 is troublesome. I'll look into it," Love finally said. "You are leaving Durian and going back to the dojo. I should be returning shortly, with Keeper Chance." He took out his phone and sent a text. "I've called for a car. It will pick you up on the east corner of the park and take you home. I'll walk with you."

"That's not necessary," Y said.

"Oh, I think it is."

Y walked silently around the pond with her father. A black sedan waited at the curb. Sensei Love opened the back door, and Y slid into the car. The door closed without so much as a *goodbye, I love you,* or *see you soon.* Just a couple of taps on the roof to signal the driver to go.

The sedan pulled away and began weaving through town, toward the highway entrance. After a few blocks Y could see a number of strip malls and fast-food restaurants ahead.

"I need to use the bathroom before we get on the highway," Y said to the driver.

The driver pulled into the lot for a Chicken Barn, and Y got out. She walked into the fast-food place and turned down the hallway for the bathrooms but chose the door that led to the kitchen instead. She quickly walked through the prep stations, ignoring any remarks, and exited out the back, where the dumpsters were.

It took her over an hour to carefully make her way back to her *borrowed* SUV near the park. By the time she reached Toby's house and slid through the basement window, it was past eight o'clock at night.

Toby and Keeper were hard at work on the folding table. Toby was on his computer, and Keeper had an odd assortment of various containers that looked highly scientific. There was a mortar and pestle, a hot plate, and a set of what could only be Toby's mom's Pyrex storage containers. Some were filled with brightly colored liquid. There were two piles of Ping-Pong balls in front of Keeper.

Y stood behind him. "Looks like you've been busy," she said, bending over and picking up a bottle to read the label. "Ammonium nitrate? Are you making something naughty?"

Keeper could feel the warmth of her next to him. "I wouldn't say naughty," Keeper said focusing on the Ping-Pong ball in his hand, "but you certainly don't want to be within five feet—maybe seven—when one of these Ping-Pong balls goes off."

Y slid a chair over to Keeper's and sat down next to him so there wasn't even an inch between them. "Did you meet with Chaos?"

"Yes," Keeper said, returning his attention to his work. He repeated the details of the meeting and kept the car shopping fiasco to himself. Keeper placed the final ball into its pile, removed his latex gloves, and turned to face Y. "What about you? Get everything done that you needed to get done?"

"More or less. Have you found anything, Toby?"

Toby sighed in frustration. "Not really. I can't find anything on a Raymond Arkamboo that fits his description. No school records, no past residences, no nothing. I know the whole point is to get inside this guy's mind, but when I look over his villain records with Chapter 403, he seems to be, for the most part, no different from any villain."

Y furrowed her brow, thinking. "I'm betting he has no real abilities beyond the cramping. Never felt a need to protect himself any other way." She turned and looked at Keeper. "What about you?"

Keeper was afraid to ask, but he did anyway. "What do you mean, *what about me?*"

"What do you have to protect yourself?" Y stood up, moved her chair to the side, and motioned with her hands for Keeper to join her. "Come on."

Keeper could feel the swell of panic moving up his chest into his throat. He wasn't sure what was happening, but there was definitely a warning siren going off in his head.

"I'll show you the basics of self-defense. How to break free from a hold, blocking, a front kick, maybe some elbow and knee moves." Y motioned for Keeper again. "Come on. Let's go."

Despite Keeper's better judgment, he rose from his chair. "You know martial arts?"

"I've had a few classes," Y lied. Truth was her father had her snap kicking before she could walk.

Y showed Keeper some basic blocking and attack moves, then moved on to breaking holds. She wrapped her hand around Keeper's wrist and was instantly pushed back, off her feet, tumbling over the sofa.

Keeper rushed to help Y up. "I'm so sorry. Are you okay?"

Y straightened her skirt over her tights and looked at Keeper. "What the heck was that? My ears kind of hurt."

Keeper lifted his shirt to show pieces of the Burmester sound system strapped around his waist. "The trigger band is on my wrist. I forgot I still had it on. When you grabbed it, you set off this little self-defense mechanism I built."

Y bent to get a closer look. "Is that a subwoofer?"

"Yes. I got the idea from Barricade. I did some tinkering with an amplifier just in case I run into a situation where I need some distance from Polyp. To be honest, I didn't even know if it would work. Toby was unwilling to be my test subject."

"It was totally awesome," Toby said from behind his laptop. "And I still stand by that decision."

Y took a few steps back. "Okay, I'm going to charge you. Give it everything you got."

Keeper held up his hands for Y to stop, but she was already in motion. "I don't think that's a good—"

Y barreled into Keeper, driving her shoulder into his chest and knocking him back, over the sofa. Together they rolled backward, flipping upside down and finally landing on the floor with Keeper on top, his mouth inches from Y's.

"Boys!" Toby's mom opened the basement door and came halfway down the stairs. "Remember, I'm going out tonight." She looked down at Y and Keeper. "Oh! Hello, Y. I didn't know you were here."

Y turned her head toward the stairs, her body still plastered under Keeper's. "Hi, Mrs. Toby's mom. How are you?"

"I'm doing great. Going out with the ladies tonight. So nice of you to ask." Toby's mom's lips pursed, and she gave her head a little shake. "Honestly, Keeper. Roughhousing is no way to show a girl you're interested."

Keeper's mouth dropped open in horror. "I . . . I'm not interested. I swear. I would never. There's no roughhousing. It was an accident."

Toby's mom rolled her eyes in disbelief. "Just take the poor girl out for ice cream or something."

"I like ice cream," Toby said from the table. "Can I come?"

"What? No!" Keeper said, trying to pry himself off Y. She wasn't making it easy. "No one is getting ice cream."

"Nonsense," Toby's mom said. "I'll leave some ice cream money on the kitchen table with the keys to the Kia. Ellen Smartle is picking me up. Take the dog with you. He doesn't like to be left alone, and if your father finds him, we're all in hot water." Toby's mom came down the rest of the stairs and started picking up empty cans and bags of chips as she approached the table. "Are you done here, Keeper? Do you need me to take any of this upstairs?"

Keeper managed to get away from Y and hurried to block Toby's mom from the Ping-Pong balls. "No, ma'am. That's incredibly kind of you, but it's not necessary. I'll make sure everything is cleaned up when I'm done. I promise."

"Okey dokey." Toby's mom turned, arms full of teenage boy trash and headed back up the stairs. "You should try that new place in Parsimmon, the Icebox Creamery. It's not far from the old factory where your grandfather worked, Toby, before I was born. I can only imagine the unsavory types of people squatting in it. Owned by the nicest fellow, Stanley Wonet, or maybe it was Bonet? Had an unfortunate accident involving mayonnaise and passed way too young."

"Mom!" Toby had his arms out, imploring the talking to stop.

"His widow abandoned the factory and moved north of the city. Went back to using her maiden name, Archambeau. Beautiful young French girl. Supposedly, she had a baby years later, out of wedlock—"

"Mom!" Toby stared at her. Desperation in his eyes.

"Okay, okay. Sorry, Jelly Bean. Don't mean to ramble. Have fun tonight. And, Keeper, please don't forget to clean up before you go out."

"Yes, ma'am."

Toby's mom closed the door behind her, and everyone let out a sigh of relief.

"Okay," Y said. "Back to business. Blast me with everything you've got, Keeper."

"I don't think . . ."

"For crying out loud, stop thinking so much," Y said, taking a stance like she was bracing for hurricane-force winds. "It's going to give you pimples and ulcers. Just do it."

"Yeah, Keeper," Toby chimed in, clearly eager to see the results. "Give it all you got."

Y didn't stand a chance. She flew backward, crashing through the paper-thin, circa 1970, faux wood wall, and laid waste to boxes of Christmas decorations.

There was the sound of someone banging on the floor above, followed by the voice of Toby's father yelling at them to turn the television down.

Keeper moved multiple boxes to the side until he found Y. "Are you okay?" he asked.

"WHAT?"

Keeper offered her a hand and pulled her out of a nest of disintegrated plastic garlands and what might have once been the family tree.

"MY EARS ARE THROBBING," Y shouted.

"You're lucky they aren't bleeding," Keeper said.

"WHAT?"

Keeper gave her two thumbs up and an encouraging smile.

"YEAH. IT WAS AWESOME."

CHAPTER 28

KEEPER, Toby, Y, and Peanut sat outside the Icebox Creamery at a small bistro table, ice cream in hand. Couples and groups of teens came and went out of the little shop, looking for a late-night treat.

"You sort of surprise me, Toby," Y said. "You don't strike me as a vanilla man."

"It's *French* vanilla. I've never had *French* vanilla before," Toby said, digging in.

Y did some careful excavating to find the cookie dough chunks in her scoop. "Spoiler alert. It's just vanilla."

Toby paused with his spoon in his mouth, disappointment registering on his face. "Yeah, but I bedazzled it with gummy worms."

"It was a nice touch," Keeper said. "Really ups the fun factor."

"Thanks, Keeper."

Toby removed a worm from its creamy, icy grave at the same time Peanut jumped up and bolted. Toby flew off his chair and flattened on the sidewalk along with his ice cream. The leash ripped off Toby's wrist, and Peanut sprinted down the street, barking, in chase of who knows what.

Keeper and Y helped Toby up, and Keeper handed him his cup of mint chocolate chip. "Here. You can have mine. I'll get Peanut."

Keeper took off at a jog down the sidewalk, calling Peanut's name. Peanut was fast. Whatever he was chasing was even faster. Every now and then Keeper would hear a bark and follow in its direction.

He passed out of the gentrified area of Parsimmon. What had been bright and clean was now dirty and run-down. The streets became empty, except for Keeper. At least it seemed that way on the surface. Keeper wasn't one for paranoia, but he couldn't help feeling like he was being followed. He glanced behind and could have sworn he saw a figure, dressed in white, disappear into the darkness.

He finally caught up with Peanut in a highly questionable area of town. There were broken chain-link fences, with DO NOT ENTER signs, on both sides of the street. Behind the fence, to one side, was a towering, crumbling brick wall of a large building. It extended down the street for at least an entire block. Small, broken windows lined the top. On the other side was an empty lot behind the fence. A construction trailer sat alone, dark and abandoned, with a sign saying CRUMP DEMOLITION on its side.

Peanut was shoving his giant body through a hole between the fence and the ground. On the other side was the moldiest cat Keeper had ever seen. Or maybe it was a sickly opossum or ratty raccoon. Whatever it was, it hissed and ran under the trailer.

The latch for the fence's door was broken. Keeper pushed it open and crossed into the yard just in time to get Peanut emerging from the makeshift doggy door.

"Come on, Peanut," Keeper said, picking up the end of the leash. "The chase is over. Time to go." Keeper looked around, quickly realizing he had no idea which way *to go* was. Something seemed familiar about the building across the street.

"Do you think this is the old factory Toby's mom was telling us about?" Keeper asked Peanut. "Let's get out of here, and I'll call Toby to come find us."

Keeper began walking, but Peanut didn't want to move. He was whining and panting and dragging. He was probably thirsty from running. Maybe there were some bottles of water in the trailer. It looked as if the demo crew had left suddenly and hadn't expected to be gone so long.

Keeper climbed the stairs and tried the door. It wasn't locked and swung open easily. Movement caught Keeper's eye, and

Peanut went after it. Great. More mystery animals.

"Leave it, Peanut! You're going to get rabies." Keeper turned on his phone's flashlight and aimed it toward the dog. He was trying to climb onto a chair. Problem was a person was duct-taped to it. The person, the chair, and Peanut were now rolling around.

Keeper approached the person and did his best to pull Peanut off. He shifted the angle of the phone's light. The woman strapped to the chair closed her eyes from the brightness and turned her head away.

"Joanne Larbole?"

The woman's eyes opened. She was clearly scared. Her hair was a mess, and her clothes were rumpled and dirty.

"I'm not going to hurt you," Keeper said. "I found your dog. We've been looking for you." Keeper reached for her. "I'm going to take the tape off your mouth."

Keeper removed the tape in one swift pull. Joanne Larbole took a couple of deep breaths.

"Thank you," she said. "Thank you. How did you know Peanut was mine?"

"Microchip. I brought him to your house, but you weren't home, and your cookie store was closed." Keeper rummaged through a drawer, looking for scissors or anything that could cut through the tape on her wrists and feet. "What happened? Who did this to you?"

"Some horrible man who smells like burnt popcorn. He was

holding Peanut for ransom. I paid him, but he wouldn't give Peanut back. He demanded more money."

Keeper played the light from his phone over the desk, looking for a box cutter. He froze momentarily when the light lit up a coffee-stained fishing catalog addressed to Todd Jones at the Porcelain Palace. Half-covered in stains was another doodle. One of the figures was tall with curly hair, teardrops raining down from its sad face. A second, smaller stick figure, was lying at its feet. It was hard to see through the dried-up coffee, but there was a good chance the smaller figure had *X*s in its eyes.

Keeper pulled himself together, found a pair of scissors in a drawer, and began freeing the Cookie Maven from her chair. "I suspect the man didn't have Peanut to give back. I found him in a park. Have you been here long?"

"Almost two days, I think," Joanne said, rubbing her newly freed wrists. "Last thing I remember is being in my home. Then I was strapped to this chair. That horrible man has visited a few times so I can have bathroom breaks. He comes with water and stale candy bars, rambling on and on about how he is going to use me to get a keeper and then execute order 626 on evil. Just the thought of him makes my intestines cramp."

Keeper froze for a moment and looked up at the Cookie Maven. This wasn't good. The mention of "Keeper" and "626" couldn't be a coincidence. Was he the reason 626 was being dismantled one by one? Was he the reason Polyp wanted Toby out of the picture? Was all this ultimately his fault? Had he somehow caused it all to happen? What in the world was his skill, and what was going on here?

"I wouldn't put much stock into any of it," Joanne said. "The man is a cookie short of a dozen. He also kept asking me how long a cape I thought he should have."

Keeper removed the last of the tape, took his new cell phone out of his pocket, and opened the map to find their location. "Well, you and Peanut are free now. We're near the cross streets of Hutchins and Stern in Parsimmon. Is there someone you can call to come get you? Maybe a friend who will let you stay with them for a couple of days? Whatever you do, don't go home yet. It's not safe."

Joanne thought for a moment. "My cousin. She's probably worried sick." Joanne took the phone from Keeper and entered the phone number. Her cousin didn't answer, so Joanne left a message and followed it up with a text.

Keeper walked with Joanne and Peanut to the corner of Hutchins and Stern. "I can stay with you until your cousin arrives," Keeper said.

"That would be great," Joanne said. "We can give you a lift home. It's not safe for a boy your age to be in a neighborhood like this, late at night."

Keeper looked up and down the street. He could have sworn he saw a flash of white again. "Thank you, but I'm going to decline. I'll be fine." Keeper had a feeling that was a total lie. He was in serious danger, but not as much as Toby and 626. He had to do something to help them.

The Cookie Maven looked at Keeper, searching his eyes for something. "Who are you?"

Keeper shifted his eyes away. "Nobody special. Just someone who desperately needs you to keep making cookies. There are people looking for the man who took you. I'll leave a note on your door when it's safe to return. I'll make sure you can see it from the road when you do a drive-by."

Joanne held tight to Peanut's leash. "The horrible man, he's upset some bad people, hasn't he? You aren't involved with those people, are you?"

Keeper thought about it. "I'm not sure how bad they really are. More like lawful evil." He gave the Cookie Maven a weak smile as a blue Nissan Pathfinder pulled up to the curb.

Joanne Larbole and Peanut climbed into the Pathfinder and tried one more time to give Keeper a ride. After the car pulled away, Keeper walked a couple of blocks and took a corner. He glanced behind to make sure no one was around. Out of the corner of his eye, there was another white flash. What in the world was it? It couldn't be Polyp. He always wore dark colors.

Keeper took out his phone and texted the names of the cross streets to Toby. Five minutes later the Kia pulled to the curb, and Keeper climbed into the back seat.

"Where's the dog?" Y asked Keeper.

"You aren't going to believe this. He's with Joanne Larbole."

Toby stopped the car in the middle of the street and turned

to look back at Keeper. "You found the Cookie Maven?"

"Yeah," Keeper said, sitting back and buckling in. "Peanut chased something down to the factory your mom was telling us about. Larbole was tied up in the abandoned demo trailer in the factory's old parking lot across the street. What are the chances? Crazy, right?"

Toby turned and continued driving. "Heh. Yeah. Crazy."

Y looked at Toby. She was certain he had figured it out. Toby knew what Keeper's skill was. It must have something to do with finding Joanne Larbole, but what? Keeper found Larbole's dog, too. Was that it? He found lost things?

"Supposedly the kidnapper wants to execute order 626 on evil." Keeper's eyes focused on Toby and Y. "And he plans on getting a keeper to do it."

Y's eyes slid toward Toby. Toby's eyes went to the rearview mirror to glance at Keeper.

"Is that like order 66 from *The Clone Wars*?" Toby asked. "Is he trying to eliminate E.V.I.L. villains worldwide? Why?"

Keeper shrugged. "I don't know. But I do know that if 'getting a keeper' refers to me, it's not going to happen. I have no desire to be used as a weapon of mass destruction against E.V.I.L., much less against the only group of people who have ever liked me and welcomed me into their family . . . not counting Tsunami."

Y mindlessly watched houses and businesses pass by her window. There were now three parties interested in Keeper's skill.

Whatever it was, it was big. Maybe she had messed up, and Keeper would be better off at the dojo. At least he would be safe there for a few years.

"Hey, Toby," Keeper said, breaking the silence. "How do you spell Arkamboo?"

Toby squinted his eyes as if it would help him remember. "A-R-C-H-A-M-B-E-A-U."

Y rolled her eyes. "That's pronounced Are-sham-bow. It's French." Y sucked in air. "OMG!"

Keeper knew exactly what she was thinking. He leaned forward a bit. "What if Polyp is the child born out of wedlock? Like your mom said, Toby. Polyp's mother went back to *using* her maiden name, but it might not have been her legal name. That would mean Polyp is not officially an Archambeau."

Toby looked at Keeper in the rearview mirror. "He'd be a Wonet, or Bonet, or whatever the death-by-mayo guy's name was."

"If Polyp has a connection to the old factory," Y said, "it might be a location that gives him comfort and confidence. That's why Larbole was there, and it would explain why we saw Polyp on the streets near the antiques store in Parsimmon. The members of 626 might be inside the factory."

"I'm going to call Chaos," Keeper said. "Tell him we have a possible location."

Toby's eyes went back to the rearview mirror. "Make sure you tell him about how you saved Joanne Larbole and reunited her with Peanut."

Keeper removed his phone from his pocket and paused. "Before we meet up with everyone at the factory, I need to swing by your place. I get the feeling I should load up on balls and get my sound barrier belt."

CHAPTER 29

CLOUDS came and went, covering the moon and stars, leaving the abandoned factory dark and dirty in the amber glow of streetlights. Keeper, Toby, and Y were the first to arrive on the building's east side at 12:45 a.m.

"What's wrong with you?" Y asked Keeper. "You look like you're going to throw up."

"I feel like I'm going to throw up." Keeper swallowed and wiped his palms on his pants. "Listen, there's something I should tell you, Y. I didn't know until—"

"Sssshh. Someone's coming," Toby said.

Barricade and Staticanator ducked under the KEEP OUT tape barrier and approached Keeper, Toby, and Y. Joy straggled in behind them.

"Hey," Barricade said, giving a nod to the group.

A gust of wind gathered years of street dust and debris up into a sandstorm, pelting the group. It cleared almost as quickly as it came. When everyone finally removed their heads from the protection of their arms, Chaos and Slasher had joined the group.

"Sorry," Chaos said. "Probably my bad. When everyone is done dusting the dirt from their hair, we'll separate into two groups. Slasher will take the recruits and Y. Barricade, Staticanator, and Joy, you're with me. I remind all of you, this is first and foremost a rescue mission for Chapter 626. The Cookie Maven has been found. Don't go charging in. Wait for the entire group to reassemble, and we will collectively come up with the best plan. After everyone is safe there will be plenty of time for hunting down Polyp and making his life miserable. Understood?"

Everyone nodded in agreement.

"My group will take the south side and move inward. Slasher's, the north."

Chaos and his group disappeared into the darkness, making their way to the southern entrance. Slasher turned to address his team. "Listen, newbies, I realize this ship has already sailed, but let's try to keep things as professional and, for lack of a better word, not weird as possible."

"Absolutely," Toby said. "Not a problem."

Slasher rolled his eyes, turned, and led everyone toward the north side. They did their best to stay in the shadows, moving between cement-block barriers, rusted-out metal containers, and piles of broken wood, metal, glass, and rats. On the north side of the factory, the metal chain-link gate was open. One door was hanging by a final hinge, and the other door lay crumpled on the ground.

Slasher approached the open yard between the gate and the building. "Tire tracks in the dust. Someone's been here within the last two weeks. I don't think we've had rain since then." Slasher picked up a piece of broken metal pipe from the ground and headed toward the factory's open bay door, following the tire tracks. "Stay on your toes,"

They followed Slasher into the loading bays. The tracks continued deeper into the building.

It became darker the farther inside they went. Slasher had his phone's flashlight out, but it had minimal range. Keeper was about to reach for the night-vision goggles on top of his head when he slammed into Toby, who had stopped walking and was frozen, paralyzed in fear. Slasher dropped to his knees, and his hands went to his head, the sight before him too much for a mortal man to see.

"Omigosh, omigosh, omigosh." The words were coming out of Y's mouth in a steady and unconscious stream. She grabbed a handful of Keeper's shirt. Before them lay the unsightly remains of Slasher's Rolls-Royce. It looked far worse than Y had remembered.

Slasher turned and looked back at them. Keeper grabbed Y by the back of her neck and shoved her face into his chest, wrapping his other arm around her back, patting it as if in consolation, holding her to him.

"It's okay. Don't look," Keeper said to Y. He shook his head in disbelief. "Who would do something like that to a Rolls-Royce?"

Slasher looked like he was fighting back hysterical tears. "I'll tell you who. A sicko. Someone seriously deranged."

"Totally," Keeper agreed. "Someone who clearly has no sense of boundaries." He released Y and pushed her back. "Should probably be locked up for the safety of society."

Slasher stood, took a shaky breath, and walked back to Keeper, Y, and Toby. "No. No. That would be too good for Polyp."

Keeper's, Y's, and Toby's mouths dropped in unison. They couldn't believe what they had just heard. Slasher thought Polyp had trashed his car.

Slasher bravely pulled back his shoulders and swallowed. Steadying himself. He pointed at the pile of luxury garbage, unable to look. "Do you know I paid $1,036 for that car? I know. I overpaid. It was worth it. I thought about slashing the price further down, but she was so beautiful. We had an instant bond. You know what I mean? I got wheel protection thrown in for free."

"Do you need to take a moment of silence?" Y asked.

"No," Slasher said. "It's very thoughtful of you, but no. What I need is to crush Polyp's knuckles with this pipe, followed by an equally devasting blow to his psyche, leaving him a quivering, gelatinous mass of emotional baggage incapable of ever raising another harmful hand to villains or to handmade, high-performance vehicles." Slasher had gone from sad to scary. His eyes were wild, and his teeth were clenched. "Let's go. I have a score to settle."

Slasher brushed past the young wannabe villains and stormed down the corridor. Looking for other hallways that led deeper into the building.

Toby followed first. Keeper and Y took up the rear, falling back slightly.

"Holy chest of horrors," Y whispered at Keeper.

"I know. I can't figure out if I'm relieved the blame is on Polyp or if I feel bad for him," Keeper said.

"I'm relieved." Y moved closer to Keeper. "Why didn't you tell me *it* was here?"

"I tried. I didn't know until after we arrived. The other side of the building, where I found the Cookie Maven, looked completely different. Plus, I have this terrible sense of direction. We were standing outside the building for fifteen minutes before I started to recognize the area.

"I used the car's last breath of life to barrel down the gate and roll to the building's entrance. From there I had to push the car inside. I was hoping the building would just collapse on it."

"No such luck." Y thought about it for a moment. Was it luck that Slasher put the blame on Polyp? After all, it was Polyp's fault they'd had to steal Slasher's car, and it got trashed. No, that was more like poetic justice. However, if Polyp was holding his kidnappees here, in the factory, then what were the chances of the car Keeper was driving breaking down right here? Y squelched a grimace. Chances were probably pretty good the car couldn't make it any farther. And it wasn't like Keeper easily drove it into the building. And it wasn't like he happened upon the kidnappees while he was hiding the car. No, luck wasn't his skill. But there was something. Definitely, something. She had to be patient and observant because Y was certain she was about to figure it out.

They followed Slasher and the light from his phone through what felt like the Labyrinth of Crete. There had to be some sort of pattern for the endless passageways and rooms off to the side, but that was lost in the darkness and decayed state of the building.

"This is crazy," Slasher said. "Too much ground to cover. We need to split up. You three go left. I'll go right. When you make it to the end, turn around and come back here to meet up. We'll move forward together."

Toby led, with Y in the middle. The building should have been quiet, but there were noises all around. Every now and then something would crumble on the building, and there was the sound of walking and scratching that Toby was confident belonged to an animal. The smell in some of the rooms was worse than ripe. More passages branched off to the right and left.

Toby stopped and aimed his phone's light down a passageway, even though it barely lit up anything past five feet. "Should we go down any of these?" he asked, turning around to face Keeper and Y.

"I don't know," Keeper said. "If we aren't careful, we're going to . . . Toby? Are you okay?"

Toby's eyes were wide open, much like his mouth. He raised a shaky arm, pointing with his phone down the hallway on the opposite side.

Keeper and Y turned to see what could only be a Minotaur. Or maybe a giant troll. Or an enraged bear. Dim light, from the moon shining through a hole in the roof, highlighted the enormous, freak-of-nature creature from behind. It was grunting and staggering toward them. Like a bigfoot defending its territory. It started to pick up speed.

"Holy snot rockets," Keeper said. "Run."

There was some panicked pushing and shoving as they turned around. Once they got Toby's legs moving, he was surprisingly fast. They ran blindly down hallways and took a couple of turns, hoping to lose the beast in the maze. It seemed to be going well until Toby slammed into something and Y slammed into Toby. The entire hallway lit up in a static electric charge, Toby taking the brunt of it.

"Toby! I'm so sorry," Staticanator said. "I thought you were a bad guy."

Toby dropped to his knees. His teeth were stuck together. "G-g-g-g-g-g."

Y went to help him up, but all of Toby's muscles seemed to be locked into place. "Keeper, give me a hand. Keeper?" Y played the light from her phone around, in circles, looking. "Where's Keeper?"

Keeper hadn't seen it coming. The hands had seemingly materialized out of nowhere, grabbing his shirt from behind and throwing him into a room. He skidded across the loose dirt and rubble on the floor until his back hit a wall. He heard a door close, and a light came on, shining into his eyes, blinding him.

"Keeper Chance, I presume?"

Keeper knew the voice. It was the voice of someone who sold porcelain products. "Yes. And you must be Raymond Archambeau."

"Please, call me Polyp. We're all friends here."

Keeper slowly got up from the floor, using the opportunity to block Polyp's view as he removed the baton from his sock. He kept it collapsed and hidden at his side. "I seriously doubt it."

"That hurts," Polyp said. "Not outside, but inside."

"I found a couple of your doodles. You're trying to off Toby."

"Who's Toby?" Polyp sounded genuinely confused.

"My friend. The one who's trying to become a villain with

me." If it wasn't stick-figure Toby, that left Slasher or . . . Chaos!

"Gracious, no," Polyp crooned. "I would never hurt your friend."

"I find that hard to believe," Keeper said. "You've been kidnapping villains and cookie makers."

"Sadly, yes. It was the only way I could protect you from that scheming martial arts grand master." Polyp adjusted the direction of his penlight so Keeper could see his sad, puppy-dog eyes. "Calls himself Sensei. He made me do it. You're the one he really wants me to kidnap."

"Why would a martial arts guy want me?"

"Why, for your skill, of course," Polyp said in his most concerned tone. "He would tell you it would be used for good, but it would be a deceptive lie. The man is terrifying. Intent on world domination. A true plague upon this earth." Polyp aimed his light back into Keeper's eyes just in case he couldn't deliver the next line with a straight face. "Chapter 626 isn't much better. They've been trying to eliminate other E.V.I.L. chapters and take over the city of Durian for years. I removed the cookies to protect you. The idea of Chaos manipulating you into being part of his evil plot makes me absolutely sick."

Keeper raised his free hand to block the light and took a step forward. None of this was passing the smell test. "Is the Cookie Maven okay?"

"Oh, yes, yes," Polyp crooned. "Very. I sent her on a week's vacation down to Florida. Made it look like she won a cookie award."

It was official. Polyp was a liar, and Keeper was in danger. He needed to get out of the room, and he needed to find the others, especially Chaos. Keeper took another step forward. "Good to know. Thank you for the heads-up on 626 and the grand master. I'll be leaving now."

Polyp matched Keeper's step. "Oh, no need to use Jedi mind tricks on me. I'm on your side, remember? My skill isn't anywhere as impressive as yours, being able to use the Force and all, but I was thinking that together we could stop 626. Maintain the balance of good and evil in Durian."

Holy Jar Jar Binks. Polyp thought his skill was the Force? Not only was the guy nuts, but he was a pathetic Palpatine without the zappy hands. Keeper snapped his baton, extending it.

Polyp heard the baton open and quickly moved his light in the weapon's direction, playing off its shiny surface. "Crikey! A lightsaber!" Polyp clicked his light off, and the room became pitch-black.

"Keeper? Keeper, are you in there?" Y's voice called from the other side of the closed door. "Hold on! We're coming!"

The sound of someone kicking furiously at the door echoed throughout the room. A cloud of dust and dirt exploded from the floor as the door came crashing down. Y, Toby, and Staticanator came tumbling in, just as Polyp escaped through a crumbling hole in the far wall.

CHAPTER 30

Y was first on her feet and rushed to Keeper, wrapping her arms around him. "Thank goodness. You're safe."

Toby followed Y, wrapping his arms around both Y and Keeper. "We thought you'd been kidnapped, and we'd never see you again."

Keeper closed his baton. "I'm fine, but I did have a little run-in with Polyp. He seems to have escaped somewhere when you took down the door."

Y walked the perimeter of the room, searching with her light until she found a hole in the wall just large enough for a body to squeeze through. "It leads to another room, but it's empty. I don't see Polyp anywhere."

"Should we try to go after him?" Staticanator asked.

"Staticanator? Is that you?" Keeper took out his phone so he could turn on the light. He counted off people. "Where's the rest of your group?" Keeper asked.

"Gone. Gone, gone, gone." Staticanator's voice started to tremble.

Keeper frowned. "What do you mean gone? All of them?"

Staticanator took a steadying breath. "We found Dr. Spot. She was in a room by herself. She was duct-taped to a chair. Who knows how long she'd been in that pitch-black by herself. Once we got her free, Chaos ordered Joy to take Dr. Spot out of the building, to safety. There's a huge wall of sandbags in the yard, on the south side. The plan was to meet up there.

"Barricade, Chaos, and I went in search of the others. Dr. Spot said Polyp separated them. We'd only been walking and searching rooms for a minute or so when I realized Chaos wasn't with us anymore. I backtracked a bit, looking for him, but couldn't find him. When I went back to Barricade, I couldn't find him, either. Barricade was gone. Gone!" Staticanator's voice was sounding distressed. "You have to help me find Barricade. I need him! Taking care of our crash of kids is a two-man job!"

"I think we already did," Keeper said. "I suspect that was who we were initially running from."

"I thought it was a zombie, come to eat our brains," Toby said.

Staticanator shook her head. "Barricade would never be a zombie. He's a totally unadventurous eater. I'm so relieved you found him and he's okay."

"Back this way," Y said. "I'll lead."

They followed Y down the hall as she took turns. She seemed to remember every detail of the terror-stricken run, which relieved Keeper since he had no idea where they were.

"You know," Keeper said, "thinking back on it, if that was Barricade, he was walking a bit zombieish. Kind of dragging a leg and listing to the side."

Toby quickened his pace to stay next to Keeper. The last thing he wanted was to fall behind and disappear like Chaos or have his own run-in with Polyp. "Maybe he twisted his ankle or something."

"Maybe." Keeper had a feeling it wasn't likely. Barricade hadn't called out to them. At least Keeper didn't think he had. Hard to say over the blood pounding in his ears and Toby's screaming.

They made it back to the area of the sighting, but there was no Barricade. Soft snapping sounds were coming off Staticanator and her hair was beginning to float upward.

"Realistically," Keeper said, "Barricade can't be far. If he was injured, he's not moving fast. Maybe he's heading to the meeting point. And if Polyp got him, good luck moving what must be at least three hundred pounds, conscious or unconscious. Staticanator and Toby, take the hallway to the left. Check all the rooms. Y and I will search the rooms in the hallway Barricade was coming down."

Keeper lowered his night-vision goggles and walked off

with Y. They checked room after room. The hallway seemed to go on forever.

"Those stick-figure drawings were of Chaos," Keeper said once he was sure they were out of Toby's earshot.

Y frowned, thinking. "Why would Polyp want Chaos dead?"

"I don't know," Keeper said, coming to a stop. "Last door. If Barricade isn't in here, I say we return to Staticanator and Toby."

Y opened the door and stepped inside with Keeper. A single lantern was on the floor, glowing, illuminating a figure, feet apart, elbows out, fist in palm. Keeper raised his goggles and took in the white bracers, tunic, and pants that didn't leave a lot to the imagination. The man was around five foot eleven and solid muscle. Not Barricade-like muscle, lean and purposeful muscle. The scheming grand master was real!

"Hello, Keeper," Sensei Love said. His eyes shifted ever so slightly to the side, acknowledging Y's presence. He dropped his arms and silently approached his prey. He stopped about two feet in front of them. His eyes focused on Keeper's. "I saw you save the woman in the trailer." His eyes moved to Y, and for some reason he was compelled to do something completely out of character. He reached out to tuck a strand of loose hair back behind his daughter's ear. It was a mistake.

Before Love could reach Y, his arm was knocked away and a foot squarely planted in his stomach, sending him flying to the back of the room. Y's feet were frozen to the floor. She blinked a couple of times in complete confusion. No one. NO ONE got the drop on Sensei Love. It went against his skill.

"Don't touch her," Keeper said. His fighting stance was balanced. His strike had been perfectly executed. "Don't ever touch her."

Sensei Love slowly and deliberately rose to his feet. What might have been some sort of smile tugged at the corner of his mouth as he glanced between Keeper and Y, but it was gone as fast as it had appeared.

Keeper couldn't figure out how Sensei played into things. Was he really scheming? Did he really have plans for world domination? Had he really asked Polyp to kidnap Keeper? Hard to say, but it was clear that Sensei was far more skilled and potentially dangerous than Polyp. A fight with Sensei was going to take up more time and energy than Keeper had to give.

Sensei Love went into a fighting stance. "We can fight, or we can talk," he said. "Either way, it's a pleasure to finally meet you."

Keeper reached into a fanny pack he had borrowed from Toby's mom, pulled out a Ping-Pong ball, and threw it at Sensei.

Sensei Love caught the ball between his two hands, flattening it as if it were a fly. The second the ball compressed, there was a clicking sound and a spark. The ball exploded, filling the room with thick pink smoke.

Keeper already had Y by the hand and was running out of the room. He slammed the door closed and took off at a sprint down the passageway, dragging her behind him. They took the corner and raced down the hallway Staticanator and Toby were searching. There was the occasional flash of light from a phone coming from a doorway on the right. They slid to a stop in the years of dirt and debris, jumped into the room, and Keeper closed the door behind them.

CHAPTER 31

"**LIGHTS** out. Lights out." Keeper lowered his goggles and tried to see through the small dingy window in the door.

Everyone was quiet while Keeper watched out the window. After a few minutes Keeper felt relatively confident that the grand master, Sensei, couldn't leave the sanctum of his falling-down factory room or wasn't interested in a chase. "Okay," he said, raising his goggles. "I think the coast is clear."

Cell phone lights flashed back on, and the figure of Barricade sprawled out on the floor was now visible.

"It's okay," Toby said. "He's just sleeping. There was a tranquilizer dart in the back of his thigh. We think Polyp put him here. There's a two-wheel dolly in the corner that looks like it's seen better days." Toby hooked a thumb in Barricade's direction. "Not sure it was made for this much weight."

"Were you running from Polyp?" Staticanator asked.

"I wish," Keeper said. "We opened a door, and inside the room was some weirdo in tight pants. He knew my name and tried to manhandle Y. I swear this place is like some sort of freaky-deaky horror-movie funhouse."

"Keeper thwarted him with a spectacular smoke bomb," Y said.

Keeper smiled. "It was no ordinary smoke bomb. I tinkered with it a bit. It's designed to ignite and explode on impact. And it's not just smoke. I filled it with poison ivy oil. Toby's backyard is loaded with the vile weed."

Y felt her body go rigid. "Seriously?"

Keeper knelt next to Barricade. "If Polyp did this to Barricade, I suspect Barricade was deposited here because it was too difficult for one person to move him any farther. Let's get Barricade back on the dolly, and the three of you roll him out of here. Take him to Chaos's meeting place behind the sandbags and wait. I'll go find Slasher, fill him in, and he and I will find the rest of 626."

It took more than minimal effort to get Barricade up and onto the dolly. Two were going to wheel and one person was going to keep him from rolling off the sides.

In the hallway, Y turned to Keeper. "Once they're safe, I'll come back in and find you."

Keeper shook his head. "No. Someone needs to stay with the rescued villains and protect them." A smile played at the corners of Keeper's mouth. "Someone with a skill like finishing fights."

Y returned Keeper's hint of a smile with a full-on brilliant one. She took a step closer, into Keeper's personal space, rose onto her toes, placed her hands on his chest, and kissed his cheek.

"That was for saving me," Y said, taking a step back.

It required an extraordinary amount of effort for Keeper to keep his hands at his sides. "I didn't save you. You're perfectly capable. I just had your back." He turned and made his way down the hallway in search of Slasher.

As he walked, Keeper took out his phone to text Slasher that he was looking for him, then realized there was no cell service. The building was a total dead zone. He turned to tell Y, but she was already gone. Keeper raised his hand, briefly brushing the spot Y had kissed, then continued up to his goggles, lowering them for night vision.

He mostly tried to listen for any signs of human activity. Footsteps or doors opening and closing. All he could hear were the rats darting along the sides of the walls. He had to find Slasher. He had to find the other missing villains. And he had to find Chaos.

Chaos's sight was blurry, and he had a horrible headache. The blurriness was probably from being drugged or physically knocked out. The headache was undoubtedly from the incessant jibber-jabbering of the only other occupant in the room.

"Oh, hello. There you are, sunshine," Polyp said, pacing back and forth in front of Chaos. "How you feelin'? Like dookie on a stick? Good!"

Chaos tried to blink a few times, but it was requiring an enormous amount of effort and he wasn't even sure he was succeeding. The best he could tell, he was slouched on a metal folding chair, his hands in front of him, taped at the wrists. He willed himself to focus on breathing.

"I have to admit," Chaos said, "that I feel bad. If I had known you were having a villainous party, I would have brought chips and dip. I feel like an ungrateful guest."

Polyp straightened himself a bit and placed a smirk on his face that wreaked of false amusement. "Oh, no need for that. Your presence is enough."

Chaos needed to buy some time to clear the cobwebs in his head and regain strength. He was banking on Polyp wanting to bore him with a fantastical tale of woe. "I'm honored? Definitely perplexed. Perhaps you would like to elucidate?"

"Don't play innocent with me, Chaos." Polyp pointed his scepter accusingly. "You've gone out of your way to ruin my life for months now. It's finally my turn to ruin yours."

Chaos managed to sit a bit more upright and shrug. "I ruin a lot of people's lives, but I don't remember pinpointing yours. Are you sure you don't have me confused with someone else?"

"Oh, the great and mighty Chaos. So humble. So condescending. So full of goose goop. Let me jog your memory. October, baseball, the Durian Devil Dogs, last home game of the season. Didn't end well. There was a massive stampede . . . and *Chaos*."

Chaos thought back on the day. It was hard to forget. Chaos, Slasher, Showboater, and Tsunami had taken Barricade to a baseball game for his birthday. A guys' day out.

Chaos had been thoroughly enjoying himself. The sun was shining, and the grass was green. He'd had two hot dogs and a beer and was working his way through a soft pretzel when he started to feel crampy. He tried to ignore it, not wanting to ruin Barricade's day, but no such luck.

"Oh," Polyp said. "Judging from that look on your face, you do remember. Well, I was two rows behind you. I had the day planned perfectly. I had trained for months. I was going to get a medal of outstanding evil villainy for one of the greatest evil events on record."

Chaos scrunched his eyebrows. "Giving me gas?"

"I had my skill reaching almost double its distance. All I had to do was get in the cramping zone, then jog around the lower concourse, heading up to the balcony, when I reached home plate. Oh, it had to be perfectly timed, but I was going to have that entire stadium fighting for the bathrooms in blind panic, minus the box seats, but that's not exactly what happened. Was it, Chaos?"

"No, not exactly."

Once the cramping had started, Chaos had tried to wait too long to head to a bathroom, and in his state of emergency, chaos ensued. An enormous flock of pigeons began attacking people for popcorn. A child managed to get his cotton candy stuck in three people's hair. Some moron began complaining that his peanuts weren't nut free and he wanted a refund. Unfortunately, the chaos Chaos was causing was blocking him from being able to get up and out of his row. He had turned to Tsunami for a little help, but Tsunami helped too much. The skies suddenly opened, and a torrential downpour dropped. People were jumping out of their seats, pushing and shoving to make it to cover. Tsunami told Barricade about Chaos's issue. Barricade forged forward, people flying right and left as a path was cleared to the bathrooms. Unfortunately, the bathrooms were full. So Chaos caused enough plumbing issues to empty a stall.

Turned out to just be severe cramping. Barricade claimed it was his best birthday ever.

"I should have gotten a medal," Polyp screamed. "They said I had 'help.' I didn't need your stinking help!" Polyp looked up at the crumbling ceiling, closed his eyes, and laughed. It didn't sound genuine. "You would think that such an outrageous turn of events would make me a little . . . I don't know . . ."

"Testy?" Chaos offered.

"I was going more for angry or perturbed. But no, I wasn't."

"Are you sure?"

"Yes, I'm sure!"

Chaos was now feeling more like himself. His vision was almost back to normal. He could see an old metal desk and file cabinet. There were camping lanterns scattered about the room. "You don't sound sure."

"If only it had ended there. Let's move forward to early December. Ballantine Bakery. It's not located in your jurisdiction, but I think you know it."

"It rings a bell." Chaos knew Ballantine Bakery all too well. It was his secret indulgence.

Once a year, on the first Friday of every December, Chaos would go to Ballantine's for homemade snowballs, decorated to look like snowman heads. He always went alone. Always ordered a dozen. And always ate them outside, on a bench in the park. He loved being surrounded by the holiday decorations and watching everyone enjoy themselves at the temporary skating pond.

Last December's outing had been a bit out of the ordinary. It was an excessively cold day. Chaos had been working on his sixth snowball when he started to not feel so well, and it wasn't his stomach that was upset. It was lower. Chaos had closed his box and hurried to the park bathrooms. He didn't want to let go of his precious box of snowballs, so he kicked the stall door open. It swung back. Chaos kicked it harder and shoved himself inside, big puffy coat, pastry box, and all. He looked down, and there was a giant brown ball floating. No time to be picky. Chaos used his foot to flush and then realized he was feeling better. He waited a couple of seconds to be sure and left.

"Do you know whose lair is under the park across from Ballantine's?" Polyp asked.

"Yours?" Chaos said, taking a wild guess.

"Wrong. I'll give you a hint," Polyp said. "She's the head of Chapter 403. That ball you flushed, I made myself. It was specially designed to explode and clog as soon as it hit a junction in the pipes. That junction happened to be right over that she-devil's living room. Thing is, I didn't put it in the toilet. I was still thinking about it until you slammed the door open, knocking it out of my hand. Yes, that's why the door wouldn't open. I was trapped behind it! I got ousted from 403 for something I didn't even do."

"But you were going to do it," Chaos pointed out. "And maybe you should learn to lock your stall door, so these types of accidents don't happen."

"That's beside the point! No one believed me that it was you. Once again, a person would think this turn of events would leave me feeling a bit . . ."

"Testy?" Chaos offered.

"Angry or perturbed!" Polyp tapped his head with the golden plunger, laughed his insincere laugh again, and continued on his verbal rampage. "I wasn't angry or perturbed. I figured it was all probably for the best. I'd get a real job. Live a normal life."

"Sounds lovely," Chaos said. "Good for you."

"It would have been good for me, but oh no! Here. Comes.

Chaos. Let's move ahead to January. I got myself a job working the front desk in a gastroenterologist's office. Figured I was safe there."

"Ah! Dr. Zimmerman," Chaos said. "I thought you looked familiar."

"Glad you finally recognized me." Polyp's eyes narrowed. "FYI, I got fired, thanks to you."

"Ooohhhh. Sorry to hear," Chaos said. "You see, I have a little gluten issue, and I was rather nervous about my appointment. I rarely have need of a doctor. Things did get a bit out of hand. I'm not sure who brought that cat, but I assure you it wasn't me."

Polyp held up his hands, one with the scepter, for Chaos to stop. "It's okay. I'm not angry. I hated that job anyway. Had to sit in a chair all day, be nice on the phone, and listen to watered-down classical music."

Chaos nodded in understanding. "The music was awful."

"I figured I would be better off with my own business. So I found one I liked. Once again," Polyp said, gritting his teeth, "I did a lot of planning for nothing. Found a great business where I would have the perfect life selling carpets in my castle."

Chaos's face fell. He had a good idea where this was going.

"Every year Floyd Mason of the Carpet Castle goes fishing and scuba diving in Honduras. Except this year. Because someone"—Polyp pointed his scepter at Chaos accusingly—"SOMEONE caused a bunch of carpets to go up in flames, causing Floyd to cancel his trip."

Chaos opened his mouth to explain himself, but Polyp held up a hand for him to wait.

"Oh, no," Polyp said. "It gets better. There I was, standing in the middle of what could have been my future, smelling burnt New Zealand wool, when I overheard a phone call. Floyd is giving his vacation to someone else who owns a business in the design district. I figure, what the heck? Any business is better than no business. So I head down to Honduras and arrange it so Todd Jones would have a little accident and break both his arms and legs. While he's in traction, I steal his identity and come back here to what is now my store. Guess what that store turns out to be?"

"The Porcelain Palace?" Chaos guessed.

"Correct. I'm back to toilets!"

Chaos grimaced slightly. "It does seem to be your destiny."

"The worst part is," Polyp ranted on, "the store was a dump. Do you know how many trucks I had to hijack and warehouses I had to raid to fill that place?"

Chaos shrugged. "A couple?"

"A LOT! Guess how many customers have come into Porcelain Palace since I took over?"

"A lot?"

"A COUPLE! I don't count your posse of losers. Guess what I am now?"

"Testy?" Chaos offered.

"Angry and perturbed!"

Chaos rolled his eyes. "Fine. I get that. However, the carpet fire was completely accidental. All right, maybe not completely accidental, but mostly. I needed advice on how to get red wine out of a silk/wool blend. The store was packed. It was taking forever. Unfortunately, I'd had bread the night before. I couldn't help myself. It was fresh and warm and delicious and covered in garlic butter. I started to not feel well, so the crowd had to be thinned to hurry things along. One thing led to another, and whoosh. Up in flames. On the plus side, virtually everyone fled. There were only a few stragglers gawking and taking videos on their phones, and . . ." Chaos stopped. His eyes fixed on Polyp. "You!" Chaos pointed accusingly. "You were there!"

"Yes, I was. The emotional pain is still very much real, if you're even remotely interested. Best part is I can't get the smell of campfire out of my clothes, so every day is a not-so-delightful reminder."

"And where does the Cookie Maven fit into all of this?" Chaos asked.

"The Cookie Maven? Oh, this is brilliant. You'll love this," Polyp said, his eyes glassing over in the excitement of his genius. "Not only was her removal for forcing you out into the open, but once I kill you and all of 626, I'll kill her and make it look like 403 did the dirty work. E.V.I.L. will have to dismantle 403 in fear of law enforcement, or worse. I'll rescue any villains willing to follow me, and we'll go after 649. The process will continue until I have control over Durian and then all of E.V.I.L. I could be wrong, but I honestly think it's time E.V.I.L.

was under new management and a supreme ruler. Namely, me."

Things were starting to come together for Chaos. The timeline, the events, it was all making sense. "I see," Chaos said, his body becoming rigid with anger. "You should know that I don't take well to threats against my chapter members. Nor do I tolerate atrocities against cookies or their makers. And it seems to me that I don't have a gluten issue. I have a Polyp problem."

Polyp held his arms out, scepter toward the sky, presenting himself. He smiled proudly. "You're welcome."

"You're going to be welcoming my boot up your keister!" Chaos yelled. "For at least six months I've been eating pizza made with cauliflower crust. Cauliflower! The devil's broccoli! The most worthless, tasteless vegetable known to man. I gave up cake and waffles. Waffles!" Chaos was vibrating with anger and trying to keep control. "And what is up with all this Scotch tape around my wrists?! It's like I'm part of a white elephant."

"I used up all the duct on other villains! The Scotch does the job. As if you've never . . ."

There was the sound of crumbling brick. An unnaturally large swarm of rats emerged through a hole in a wall and ran across Polyp's feet, looking for a way out.

Polyp freaked. He tried to find a rat-free spot in the room, but in his panic to get away, he kept stepping on angry rats, making him lose it even more. Chaos wasn't bothered by the rats. He raised his wrists to his mouth and started using his teeth to break apart the tape.

The rat stampede wound down, and Polyp kicked at a few straggling rats and made for his archnemesis. "I don't think so, Chaos. . . . GAAAH!" A giant, moldy opossum jumped out of an open drawer in the file cabinet and ran at Polyp. The cabinet fell to the floor, sending up a cloud of ancient dust and dead roach parts.

Polyp fended off the opossum with his plunger until the animal saw an escape in the wall. "You think some bloated marsupial is going to save you?" Polyp yelled. "Your reign is done!"

Chaos removed the last of the tape from his wrists and dropped it to the floor. His voice was calm, his eyes focused. "On the contrary. I'm just getting started."

CHAPTER 32

KEEPER felt the factory shake before he heard the rumble. Chunks of plaster disintegrated from the vibration and rained down on his head. Keeper was sure he was on the correct passageway, but which of the intersecting hallways was the one where his group had originally parted with Slasher was a mystery.

The rumble stopped and was replaced by a different sort of rumble. Keeper looked down the hallway to his left. It was like the ground was moving, or shaking, or omigosh, rats!

Keeper hurried out of the way and watched as the largest mischief of rats this side of the sewers of New York charged down the passageway. A few strayed off in his direction, but most of the mischief stayed together on their quest through the old factory. Keeper wasn't sure where the rats had come from or where they were going, but it was a plus that they weren't heading in his direction.

Keeper continued making his way down the corridor until it came to an end. In typical maze fashion, the hallway split. He looked to his right and then left. For a brief moment he could swear he saw a glint of light. Keeper turned and stuck to the wall. He couldn't tell how far down the light had come from, so he stopped at every door, listening before he crossed its path, and moved on. Eventually he came to the door that had contained the light and now held voices.

"For the love of nickel and diming, take it off!"

"Never!"

"It's just a cape."

There was the sound of a gasp in abject horror. "How dare you! I would never tell you your car was just a car."

"Okay, okay. I'm sorry. I'm just getting a little nervous here. That rumble had to be Chaos's work, and I can't see anything. How in the world did you manage this?"

"I don't know. Frog! Get over here and hold the light for Slasher."

There was a sad and pathetic attempt at gunking.

Keeper stepped into the room and raised his goggles. "Hey."

There was a collective scream, followed by Slasher's light in Keeper's face, and then a round of relieved *thank you*s to the world of Moriarty.

Keeper took out his phone and pressed the flashlight icon.

"I was going to text you, Slasher, but there's no cell service in here." Keeper's light landed on Frog. He was curled into the fetal position and rocking back and forth. "What's wrong with Frog?"

Showboater rolled his eyes and flapped his arm in overexaggerated exasperation. "What do you think's wrong with him? He tripped over his giant frog feet and twisted his ankle, or something."

"It was dark. I couldn't see. My large feet are hereditary. Stop judging!" Frog said from the floor.

Showboater shook his head in disbelief. "I told you to just wear sneakers and dye them green. There's no arch support in those neoprene boots."

"Barricade, Staticanator, Joy, and Dr. Spot are all outside, south end, behind a pile of sandbags," Keeper said. "Toby and Y are with them. It was a meeting place picked by Chaos."

"And where's Chaos?" Slasher asked.

"Missing."

There was another rumble throughout the factory, this one more severe than the last. Everyone covered their heads as debris rained down.

"I don't know if Chaos found Polyp or Polyp found Chaos," Slasher said. "Either way, this building can't handle it."

Keeper went over to Slasher and Showboater and directed his light on Showboater's cape so Slasher could see. It was hopelessly tangled in a piece of old machinery, or maybe it was a piece of a piece of old machinery. Regardless, it was a bleak situation.

The building shook again. A large chunk of the ceiling fell to the floor, releasing a massive intrusion of freaked-out cockroaches. They scattered, looking for new hiding places, their little antennae searching for someone's pants leg to climb up.

Keeper and Slasher exchanged a look. Someone had to make the executive decision. Keeper nodded once, giving the go-ahead.

Slasher took out his multi-tool and began sawing away at the cape's fabric. He tried to stay as close to the machinery as he could, taking off as little fabric as necessary, but desperate times called for desperate measures.

Showboater's cape went free, and lines of sequins released themselves, falling to the floor into a grave of dirt and rat droppings. Showboater's eyes rolled back in his head, and he began swaying. Slasher grabbed him by the cape around his neck and gave him a good shake.

"Get it together, man," Slasher yelled in Showboater's face. "This is a crisis situation! If you want to be buried in this cape, fine, but today is not that day. You can rebuild it. You are the Showboater!"

Showboater swallowed and took a deep breath. "Yes. Yes, I am. Thank you." He looked down at the pile of bedazzlement, now being examined by a few select roaches. "I made this cape from a *Moulin Rouge* costume I stole when the off-Broadway troupe came to town. It was a collectible and the gaudiest thing I own."

Slasher rested a hand on Showboater's shoulder. "It was truly flamboyant."

Showboater fought back tears. "Not that anyone would notice."

"I noticed. And it will be flamboyant again. Come on. We need to get Frog out of here."

Slasher and Keeper directed their lights toward Frog. Under all the green, he was looking pretty white.

Showboater pulled his shoulders back and used his most authoritative tone. "Time to get up, Frog! This place smells bad, and I don't even want to think about what you're rolling around in on the floor."

"GORP-gorp-gorp," Frog tried to croak. "Just leave me here to die. I've hopped my last hop. Write something like 'he was a good frog' on my tombstone. I never even had tadpoles."

Showboater shook his head and looked at Slasher. "Always so much drama." Showboater reached down and pulled Frog up by one of his arms and placed it around his shoulder. "Let's go."

How the members of Chapter 626 had managed to survive in the real world up to this point was a mystery to Keeper. Maybe it was a herd mentality type of thing. Except they seemed to be falling apart pretty fast.

"You should help Showboater," Keeper said to Slasher. "He can't carry Frog out by himself."

Slasher shook his head. "I'm not leaving you in here on your own."

"Don't worry about it. I'm fine," Keeper said. "Hopefully the next villain I find will be in good enough shape to help me finish searching."

Slasher looked Keeper in the eye, then turned and placed Frog's other arm over his shoulder. "We'll take Frog to the south side meeting place. Remember Chaos's orders. Save Chapter 626. Find Tsunami. Find Chaos. Get everyone to safety. Forget Polyp. You don't need to save him. You don't need to stop him. You don't need to be a hero."

"Don't worry, sir. I have no interest in being a hero."

Hints of an evil smile played across Slasher's mouth. "Happy to hear it. Hopefully, when this is all done, you'll still have interest in being a villain."

CHAPTER 33

KEEPER figured Chaos would be easier to find than Tsunami. If Slasher was right about the rumblings, all Keeper had to do was follow the disarray. He went back to the hallway of rats. There were far fewer of the rodents, but a few stragglers were scurrying along, trying to find their mischief. Keeper followed the hallway in the direction the rats had come from.

When he reached the next intersection, Keeper placed two bricks in the middle of the path, pointing in the direction he was heading. He chose the right side first, checking every door. The night-vision goggles sped things up, but the fear of lurking senseis and other types of monsters, like gelatinous cubes or demogorgons, slowed things down.

Keeper came to a second intersection. There weren't any bricks to mark the path, but there was enough dust and dirt on the floor to draw an arrow with his boot, pointing in the return direction. He chose a new passageway with a singular tall door at the end. The door led to what Keeper thought was a giant room. The ceiling was high, and he could sort of see a metal catwalk. He raised his goggles to his forehead and realized he couldn't see because the room was filled with a thick fog. There were high, broken windows letting in moonlight and pigeons, but the light couldn't penetrate the fog that held around seven feet high.

"Tsunami?" Keeper stage-whispered, walking into the cloud. "Tsunami? Where are you?"

He thought he heard a sound of some sort, but it was hard to say. There were a lot of indistinguishable sounds in the factory.

"I can't find you in this fog," Keeper said, waving his arms about in front of him while he moved forward. "Tsunami?" Out of the corner of his eye, Keeper saw something. It was there, then gone. It was possible it was pink. Now it seemed to be on the other side of him. It was so quick and silent, Keeper wasn't sure whether it was all in his head. Wait! What was that sound? Keeper started stumbling forward, looking back even though he couldn't see anything. Soon he was almost running, until he fell.

Keeper picked himself up and looked back to see he had fallen over Tsunami. Tsunami was duct-taped to a chair with tape over his mouth and eyes. Obviously, he hadn't been a good guest.

"Thank the Sith Lords," Keeper said. "I hate to tell you this, but I don't think we're alone in this room."

There was a muffled response out of Tsunami, and Keeper rightfully guessed it was best that it was muffled. He grabbed hold of the tape going across Tsunami's eyes and ripped with one swift motion.

Keeper felt his mouth drop. He heard himself suck in air. He tried to force himself to blink. Keeper stared at Tsunami, then looked down at the tape. Two perfect eyebrows were attached to the tape. There were no eyebrows attached to Tsunami. Maybe he wouldn't notice.

Tsunami's eyes shifted to the tape and then tried to look upward to where his eyebrows used to reside. A steady stream of profanity was contained behind the duct tape across his mouth. Keeper grabbed hold of the tape and ripped. For the most part, the tape just left Tsunami's cheeks and upper lip red and sticky.

Keeper looked down at Tsunami, not knowing what to say. Tsunami stared daggers up at Keeper, with seemingly plenty to say.

Keeper gently laid the eyebrows onto Tsunami's lap. "Sorry."

Tsunami kept staring at Keeper, clearly thinking vengeful thoughts. Keeper quickly moved around to the back of the chair and cut the duct tape on Tsunami's hands, followed by his feet.

Tsunami felt his last foot go free and immediately stood. "Took you long enough."

"You're welcome," Keeper said, straightening up.

"I didn't say thank you. It's your fault I'm here." Tsunami leaned back and cracked his back. "Did the guy find you?"

"Depends," Keeper said. "Was the guy more like a martial arts guru or more like an irritating lump?"

Tsunami looked at Keeper as if he had grown a second head, and it wasn't any smarter than the first. "What in the world would a martial arts guy want with you? Could you be any more full of yourself? I don't know who it was. I had tape across my face, remember? Polyp kept calling the guy Sensei."

"Sensei is Japanese for teacher," Keeper said. "You should know this. Your name is Tsunami. That's also Japanese."

"Well, then maybe he's a teacher. Looking to teach you a lesson . . . GAH! What was that?"

Keeper whipped around to look behind him. "What? Where?"

"I—I don't know. I swear I saw something. The fog's too thick."

Keeper looked around frantically. "Let's just get out of here and go find Chaos. He's the last missing member, and I think he's in danger."

"Polyp got Chaos? Why the Medusa are you standing around chatting with me like it's teatime?" Tsunami took a couple of steps forward, his eyes darting around, trying to see. "You first."

It was all Keeper could do to not duct-tape Tsunami back to the chair and leave him. At the very least, Keeper was regretting removing the tape from Tsunami's mouth.

They crept through the fog easily. The room seemed to be empty, with the exception of Tsunami and whatever else was moving around. At one time the space was probably used for production and had machinery or tables.

As they neared the outskirts of the room, the fog thinned. The outline of a door was visible. Unfortunately, so was the outline of a man in a white tunic with a splotch of pink staining it.

"It's him," Keeper said. "Sensei."

Tsunami squinted. "Is he wearing pink?"

Sensei Love released from his at-ease stance and took a step toward Keeper and Tsunami. The fog seemed to part in front of him, as if it was fleeing in fear.

Keeper reached into his pack and pulled out a couple of balls. "Get ready to run."

Sensei Love raised his hands for Keeper to not panic. "I don't . . ."

Before he could finish, the balls were launched. Love easily avoided them this time, but Keeper hadn't been aiming for him. The miniature bombs hit the door behind Sensei, exploding in thick clouds of blue and green.

Keeper and Tsunami took off at a sprint for the opposite side of the room.

"You brought smoke bombs to a rescue?" Tsunami said, working to keep up with Keeper's long legs. "Smoke bombs? You couldn't bring something useful, like, I don't know, bear Mace?"

"I filled them with poison ivy."

"Hya, hya, hya. Okay. That's not bad."

They pushed and shoved each other through a door and continued running, full-bore, down a hallway. Keeper lowered his goggles and saw his arrow in the dirt. "This way."

They kept going until they found the brick arrow, turned the corner, and tried to run faster. Keeper's lungs were starting to burn, and Tsunami was stumbling and wheezing, when another rumble ran through the decrepit building. Keeper came to a sliding halt and put his arm out to block Tsunami. A door on the right fell off its hinges, landing in front of them. A chunk of ceiling crumbled above them, releasing a nest of spiders. Keeper and Tsunami brushed at the creepy-crawlies and shook out their hair and shirts. The spiders were probably gone, but the feel of their little feet would last through years of nightmares.

"Looks like we found Chaos," Keeper said.

Tsunami shuddered involuntarily. An inevitable side effect of falling spiders. "You think?"

CHAPTER 34

CHAOS and Polyp were rolling around on the floor in what could only be described as the world's worst and most pathetic, middle-aged-man ultimate fight. There was a lot of slapping, name-calling, and attempted headlocks. There was cramping, then chaos, cramping, chaos, cramping, chaos. The factory walls rumbled, and debris fell like confetti.

Tsunami's eyes went from Chaos to the ceiling and back again. "I've never seen Chaos like this. He isn't going to walk away from this fight. Assuming the building doesn't just collapse on all of us, it's going to take something substantial to pull Chaos away."

Polyp was on Chaos's back, beating him with the golden plunger. Only the top had broken off, and now it was just a painted aluminum pole. Chaos got himself onto all fours, grabbed a handful of dirt and threw it into Polyp's face. Polyp staggered backward, even more berserk. He threw his scepter at Chaos and missed. The scepter bounced off the floor, returning to spear Polyp.

"Everyone has a tipping point," Tsunami said. "When it comes to Chaos, you don't mess with his family. And waffles. The guy really likes waffles."

"I've never had a waffle."

Tsunami looked as if he had been struck by a bolt of enlightenment. "Seriously? No wonder you're such a loser."

Keeper closed his eyes for half a millisecond and tried to pretend Tsunami wasn't there. "Listen, I made—"

"Pretty smoke bombs?" Tsunami said, rolling his eyes. "That's great. If you're in high school. Which you are. Leave this Polyp problem to me. I have some real skills." Tsunami interlocked his fingers, stretched his arms out, and cracked his knuckles. "Stand back. I'm not being held responsible if you get yourself hurt."

The sound of walls crumbling echoed through the room. Another piece of roofing fell. It narrowly missed Polyp and Chaos, landing on a metal desk, smashing a lantern to oblivion, and pelting Keeper and Tsunami with rusty shards.

Keeper lowered his goggles. Not because the remaining lanterns had gone out, but because a wind had begun to blow around his feet. It was only a matter of time before what was now struggling to lie at rest on the floor would be flying through the air.

A small dust sprite began to form near Chaos and Polyp. Keeper had a sinking feeling growing in his stomach. "Um, Tsunami. Considering Chaos's chaos, I'm not sure a miniature tornado is a good idea in this situation," he said.

Tsunami's eyes were focused and unblinking. "There isn't going to be anything miniature about my tornado, kid. Hya, hya, hya!"

Keeper looked up, through the newly formed hole in the roof. Dark clouds began to cover the moon. Rain began to fall, and the windstorm grew in strength. Small chunks of brick and roofing rose and battered at Polyp and Chaos, getting their attention.

Polyp's attention turned to Keeper. "See. It's just as I told you, Keeper. You must join me before it's too late. Chaos is out of control. He's trying to kill me. Help me, Keeper. Help—CRAAHHHK!" Dirt, debris, cockroaches, and who knows what else were flying into Polyp's mouth. It was the price one paid for ranting and raving in a tornado that had moved from miniature annoyance to what-the-Gargamel.

Chaos grabbed at a folding chair as it went sliding past him on the floor. He picked it up and swung it as hard as he could, walloping Polyp in the stomach.

"What's he talking about?" Tsunami asked. "And why is he so interested in you?"

Keeper watched the tornado pick up pace. "Polyp thinks my skill is that I'm one with the Force."

"Hya! Hya! Hya!" Tsunami stopped laughing and shifted his eyes to Keeper. "Is it?"

"No."

"Hya! Hya! Hya!"

The wind radius was growing. Candy bar wrappers, rodent droppings, and tape remnants were plastered against Keeper's legs.

"Maybe you should tone down the tornado a bit, Tsunami," Keeper suggested.

"Tone it down? Who do you think I am? I don't control the weather. I just make disasters happen."

Keeper motioned with his head for Tsunami to look to the side. "Then maybe you want to make a little less disaster happen before you blow us all sky-high."

Tsunami eyeballed the boxes against the wall. They read CRUMP DEMO C4. "Ah, fuuu . . ."

Thunder crashed, and the room lit up from a bolt of lightning. The factory shook, and the crumbling increased in intensity. Some of the debris made it to the floor, and the rest was caught up in the ever-growing tornado.

"New plan," Tsunami said. "We each grab one of Chaos's arms, pick him up, and start running like the *Millennium Falcon* leaving Mos Espa."

Polyp recovered from the chair and charged Chaos, driving him back. The backs of Chaos's legs hit the fallen file cabinet, and Chaos went down. Polyp was poised to pounce when Keeper whipped his extended baton across Polyp's calves.

"GAAAHH!" Polyp fell to his side, grabbing at the searing pain in his legs.

Keeper and Tsunami each took hold of one of Chaos's arms and yanked him up.

"Ha! I've got you now, Polyp," Chaos yelled over the howling wind and the sound of rock pummeling the metal desk. "Feel the wrath of Chapter 626!"

Keeper and Tsunami were dragging Chaos as quickly as they could toward the door, their heads down against the wind.

"I hate to tell you this, Chaos," Tsunami yelled over the storm. "The wrath of 626 fled from certain death and vacated the building. We're all that's left. A little help getting out of here would be appreciated."

Chaos looked around the room as Keeper and Tsunami fought to make it across. "Holy wombat cubes!" Chaos said, ducking a lantern in flight. "Did I do this?"

"Yes. Yes, you did," Tsunami said. "You're completely out of control."

An ancient metal typewriter flew between Keeper's and Chaos's heads. The strength of the storm increased, creating a wind tunnel. The wind shoved Keeper, Chaos, and Tsunami forward, into the hallway, plastering them against the wall. Abandoned factory garbage pelted them.

They inched their way clear of the onslaught and took off

running. Keeper grabbed a handful of Ping-Pong balls from his pack and threw them back through the doorway just in case Polyp was following.

With the addition of the smoke from the smoke bombs to Tsunami's storm clouds, it soon became too dark to see. The rain was getting heavier. The rumbles grew stronger and more frequent, but Keeper couldn't tell if the noise was coming from the building or the sky. He switched on night vision and led everyone down the hall to the cavern where Polyp's car was parked.

Chaos pulled out his phone and turned on the flashlight. "To the right," Chaos said. "When it dead ends . . ."

Chaos's phone went flying as he was yanked back off his feet. Polyp had Chaos by the cape and was dragging him back into the building.

"Chaos!" Tsunami took a step forward to race after Chaos, but Keeper held on to him.

"Don't touch Polyp!" Keeper yelled. "He's covered in poison ivy oil from my smoke bombs."

Polyp and Chaos froze. Their heads snapped up, staring at Keeper, taking it all in. Wondering if they had heard correctly.

"Hya! Hya! Hya!" Tsunami's hyena laugh echoed through the building.

Chaos released the clasp of his cape and scrambled forward. The rain poured down at monsoon level, and a strange roaring noise gained volume.

"Don't worry, Chaos," Tsunami called out. "I got this one."

It was hard to hear anything over the growing roar, but Keeper was pretty sure he heard Chaos say "Oh, dear Megatron." Chaos was now up on his feet and sprinting, Polyp close behind. A flock of birds, riled from their sleep and overcome with an urge for chaos, swept into the room and swarmed Polyp. Chaos kept running. The metal catwalk and a beam fell from the ceiling, landing on a corner of Polyp's car. The car flipped and came down between Polyp and Chaos.

"You missed me!" Polyp yelled.

Then it happened. The roaring sound showed itself. A tidal wave of water carrying anything and everything it could get ahold of in the empty hallways and abandoned rooms burst through the opening they had just come through. It smashed Polyp against the car, covering him, as it rose in a giant wave, increasing in strength and volume.

"Hold on to me!" Keeper yelled, grabbing the trigger band on his wrist. Chaos and Tsunami wrapped their arms around Keeper's chest, their faces behind his back, not wanting to watch their demise.

The invisible force from Keeper's amplifier belt held back the initial hit of water, but the weight of the water was greater than the weight of the three villains. The push of the water against Keeper's barrier propelled them backward at an alarming rate. Their feet skidded on top of pebbles and dirt until they were airborne, crashing through the decaying wall at the far end and landing in the yard outside. Water and grime came rushing out, over them, looking for an escape.

It lasted only a few seconds, but it seemed like forever. When the water stopped spreading out around them, soaking into the ground, Keeper finally took a breath. His back was killing him. He was lying on top of Chaos and Tsunami, looking at the night sky.

A face appeared in front of Keeper, and hands lifted his goggles back to the top of his head. "Hey," Y said. "What took you so long?"

"A few minor complications."

Y gave Keeper a hand up and then Chaos. Chaos brushed himself off and looked down at Tsunami. A small cloud formed and rained on Tsunami's eyebrowless head.

Chaos rolled his eyes. "Really, Tsunami?"

"I'd do better," Tsunami said, "but the kid stole my thunder."

The sound of ripping metal penetrated the air, and the barometric pressure pushed at their eardrums. "For the love of the Witch-king!" Showboater exclaimed. "Find cover!"

Slasher and Chaos picked Tsunami up and dragged him behind the stack of sandbags waiting on the factory's implosion day. Barricade was there, still tranquilized. Dr. Spot didn't seem any worse for wear.

Everyone poked their head up over the sandbags to look at the building. Tsunami's tornado could now be seen, shredding the building from the inside and extending up, through the missing roof.

Chaos's eyes narrowed, and he turned toward Tsunami. "That," he said, pointing back at the tornado, "is *not* my work."

"Hya, hya, hya."

The ground began to shake, and the factory began falling in on itself. It was hard to say if it was from an explosion, the tornado, or both.

The villains huddled together, their backs to the sandbags, their arms covering their heads. A massive wave of dirt, debris, and sound swept over them and out into the town.

When the coast seemed clear and quiet had returned, Chaos straightened, shook chunks of cement and brick from his hair, and looked back at where the factory used to stand. He was silent for a minute, lost in thought. "I suspect that's the last we'll see of Polyp," he said. "What a tragic waste." Chaos stood, staring, for a few more seconds. The sounds of sirens could be heard in the distance, approaching the scene of the unnatural natural disaster. Chaos turned to face his chapter. "Who wants waffles? Slasher's treating."

A giant hand rose from the ground, wanting waffles.

"Ah, Barricade," Chaos said, smiling and kneeling down to see him. "Good morning. You missed all the fun."

CHAPTER 35

IT was a week after the factory showdown, and things had returned to normal. Keeper was back home with his nana, and the repercussions for the sudden sleepover hadn't been as bad as Keeper had feared. Nana must have enjoyed her time off from Keeper as much as he had enjoyed his time off from her.

Keeper, Toby, and Y stood across the street from Joanne Larbole's house. It was just after midnight. The curtains were closed, and the porch light was out. The house and the street were dark and silent.

Three days ago, Keeper had taped a note to Larbole's front door, as he had promised, and left the box of money in her backyard. The note let her know the problem had been taken care of. It was safe to return home and go back to making cookies.

He also advised that she forget about him and the whole ordeal. It never happened.

But to date, the Cookie Maven store still hadn't reopened. Keeper, Toby, and Y had stopped by to see if the money box was gone and if there was any sign of Larbole being back in her house. The box they'd dropped off was gone, but three other boxes had appeared on the front porch.

"What do you think is up with the boxes?" Toby asked.

Keeper shrugged. "Only one way to find out."

They waited a few more minutes before crossing the road, just to be sure no one was watching, and silently climbed the steps to the front porch. Three medium-size boxes were stacked on top of each other. A note was taped to the top box.

Y removed the note, opened it, and read it. She studied the text for a minute and then passed it to Keeper. "I believe this is for you."

Keeper read the note. *For my hero who desperately needs cookies.* Keeper slipped the note back into its envelope and shoved it into his pocket. "I'm no hero, but I do desperately need cookies. Everyone grab a box."

They carried the boxes down the street and piled them into the back of the Kia. Y looked at Keeper. "I guess you're all set to become a villain now. To be honest, I wasn't sure you would still want to join E.V.I.L. after everything that's happened."

Keeper shrugged. "Oddly, I think I was more on the fence before all the craziness. Now I find that I . . . I like Chapter 626."

Toby raised an eyebrow. "Even Tsunami?"

Keeper smiled in the night. "Maybe not Tsunami. But every family has a Tsunami, right?"

Toby nodded. "My Aunt Carol."

Keeper looked at Y. "What about you? Do you have a Tsunami in the family?"

Y thought about it for a moment. "Probably my dad."

Keeper frowned. It was the first time he'd heard something like this from Y. She was so confident and strong. Surely she'd had an amazing childhood. "Your dad is like Tsunami?"

Y smiled. "He means well, but we have conflicting personalities."

"I get it," Keeper said. "My nana and I have conflicting personalities too, but she doesn't mean well. She's a hobgoblin."

That got a laugh out of Toby and Y.

"She is one in a million," Y said. "Let's get these cookies to Chaos so you can have your ceremony."

The following night Y sat alone on a bench in the old theater district. Somewhere in the vicinity, E.V.I.L. was welcoming two new villains. They would always be Keeper and Toby to Y, but by the end of the night they would have villainous names and fake identities.

Sensei Love sat down next to Y. Y glanced to the side, noticing the two bandaged hands that looked more like giant Q-tips.

She refocused on her own hands, folded in her lap, trying to not smile at the absurdity.

"There was poison ivy in that ball," Love said.

"I know."

"Mature people don't fill Ping-Pong balls with poison ivy."

Y was now trying to stifle laughter. "I know."

"It's really quite uncomfortable."

"I can only imagine."

They sat in silence for a few minutes until Sensei Love broke it. "Keeper Chance has a very special skill."

"I know."

Sensei Love looked at Y and then back out into the night. "Right and wrong can come in many shades of gray. As we grow older, our experiences and needs, whether real or imaginary, shape our opinions and actions. Should we become the type of person who can't respect or understand other's experiences and needs, we can unknowingly make bad decisions." Love looked at his daughter again. "Even the best of us make mistakes. That includes me.

"Back in the factory, Keeper Chance thought you were in trouble. I never sensed him coming. I suspect you taught him those moves. He would have won that fight to save you."

"I know." Y focused even harder on her hands. The thought of Keeper fighting her father to free her from her tower was the stuff her fairy-tale fantasies were made of. Not that Y needed anyone to free her. She was perfectly capable. It was the notion that someone would want to . . .

"If Keeper's skill is used in the wrong way, it could be disastrous," Sensei Love said. "He's ruled by his heart."

They sat in silence for a few more minutes. Y thought about what her father was saying. She believed in Keeper, but if someone truly horrible tricked him . . .

Love rested his arm on the back of the bench. "People who need saving will be attracted to him."

Y looked up at her father. "Are you saying I need saving?"

A smile tugged at the corners of Sensei Love's mouth. "No. Not at all. I think you're just attracted to him. It's probably the hair." Love ran a bandaged hand over the top of his bald head. "I'd kill for hair like his."

Y smiled and glanced back at the theater, wondering if Keeper and Toby were eating cookies yet and whether they would save any for her. "He isn't in *bad* hands with Chapter 626," she said.

"No, but they aren't exactly *good* hands either." Sensei Love paused and surveyed the streets with Y. "Someone who understands the delicacy of the situation, has an unwavering devotion to the boy"—Love's eyes momentarily shifted to look at his daughter—"and her mother's allure, should probably stay and watch over him."

Y caught her father's eye, incapable of finding words. He was going to let her stay. "Probably, that would be a good idea."

"What's not a good idea is you mooching a room from Chaos. I know that's where you've been hiding from me. He told me. I've extended the rent on the condo for a year. I can't stay, but I'll have trusted associates looking in on you daily. You should be safe there on your own." Love looked up at a dark sky. "You should also probably make these streetlights a bit brighter, for safety's sake."

Y felt her body go rigid. Did he know about her skill?

"Not only am I your father, but I've been living with you for sixteen years. I know exactly what you can do. Seems the real question is what can't you do?" They sat in silence for a few more minutes until Sensei Love finally stood. "I should get going. I've been away from the dojo for too long. I'll tell your mother you won't be returning."

"Maybe I could make a few trips back to visit," Y said. "Maybe I could get an outfit? A Vogue Love original?"

Sensei Love raised an eyebrow and smiled. "You'd be stunning in it."

CHAPTER 36

KEEPER and Toby stood on the empty theater's stage with Chaos. Villains, sidekicks, and henchmen speckled the audience seating.

"I would like to thank E.V.I.L. member Showboater for providing us with this worthy location to celebrate this day," Chaos said, then waited for the polite applause to die down. "I have welcomed a number of amazing, and talented, villains into our fold, but I can't say I have ever done so with more pleasure than I do today. Keeper Chance, please step forward."

Keeper approached Chaos.

Chaos held out a silver medallion, a little larger than a quarter. "While you may still be waiting to find your skill, we have witnessed an amazing genius for inventing and creativity that should not go unrecognized. On behalf of the Evil Villains

International League and Chapter 626, it is an honor to give you the name Tinkerer and to welcome you into our family."

Keeper accepted the medallion and shook Chaos's hand. He went back to his spot next to Toby amid applause and a number of resounding *huzzah*s from Showboater.

"Toby Boggs, please step forward."

Toby stepped forward to join Chaos. He was practically vibrating with excitement.

"Your abilities to hear and smell are impressive and unique, but I think I speak for all of Chapter 626 when I say there is no better tracker in all of Durian and its surrounding areas. You are a triple threat. On behalf of the Evil Villains International League and Chapter 626, it is an honor to give you the name Beagle and to welcome you into our family."

Toby enthusiastically shook Chaos's hand and took the medallion. He turned it over several times, admiring it. His new name and chapter number were embossed on one side. The other side proudly displayed the E.V.I.L. logo—a duck wearing a sock, surrounded by a triangle, and the league motto: *Unum impilium arcanum facit. Duo impilia par faciunt.*

There was more applause and several *huzzah*s until Chaos held up his hands for quiet. "The obligatory ceremonial rigmarole is done. I invite everyone to the stage for cookies, courtesy of our new villains, champagne, courtesy of the house I'm currently calling my lair, and grape soda, courtesy of the senior members."

The stage filled as Chapter 626 enjoyed cookies and offered congratulatory words to Keeper and Toby. Chaos hung back, watching until Keeper approached the cookie table alone.

"Tinkerer," Chaos said, coming up behind Keeper. "I was wondering if we could have a word in private?"

Keeper straightened and put his cookie back down on the table. "Of course, sir."

"Chaos," Chaos said, rolling his eyes. "My name is Chaos." He motioned for Keeper to step backstage, behind the curtain, and they found a quiet corner.

"Villainy," Chaos said, "like any other trade, is learned and requires practice. There is a year of, let's call it apprenticeship, before you're allowed to go off on your own. There are a few things you should learn while you are finishing up high school. Things that we think will come in handy to you as you perfect your career. We'll set up some lessons over the coming months."

"Thank you, si . . . Chaos. I really appreciate any help and advice you, and the others, have to give."

"Excellent. In that case I suggest you stop skipping physical education and show up on time. Show Coach Martin, but no one else, your medallion."

"I knew it!" Keeper said. "I knew something was up with him. He's a villain, isn't he? What's his name? Dracula?"

"No," Chaos said. "His name is Fungus. He's with chapter 649. Commutes during the school year for the job. I strongly advise that you don't walk barefoot in the locker room or let him touch your bare skin. Other than that, Fungus makes a killer casserole and is quite good at pinochle."

"He's a villain and has a job?"

Chaos shrugged. "It makes him happy. After many years of an accomplished career in villainy, Fungus felt like he needed a second career. He chose to stay with his chapter, keeping villainy as his summer job and weekend escape.

"One other thing. You strike me as the type of villain who would, once you've graduated from high school, rather have his own lair over living with your nana or in Toby's parents' basement . . . with Toby. Am I correct in that assumption?"

"To be honest, I haven't really thought about it. I've never been on my own."

"Well, I've thought about it. There's an old, abandoned villain's lair that I think would suit you well. The lair isn't for everyone. It's underground and needs cleaning and updating. Will probably take a year of work. However, I think between you and Toby, the job can be done. If I'm remembering it correctly, there is even a lab."

"What happened to the villain?"

"There was an unfortunate explosion."

"Omigosh."

"No worries. That part has been cleaned up," Chaos said. "I'll text you directions and meet you there next Saturday, at noon. The lair has two bedrooms, I think, if you want to invite Toby to be a roommate. However, that might cramp your style if you have a girlfriend."

Keeper wasn't sure if that last part had been a question or a generalized statement. "I . . . I don't have a girlfriend."

"No? Well, I feel fairly confident that there is a young woman out there who will not want to let you go." Chaos put his arm around Keeper's shoulders and directed him back toward the party. "Until then, let's stuff our faces with cookies."

TWO MONTHS LATER

"**SONOFA** . . . Rotten . . ." Todd Jones fumbled with his keys, trying to single out the one that would open the back door to the Porcelain Palace. He hated Honduras. He hated fishing. He hated vacations. He hated the wrist cast on his right arm, the full-on shoulder cast on his left arm, complete with an immobilization brace that kept it up and out like a chicken wing 24/7, and he hated the boot brace on his left leg. He also hated the boot brace on his right leg. Most of all he hated the ridiculous gold mountain, topped with a hideous gold toilet, that sat in the middle of his pathetic, failing store.

The golden mountain had been his ex-wife's idea. So was the idea of a store that only sold porcelain.

"She had nothing but bad ideas," Jones fumed to himself.

That wasn't entirely true. Jones's ex-wife also had his money, his house, his friends, his cat, and his dignity.

For two months, Jones had resided in a hospital bed in Honduras plotting how to destroy that gold mountain, along with the store, and collect some insurance money to pay off his bills.

He had spent another two months in Honduras plotting while he battled it out with the US embassy, trying to recover his stolen passport, phone, credit cards, cash, driver's license, and identity. Good times.

Jones finally shoved his broken body through the back door and wobbled his way to the door that led to the showroom. He didn't notice the cot and sleeping bag. He did notice that there were some crates, but they might have always been there. He'd been gone too long to remember. He did remember that the showroom was pretty much a wasteland. Between distribution and fulfillment issues, and lack of capital, there was only a scattering of sinks, one tub, and a handful of low-grade toilets.

Jones opened the door to the showroom, ready to look at the golden mountain with disdain. "What the . . . ?"

The showroom was packed. Displays, model rooms, hardware, and high-end shower packages. He had, of course, heard about elves who filled up shoe stores, but who would have thought there were ones for porcelain products?

Jones's eyes glassed over. He might not have to burn the store down after all. "I need to go on vacation more often."